Exquisite Prey

Dark Blood Clan Book 1

T. RAE

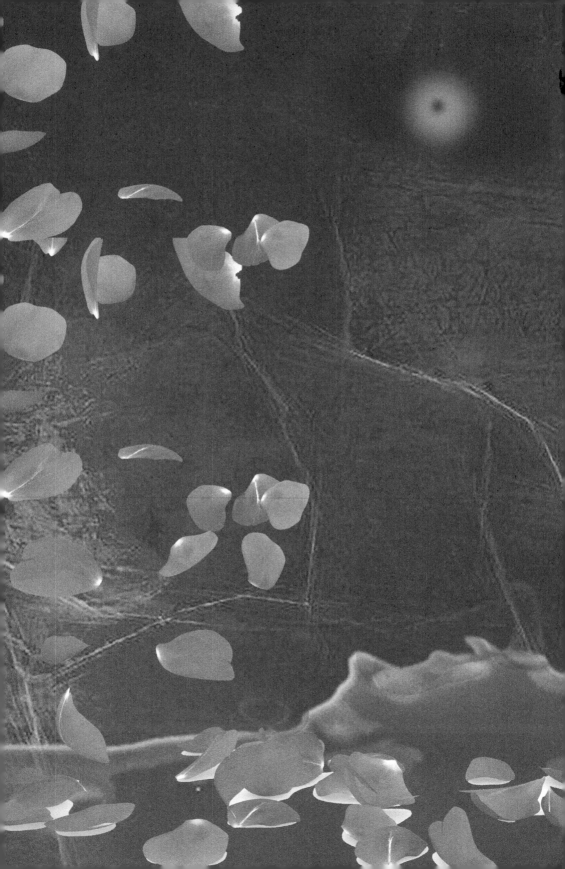

T. Rae

ExquisitE PREY

Dark Blood Clan
Book One

Equisite Prey

T. Rae

Author Note

As a new author, your rating and review means the world. If you enjoyed this book, please consider supporting it by leaving your thoughts in a review. If it wasn't to your liking, please feel free to toss it in the bin and never think about it again.

Trigger Warning

This book may contain triggers for some readers. This book may not be for you if you're uncomfortable reading taboo subject matter, gore, explicit/graphic situations, and disturbing content. You've been warned.

Exquisite Prey

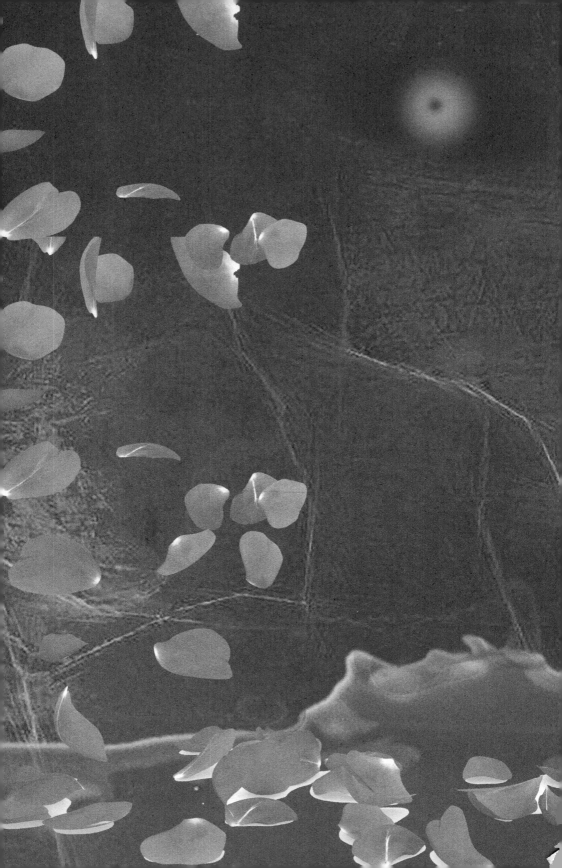

Dedication

I want to give my husband and daughter special thanks for their unwavering support, patience, and time. This book is dedicated to my mom for loving me, no matter what. I wish you were here to read it.

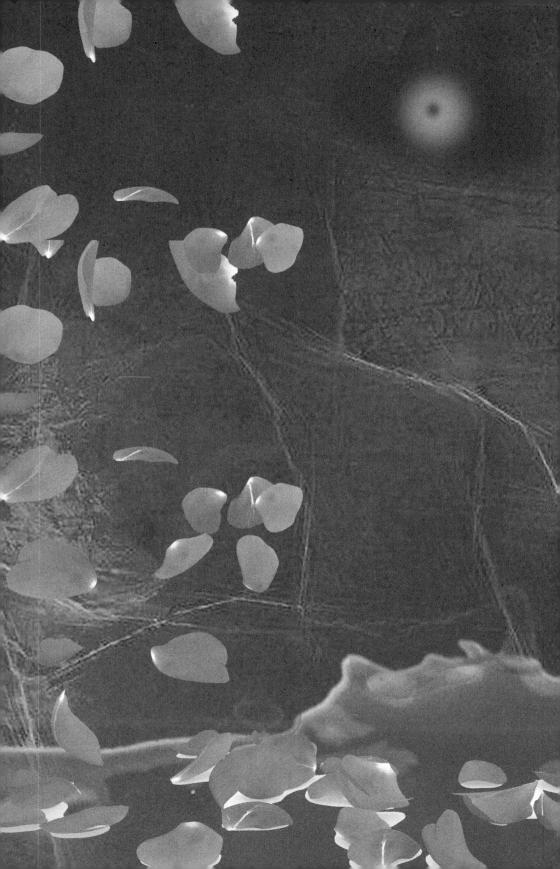

Play List

White Rabbit–David Diebold and Kim Cataluna

Fall With Your Knife–Peter Murphy

Headhunter–Front 242

Worlock–Skinny Puppy

Sex On Wheelz–My Life with the Thrill Kill Cult

Reise, Reise–Rammstein

Out of Control–She Wants Revenge

So What–Ministry

Juke Joint Jezebel–KMFDM

Lifeline–Front Line Assembly

Hurt–NIN

More–Sisters of Mercy

Cities In Dust–Siouxsie and the Banshees

Down In It–NIN

She's Lost Control Again–Joy Division

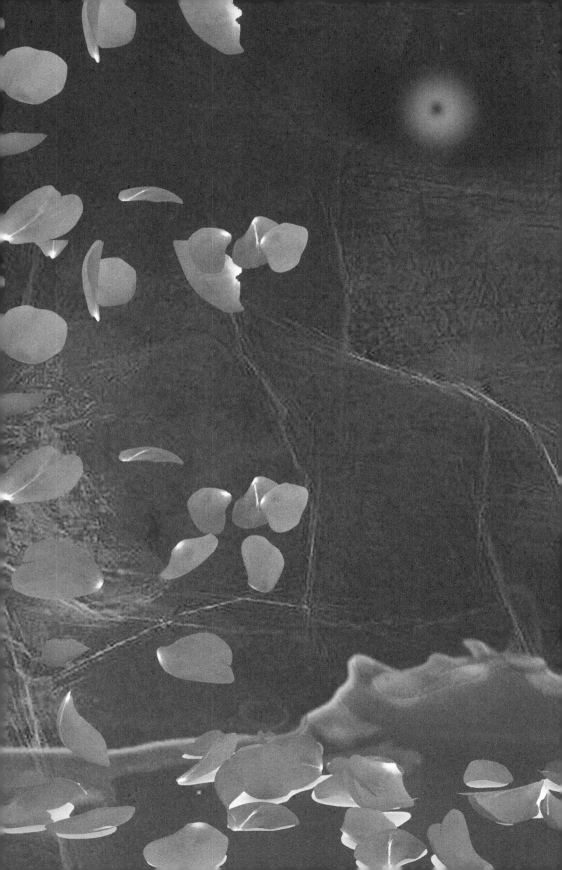

Chapter
One

One

Fine Wine & Fancy-Ass Popcorn

October 19th, 1996 - 11:59 PM

E vaine sat at a large wooden table in the middle of Columbia University's empty library. For her fellow students, Friday night meant fun, parties even, but for her, it meant more research, more note-taking, and worst of all, more writer's block. *Why does this always happen during a deadline?* Like her brain said, nope, and went on vacation. *There's no way I'm gonna pass if I can't write this freaking paper!* As it was, she needed an A+ essay to ensure her perfect GPA, and there was no way she would let one class pull it down. She'd worked too hard to have her impeccable record smudged.

She sighed and tapped her pencil on the table, flipping through the Devil in Massachusetts. "Why witches?" Because the dark beauty of the world drew her curiosity, and when she was a child, her interest in the macabre freaked her mother out. By age ten, Evaine saw a psychologist once a week because her mom thought she was crazy, like her great grandmother Rosalyn. Evaine was a clever little girl and quickly learned what to say to Doctor Evans. Still, her mother insisted that Evaine continue to see the good doctor until she turned eighteen. Then, Daddy put his foot down and told her Evaine was a grown woman who could make her own decisions. Her mother didn't like that.

Her mother also didn't like it when Evaine moved out into her own apartment. Maybe not on her own because she shared it with her best friend Jacob, who she'd known since elementary school, and her boyfriend, Gage. Mother said she was living in sin, but after three years of dating, Daddy disagreed. Besides, she was head over heels for Gage, so that made it all right.

"Library's closing in ten minutes, Evaine," the elderly woman running the help desk said from behind her. The sound of her name jolted Evaine from her stray thoughts, flinching before she turned in her seat and smiled at the short, gray-haired woman. "Thank you, Mrs. Anders."

"Are you planning to check any of those books out? If so, bring them here, and I'll take care of them while you put your supplies away."

Evaine stood and smoothed her long velvet skirt before picking up The Witchcraft of Salem Village. "That would be great." As she crossed the space, her shoulders and back protested, stiff from sitting for so long; the brush of her heavy skirt was loud in the utter silence. "Thanks so much." Evaine laid the book in Mrs. Anders' outstretched hand.

"My pleasure, Dear." Mrs. Anders pushed her glasses up her nose and smiled before jutting her chin out. "Pack up and come to the front. We'll walk out together. Safer that way."

"Okay." Evaine padded back to the piles of research and notes spread across the table. She'd kicked off her shoes hours ago, and the carpet felt rough under her feet, even with her thick stockings. Evaine bent to grab her black Mary Janes from the floor before slipping into her seat. She wore the shiny patent-leather shoes so often that they didn't even need to be unbuckled anymore; they slipped right on.

As Evaine shuffled her loose research into a neat pile, she noticed a single red rose sitting between her books and messenger bag, which hadn't been there before. A wave of dread slithered through her gut. *Where did it come from? Who left it?* She'd only turned her back for a moment. Evaine picked up the stem and rolled it between her fingers. The bloom was beautiful, but the thorns dug into her flesh, making her bite her lip as she glanced around the large empty room and didn't notice anything out of the ordinary. She shrugged and set it next to her bag before shoving the pile of notes into a manila folder she'd lifted from her dad's office last week. And then she stuffed the folder into her messenger bag, followed by her legal pad, which was also stolen from Daddy, and a couple of books she'd checked out last week.

Packed up, Evaine grabbed her long, dark, purple velvet jacket from the back of the chair and slipped it on over her fitted, long sleeve black T-shirt, pulling her long fire-engine-red curls from the collar before pushing the chair in. Like a bloody beacon, the rose sat on the empty table, calling to her curiosity. Evaine gave it one last glance, her eyes scanning the many rows of books before heading to the front of the library to meet Mrs. Anders.

"Here you are, Dear." Mrs. Anders handed off the tome as she reached the sizable horseshoe-shaped desk at the front of the expansive library.

"Thank you." As Evaine added it to her bag, she felt the weight of someone's gaze on her back. Goosebumps prickled her arms, and a shiver ran down her spine. It was so overwhelming she glanced behind her, half expecting to see someone standing there.

"All set then?" Mrs. Anders gathered her jacket and purse.

"Yes, Ma'am." Evaine swallowed the lump in her throat, adjusting the strap on her shoulder as she did her best to ignore the urge to run out of the library because she had a distinct feeling whoever was watching her would give chase if she did.

"Let's leave then, hmm?"

"Yes, let's." Evaine followed the kind, elderly woman out, a sharp blast of cold air hitting her face when she stepped out on the stone steps, making her shiver as she watched Mrs. Anders lock the heavy wooden doors.

"Are you taking the subway tonight?" Mrs. Anders turned around and shoved the keys into her purse.

"No, Ma'am. I was going to walk. It's just a few blocks." Evaine's voice held a hint of dread. Still trying to shake the unsettling feeling, she followed the short, round woman down the steps.

"Doesn't seem very safe; a young thing like you to be walking these streets after midnight."

Usually, Evaine didn't mind the short walk. But tonight, she had no desire to tempt fate, even with mace in her bag. "It's just a couple of blocks if you wouldn't mind giving me a ride. I'd really appreciate it."

Mrs. Anders nodded, making the pulled-up salt and pepper curls bounce as she pulled another set of keys from her purse. "Absolutely, Dear. I'd be happy to give you a ride home." And walked toward the only car in the small lot.

It only took minutes before Mrs. Anders pulled up to the curb in front of the tall brick building Evaine called home. "Thank you again for the ride, Mrs. Anders."

The woman's smile was genuine. "No problem, Dear. I'm sure I'll see you soon."

"Goodnight." When Evaine slipped from the warm car, a harsh gust of icy wind whipped the bottom of her jacket around her velvet-covered legs and made her shiver as she closed the door. The blustering wind made Evaine struggle as she pulled the heavy glass door open and then yanked it closed once inside the lobby.

"Good evening, Miss Maire," the uniformed security officer behind the desk said as she passed.

"Hello, Stan. Having an exciting night?" They were in a safe neighborhood, and nothing much happened in their building. Still, it was nice to have him around.

"Never want too much excitement. Can't get through my movie if there's too much excitement." Stan shot her a genuine grin.

He isn't wrong.

"Well, enjoy then." Evaine smiled as she crossed to the elevator and hit the button with her chilled fingers, the doors sliding open immediately like the car was waiting for something to do. She stepped inside and pushed the four.

Sometimes, she still didn't believe she was on her own because she expected to stay with her parents through school. Her father surprised her when he handed her the keys to her place right before her first year at Columbia and told her she'd earned it with all the hard work she'd put in through her years of private school and personal tutors. It was crazy to think four years had already passed, and she was finishing college. Evaine often wondered how things would change when she was done with school and couldn't imagine spending every day without Gage and Jacob. Unfortunately, change was inevitable, especially now.

When the doors opened with a ding, Evaine stepped into the well-lit hallway and crossed to her apartment. As usual, she reached for the knob instead of digging for her keys and found it unlocked.

"Jacob Michaels! How many times have I told you to lock the damn door? Someone's gonna steal your ass one of these days." Evaine hung her bag on one of the silver hooks on the wall next to the table and pulled off her coat, draping it over her bag.

"Let 'em try," Jacob said from the couch. "I don't give a fuck."

"I do!" Evaine took off her shoes and set them against the wall with all the others before crossing the open living room to sit next to Jacob on the plush leather couch. Most of the community stuff in their apartment was hers, except for Jacob's music equipment, PlayStation, and a pile of games.

"I know you'd miss me, Princess." Jacob flashed her a smile before leaning into her and pursing his lips. "Give us a kiss."

It was more an order than a request, but Evaine obliged, giving him a quick peck and then sniffing the air. "Is that popcorn I smell?"

"Of course." Jacob stole another quick kiss. "You know Daddy takes good care of his Princess." He smirked when he made the words sound dirtier than they should have.

"Yuck!" Evaine smacked his shoulder and laughed as a frown distorted his handsome face.

"No need for violence, My Little Psychopath." Jacob rubbed his shoulder and combed his fingers through his long black hair.

Evaine caught a peek at the shaved sides of his mohawk. "You shaved your head!"

"I cleaned them up with the buzzers this morning. They were getting way too long and sticking out everywhere." He grinned and pulled his hair back into a ponytail, showing her the perfect strips of fresh, stubbled skin.

Gods, I love a man with a mohawk! Her best friend was already so pretty that he made mohawks even sexier by existing. Her fingers itched to glide over the fresh stubble. When she reached out and stroked the side of his head, Jacob purred like a cat as she petted him, leaning his head toward her and closing his eyes.

"Nice, huh?" Jacob asked.

Whenever she rubbed his shaved head for a long time, her fingers tingled, and this time was no different; there was a subtle tactual tingle on her fingertips when she pulled her hand away and rubbed them together.

Jacob opened his eyes, frowning. "Done already?" When she nodded, his hair fell back, and he kicked up a well-groomed eyebrow. "Hungry?"

"Starving."

"It should be done." He stood and stretched like a satisfied feline, pulling up the hem of his black Joy Division T-shirt enough to give Evaine a peek at his defined abs and that tight V as it lost contact with his low-hung black cotton pajama pants.

The view was worth appreciating because she knew how hard he worked in the gym downstairs to keep it that way and pulled her legs under her, pooling her skirt in her lap and curling deeper into the couch. "Yum." Evaine's stomach growled at the thought of food. "I missed dinner. Come to think of it, lunch too."

"Would the Princess like wine with her fancy-ass popcorn?" Jacob asked from the kitchen.

"Mmm. Yes, please," Evaine said over her shoulder as she reached for the remote and flicked on the television. Friday late-night re-runs of Springer were on channel fourteen. It was Jacob's trash tv of choice, his guilty pleasure, and she could admit she didn't mind watching the shit show, either. Watching the guests fight it out on stage was always fun, especially when Steve had to break them up.

Jacob returned from the kitchen with a bottle of wine shoved under one of his muscled biceps, two large wine glasses in one hand, and a bowl of popcorn in the other. He gripped the wine opener between his straight white teeth and jutted his chin, mumbling something that sounded like "take it," around the metal of the opener before dropping it in her lap so he could set the bowl and glasses down on the table, and wrap his hand around the neck of the bottle and pull it from under his arm before dropping into the seat next to her. "Dinner is served, Princess," he said in his best butler tone.

"Why, thank you, Jeeves." Evaine handed him the bottle opener and leaned forward to steal a handful of movie-buttered heaven. Daddy sent over an early birthday gift, a small popcorn maker, like the ones at the movie theater. It came with a large case of corn and butter toppings and made the best popcorn shy of Coney Island, quickly becoming their favorite dinner. They'd gone through half the box in a matter of days and were down to only a few packets of the extra butter because they both loved their popcorn smothered in butter and coated in salt.

"Yum," Evaine chewed the salty, buttered puffed kernels. "This was the best gift ever."

Jacob hitched an eyebrow as he poured the red wine and frowned. "Hey now, Princess. I haven't given you my gift yet." A smirk sneaked across his full lips as he tried to keep a straight face. "I assure you. It is the best birthday gift ever." Jacob oozed confidence and raw sexiness. A toothy grin broke across his face as he shrugged. "At least, that's what I've been told on several occasions."

Evaine cocked her head. "Do they make bows that small?"

Disbelief washed over Jacob's handsome face, his mouth gaping open before his black eyebrows furrowed, the ring in the left catching the light. He jerked the wine glass back before she wrapped her fingers around the stem. "Did you just insult the size of my cock?" His lips pursed. "I fucking think you did!" And then he chuckled and set the glass on the table out of her reach. "Fuck that! No wine for you, Miss Thing."

"But." Evaine pushed her bottom lip out in a slight pout. "Even if I say sorry?"

"Nope." He popped the P as he sat back and sipped his wine, giving her his best side-eyed glare, which really was impressive.

Evaine smiled sweetly and pinched her thumb and pointer finger together, leaving about an inch of space between them. "But it was just a little joke."

The wine went down the wrong pipe, making Jacob choke as he laughed and spilled it down the front of his shirt. He shot her a dirty look, using the same hand gesture, "And you're just a little bit of a bitch!" his hand scrubbing across his mouth before brushing the red wine off the white lettering of his T-shirt.

Evaine stuck out her tongue as she chewed her popcorn before turning her attention to the show. "Look, I put Springer on for you. Doesn't that make up for it?"

Jacob licked the wine from his fingers. "Maybe a little."

The jingle of keys drew their attention to the front door as Gage slipped inside and pulled his leather jacket off, hanging it next to hers before he hiked up his black Bauhaus T-shirt and adjusted the long-sleeved black-and-white striped T-shirt under it, smoothing it back down over his abdomen and running his hand through his messy purple hair as he crossed to the couch.

Gods, the boy is gorgeous, like Propaganda Magazine gorgeous! Every time she saw him, she wondered how the hell she ended up with him, how she was lucky enough to find a considerate, kind, and intelligent boy wrapped in such hot-ass packaging.

"What are you two up to?" Gage leaned down and kissed the top of Evaine's head, his chilly fingers slipping between the fire-engine-red tendrils at her neck to caress the sensitive spot at the nape.

The harsh scent of cigarette smoke wafted off his clothes from a night of bartending at Eucharist and burned her nostrils. Evaine shivered and smiled up at him. When his hand slid from her shoulder, she grabbed his index finger and pulled it back, kissing his knuckles. "We were just discussing the minuscule size of Jay's cock."

"And how you're still a bitch!" Jacob snapped with indignation.

The corner of Gage's mouth ticked up, the silver ring in the middle catching the light. His mint-green eyes sparkled with humor as he flicked a glance at Jacob before settling them on Evaine. "I'd prefer it if you only talked about my cock, Baby."

"Oh, trust me. She talks enough about your cock." Jacob laughed as he reached for Evaine's glass of wine and offered it to Gage, who smiled wide and downed it in two gulps.

"Long night?" Evaine asked when he set the glass back on the table.

"Kinda. Busy, for sure. Working on my final project. And Matt wasn't happy about me leaving early tonight, but he'll get over it." Gage lifted his arm and sniffed the bend of his elbow. "I really stink and need a shower." His black eyebrows hitched up under the long bangs of his purple mess of shaggy hair. "Wanna join me?" He tugged her toward him, flashing her a smile she couldn't resist if she wanted.

"I'm not sure about her. But you know, I'll join you anytime." Jacob downed the last of his wine.

Gage smiled, the genuine grin making his eyes sparkle, his cheeks flushing slightly. "I'll keep that in mind, Jay."

"Stop trying to steal my boyfriend, damn it." Evaine grabbed the throw pillow behind her and chucked it at Jacob before pushing off the couch. "How many times do I have to tell you, hmmm?" She pinned her body against Gage's and pushed up on her toes, wrapping her arms around his neck. "Don't make me have to pee on him," she shot over her shoulder.

Gage wrinkled his nose as he crouched lower and planted a quick kiss on her lips before encircling her waist and pulling her off the floor for a couple of ticks. "I love you, Baby, but there will be no pissing on me. That's where I draw the line."

"What's that the thousandth time he's told you?" Jacob poured more wine into his glass and sat back against the couch.

Evaine's eyes caught Gage's as he smirked, and she pushed out her bottom lip in a pout. "You're no fun."

Gage leaned down, curling his tall, thin body into a C, and caught her lip between his teeth. She squeaked softly when he nipped it before kissing the same spot, his tongue sliding along the abused skin. When their lips parted, he said, "I'm plenty fun. Come shower with me, and I'll show you."

"How can I resist?"

"You can't." He pulled her toward the bedroom. "Night, Jay," Gage said over his shoulder when they reached the closed door.

"Sure. Fine. Just leave me here with my sad little popcorn and red wine so you can go fuck. I see where I rate," Jacob whined.

Evaine turned enough to give her friend a quick wave. "Poor baby."

Jacob stuck out his tongue and sipped his wine.

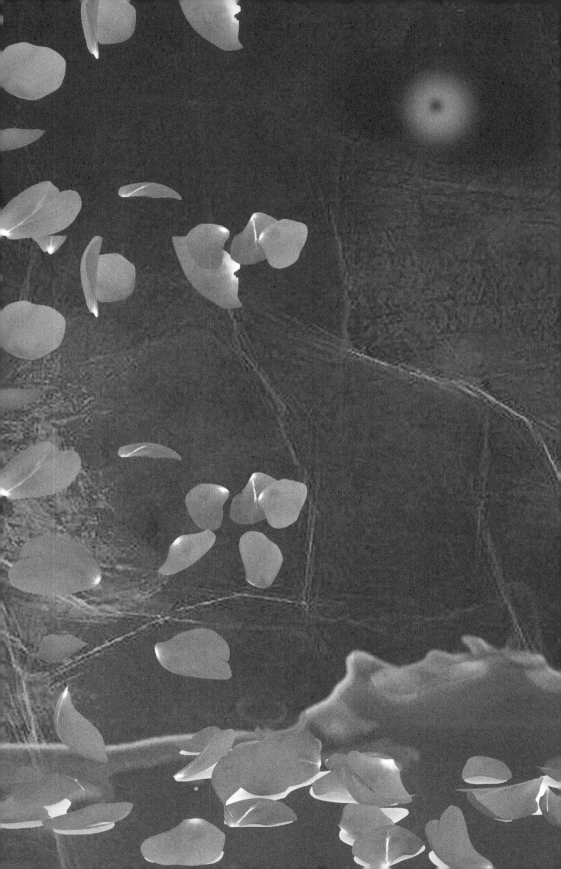

Chapter
Two

Two

Deadlines & Dinner

The alarm on Evaine's nightstand blared to life for the third time. Even without a shower, she cut it close and needed to get out of bed. Still, she quickly decided to forgo getting coffee and wearing makeup to sleep for another ten minutes and groaned as she rolled away from Gage's heated body long enough to smack the large black button on her alarm.

"You're gonna be late." Gage's thin metal bracelets jingled as he threw his arm over his face and buried his eyes in the crook of his elbow.

"Just a few more minutes, promise." Evaine snuggled against him, resting her head on his chest, and threw her leg over his to get closer, her fingers following the cut line of his abs. She loved that she fit perfectly into his side and that he always ran much warmer than her. Even with the thick velvet comforter on the bed, she was always cold. Gage kicked it off most nights, and she stole it to build her cocoon, so it worked well for them.

She felt a shiver run along Gage's body. "Cold feet," he said, mostly asleep, and draped his other arm along her back, his long fingers brushing her hip before settling against the outside of her thigh. His touch made her skin tingle and her stomach flutter.

Evaine hummed in agreement and pulled the blanket up around her neck, tucking it under her chin and drifting on edge between dozing and dreaming until the alarm blared to life again. As it screamed, Gage shifted, rolling on his side, and kissed the top of her head before giving a half-hearted push against her shoulder, making his bracelets jingle. "I love you, Baby. But get the fuck outta bed, so I can sleep. I gotta work tonight."

"Yeah, yeah." Evaine crawled out from under the covers and hit the button on the alarm to ensure it wouldn't go off again until Gage needed to get up. "Sleep tight, Grouch." She leaned over the bed and kissed the side of his head, and he mumbled something that didn't sound like English before Evaine straightened out and stretched her hands over her head, her spine protesting and her muscles complaining on her way to the bathroom.

As she washed her face and brushed her teeth, tension settled in her shoulders. By the time she finished dressing in her comfiest black leggings and tank top with a sheer black shirt that hung to her thighs, she couldn't deny the knots coiling under her skin. *I'm doomed!* Self-doubt chewed at the back of her brain, and she tried to shake it off as she headed back to the bathroom to pull her fire-red hair into a messy bun on the top of her head.

"Good enough." She sighed at her reflection, the bags under her eyes glaring back at her before she went to find her black combat boots.

Today's gonna suck! Evaine was so far behind on her essay, which meant six hours of class, followed by three more hours of library and research. If she was lucky, she'd get most of the research done and then put together her rough outline. Maybe she'd even get a first draft finished by some miracle.

Wishful thinking. It doesn't hurt to dream.

Evaine broke her record by being dressed and out the door in fifteen minutes. *Not too shabby!* It left her enough time to pop into the coffee shop and grab the largest size they had before heading to campus.

In class, her professors reviewed what would be on her two finals. Evaine took notes, despite how badly she struggled to focus. *Damn!* This paper needed to be done so she could have at least a day to study for her exams. Bs weren't acceptable. In fact, anything below an A+ wasn't acceptable. Her Lit II teacher allowed them to use class time to work on their projects, which made sense, considering it counted as their final exam, and that gave her time to do research and block out a loose outline, making her feel better about everything.

As Evaine headed across campus to the library, her cellphone rang, and she stopped at a bench to dig it out. Daddy insisted she needed a way for him to reach her, no matter what, and was the only one who called her on it.

By the time she dug the black brick from the bottom of her bag, it had stopped ringing and chimed at her to let her know she had a message. She arrowed through the simplistic screens to find her dad's direct office number and hit the green phone to dial back to him. It only rang once before she heard the deep, smooth voice that reminded her of the nights he'd read to her before bed. "Chandler Maire speaking."

"Hi, Daddy. You called?"

"Princess. Why didn't you pick up? I've asked you to keep that phone on you for emergencies, Sweetheart." Concern mixed with a hint of annoyance.

"I know, Daddy. I was in class." *It's just a little white lie.* And better than hearing the extended version of this particular lecture. Evaine pushed from the bench and started toward the library again as her dad said, "Oh, so sorry. I thought class ended at two today."

"It did, but I was talking to my professor about my final paper." *Just a tiny fib.*

"How is it coming?"

"Pretty good so far." *Okay, so, three.* "I'm headed to the library to finish the rough outline and finalize details on the trials themselves. I got a good bit of the research done in class, so that helped."

"Good. I'm sure it will be an easy A by the time you finish it, Princess."

"A+,"

"Of course, A+." Chandler chuckled and cleared his throat. "Now, Evie, the real reason for my call."

"Yes, Daddy?" Evaine bounced down the concrete stairs and across the grass into the parking lot in front of the library.

"I need you to do me a favor."

She chewed the edge of her long Merlot-colored thumbnail as she paced the sidewalk in front of the stone steps that led back to her own personal ring of hell. "What's that?"

"You know that normally we don't mind the boys coming with you to Sunday dinner, but I've invited an important new client to join us this weekend. So, I need you to come alone."

Evaine's head bobbed, even though her dad couldn't see, and when he didn't continue, she said, "Okay."

"I also need you to put your best foot forward for me, Princess. This man is affluent and offers a significant opportunity for my office if he's willing to invest, as well as for this family. So we're rolling out the red carpet. Pulling out all the stops."

Evaine flinched as she pulled a piece of skin from her cuticle and shook her hand when the cool air burned the wound. "I understand, Daddy. Best foot forward. I can do that."

"Wonderful, Princess." There was a delight in her father's laugh.

"I'm at the library, Daddy, and I've gotta get back to that A+. Okay?"

"Just remember, dinner is at seven. Your mother's looking forward to seeing you, so try to get here at six-thirty if you can. Good luck with the paper, Sweetheart."

Though Evaine's relationship with her mother wasn't awful, she was pretty sure her mother wasn't giving much thought to catching up with her daughter, being wrapped up in whatever charity or organization held her fancy that week. Still, Evaine sounded slightly terse when she said, "Send my love. See you at six-thirty."

"See you then, Sweetheart."

"Bye, Daddy." Evaine hit the red phone button to end her call and bounced up the stairs to the heavy wooden doors.

At this time of day, several students spread out among the long wooden tables and uncomfortable hard-backed chairs. Some studied in groups with books piled around them, while others preferred to study alone.

Evaine's favorite table in the back corner had one student sitting at the end. After last night's experience, she wasn't sure she wanted to sit there again, but quickly realized it was the best spot and took the opposite end, spreading out her research and books as she pulled them from her messenger bag.

Organization was a disease for her, and it showed when she piled the books on the left side and the manila folders on the right. A smile broke across her face as she pulled her legal pad and pen out last. Gage's art covered the front page. *Kick-Ass, Baby!* in his signature fancy sprawling letters with swirls and curly Qs.

Gage was the cornerstone of her current support system, filling the hole where her mom and dad had been for most of her life. Not that they'd gone far. Evaine was fortunate to have him and Jacob. There was no denying she was a spoiled little rich girl who enjoyed getting her way. She had no delusions about her charmed life. Sometimes, she couldn't figure out why they both put up with her. Evaine wet the end of her thumb with her tongue, rolling the yellow-lined papers over the top until she found the spot she'd left off and tucking them under before setting the pad on the table. Her eyes skimmed the last few paragraphs, and then she continued to formalize her outline.

Time flew by, and the next time Evaine looked up, more than half the students were gone, including the girl at the other end of her table. Evaine shook her pen hand, her fingers cramping from the abuse. The only saving grace was the relief creeping into her as she got closer to completing the first draft of her paper. As she brought the tip of her ballpoint pen back to the thick yellow pad, a shiver ran up her spine as a sense of being watched overwhelmed her. Evaine flicked her eyes up and scanned the room but had no luck finding the source of her discomfort, leaning back in the wooden chair and rolling her shoulders as she took an extended moment to check her surroundings. Everyone seemed engrossed in their studies. Still, she felt someone watching her.

Determined to finish as much as possible, Evaine shook off the feeling and returned to her task because she didn't want to be there after midnight again, especially with the creepy feeling sliding down her spine.

With some effort, she found her groove again and wrapped her outline up after another hour of work. Evaine realized the sun was setting, glancing out the large window behind her, and looked at the silver marcasite watch wrapped around her wrist to check the time. "Five already?" She glanced around the practically empty room.

The silence was almost deafening, causing Evaine to jump in her seat when her cellphone rang for the second time today. It was easy to find because she'd stuffed it in her coat pocket. Still, the ringtone echoed across the vast space, earning her a frown from the woman working the desk today, who was not nearly as friendly as Mrs. Anders.

"So sorry," Evaine whispered and then hit the talk button and, in a hushed tone, said, "Hello?" It still seemed too loud, making her cover the end of the phone with her hand to dampen her voice even further.

"Hey, Princess! Where are you at?" Jacob asked.

Heat spread across her face as embarrassment washed over her, and she lowered her voice. "Library."

"Damn, still?"

"What do you want, Jay?" she snapped.

"Grouchy much?" Jacob huffed. "Gage and I are heading to Harlem Shakes to get dinner before he goes to work. We thought maybe you'd join us, but if you're gonna be a B. I. T. C. H. about it."

"Really, Jerk?" Evaine couldn't keep the smile off her face. *Gods!* She loved her best friend, even when he was a pain in her ass.

"Well?" Jacob asked.

The woman at the desk glared at Evaine. "Okay. I'll be there in fifteen minutes or so. I gotta go. Bye."

It took a few minutes to pile her things into her bag and get out the door. She cut across the campus toward Harlem Shakes, one of their favorite hang-outs because they had the best burgers and awesome shakes. Despite the cool night, she really, REALLY wanted a shake. She just couldn't decide between chocolate or vanilla but would have to figure it out before she got there.

The cool wind whipped against her body, and she pulled her velvet jacket around her, gripping the collar to keep it off her neck. She should've grabbed a scarf this morning but forgot in her rush to make it to class on time. Fortunately, she was only two blocks from the diner. So she wasn't too miserable. Although, her stomach started growling about three blocks back at the idea of eating for the first time today. Gage was going to give her shit, but she didn't care because she wanted the biggest burger they had, with a side of fries. Or maybe onion rings.

"Yeah, onion rings for sure." A gust of wind pushed against Evaine, making her eyes water and her nose run. Fall was her favorite season, and Halloween was her favorite holiday. Every year since middle school, her dad let her host a costume party for her birthday. At first, the parties were lame, but they improved as she got older. Now, they were huge, and she hired a planner to take care of the extensive guest list and details, so all she had to do was show up in her costume and have fun. This year she was going as Morticia and Gage as Gomez from the Addams Family, and Jay decided on the Crow.

As Evaine waited on the street corner for the light to change so she could cross to the diner, she had the sense of being watched for a second time that day, and it sent a shiver down her spine that had nothing to do with the weather. It made her clutch her bag and shove the strap up her shoulder, her fingers itching with the desire to grab the mace. She resisted, and when the light changed to red and the walk sign lit, she blew out the breath she'd been holding and stepped into the crosswalk. People crowded the streets, and Evaine was twenty feet from Jay and Gage. In fact, she could see Gage's messy purple hair through the window.

Relief washed over her as she crossed the threshold and stepped into the bright lights of the diner. Evaine smiled when she caught Jacob's eyes. He waved her over with a loud, "Princess!" Her face heated as she slipped out of her jacket and into the booth next to Gage.

"Hey, Baby." He smiled and bumped her shoulder.

"Hi." She loved how his messy bangs hung in his mint-green eyes and how his shirt wrapped around his muscled arms, flexing under his long sleeves as he moved against her. She had issues, or maybe more of an obsession, and was coming to terms with it.

"How was class?" Gage sipped his black coffee before licking his full bottom lip, his tongue brushing along the silver ring that sat dead center.

Damn! She loved his lip ring, and even more so his tongue, and sucked in a breath, pushing thoughts of what he could do with it out of her mind. "It wasn't too bad. I got a lot more done today. I'm feeling good about it."

"You worry too much," Jacob reminded her for the millionth time.

"Says you, Mr. Cool," Evaine said with a sharpened edge.

Jacob cut her off with a dramatic wave of his hand. "Pish."

The waitress stepped in front of the table and saved him from Evaine's wrath when she said, "Hi, guys. Are you ready to order?"

"I am." Evaine glanced to Gage, who nodded and took another sip of his coffee.

"Ladies first." The waitress placed the tip of her pen on the small pad in the palm of her hand.

"Could I get a double cheeseburger- fully dressed, a side of onion rings, and a large chocolate shake with extra whipped cream, please?"

When she flicked her eyes in his direction, Gage shook his head.

"What?" she asked sheepishly. "I'm hungry."

He smirked. "Okay then." His eyes broke from hers and landed on the waitress. "I'll have two eggs over easy with a side of bacon and whole-wheat toast."

"That's not much better than mine," Evaine said in a chiding tone.

"Which is why I didn't say shit." Gage leaned into her shoulder and stole a kiss when she looked up, making her lips tingle.

"And you?" the waitress asked Jacob.

"I'm gonna have a burger too. Just a single- fully dressed, but no ketchup."

"Do you want fries with that?"

"Yeah, that would be awesome. Can I also get a refill on my pop?" He picked up his glass, sucking the last of his soda through his straw.

"No problem." The waitress scooped the un-used menus from the table's edge, smiling at them before heading toward the blue and white counter that looked like it belonged in a fifties malt shop. Several customers sat on the round leather stools that lined it. Others scattered around the booths against the walls and tables in the middle of the diner. It wasn't a big place, but it was always busy.

Jacob leaned back in his seat and crossed his arms, a dramatic huff pushing between his lips as he eyed them across the table. "So! Are you gonna ask me how my day went?"

"Today was your last performance, huh?" Gage was always so good at remembering people's stuff. Another thing she appreciated about him as she said, "Oh, that's right," because she sucked at it.

Jacob nodded, dropping his hands in his lap and frowning. His long hair hung in his face, hiding his sea-green eyes.

"How did it go?" Evaine feared the worst.

Jacob's smile hinted at wickedness when he whipped his chin up, his eyes sparkling with sin. "It was fucking AMAZING!" He slammed his hands on the tabletop hard enough to draw everyone's attention and made her jump, his silver rings glinting in the harsh overhead lights. "I fucking killed it. Even Professor James had to admit it was good. And you should've seen the pain on that fucker's face when he did. The only thing that would've made it better would've been making him choke on my cock while he groveled."

Gage chuckled. "You've thought a lot about this, haven't you?"

"Maybe a little too much," Jacob said with sin still written across his handsome face.

Evaine giggled.

Unsure of what to say, Gage shrugged and gave Jacob a nonchalant "Huh." Then he paused as if he was trying to shake off the visual. "I'm not surprised. It was an awesome piece."

"It really was." To be honest, she'd been so wrapped up in her shit that she wasn't even sure she'd heard the finished piece yet, but she knew Jacob was talented and was sure he nailed it.

"Here you go. Shake for the lady, and refill for the rock star." The waitress shot Jacob a flirty smile.

"Thank you, Sweetheart." Jacob flashed his best grin. Too bad she didn't have a chance with him. Though he didn't bother explaining that because he loved the attention, no matter who it was.

"Your food should be out in a couple of minutes." She walked away.

The three chatted more about Jacob's performance, and Gage filled them in on the B+ he earned on his final for Art History. He seemed satisfied, which made Evaine's eye twitch.

When the waitress returned with their food, a comfortable silence fell over them as they devoured it. Most days, the boys finished before her, but she won hands down tonight. Inhaling her burger and onion rings, she opted for water to wash it down because another shake was out of the question with the health-nazi sitting next to her.

With her last bite, Evaine rubbed her extended belly through her sheer black shirt and broke the silence. "Oh my god, I'm so full. I'm gonna pop."

Gage threw his napkin over his half-eaten breakfast and slid his arm around her shoulders, pulling her into the curve of his body. "You pretty much ate a whole cow, Baby." He kissed the top of her head as his long fingers stroked her arm through her shirt.

"I did, and it was yummy." She giggled.

"I'd have to agree." Jacob sipped the last of his soda.

"What time is it?" Gage asked her, still stroking her arm with the tips of his chipped black fingernails.

She frowned and glanced at her watch. "Almost Seven."

"Yeah, I gotta get going, or Matt will ride my ass all night. We have a band playing tonight, so we're opening the doors early. But the upside, I should make some good tips."

Evaine slid from the booth to let Gage out, wrapping her arms around his neck and kissing him goodbye.

"See ya later," he said against her lips. His hands slid along her sides and down her hips, cupping her ass as he pulled her off her feet and stole another kiss.

"Love you," she whispered, the heated metal of his lip ring tickling her.

"Love you too, Baby."

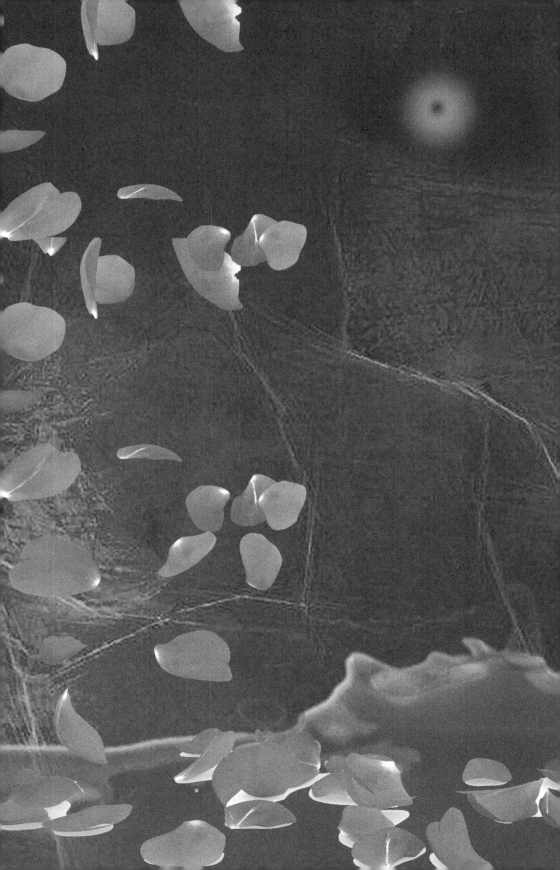

Chapter
Three

Flowers & Fighting

Evaine and Jacob took the long way home to work off their burgers, enjoying the crisp night air and the bustling city streets. It was one of the things that made her at home in the big city. She loved the noise, and even when her family vacationed in the Hamptons every summer, she couldn't wait to get back to it.

On the elevator, Evaine said, "Oh, I forgot to mention it earlier."

Jacob's hip rested against the railing, his shoulder against the mirrored wall, and his arms crossed over his chest. He cocked his head in her direction, his pierced eyebrow hitching up under his black hair. "What?"

"My dad called and said no-go for dinner on Sunday. He has some big wig client he's trying to impress, and he doesn't think you boys will make a good first impression." Evaine rolled her eyes.

"No biggie."

When the door opened, he followed her out.

"I figured, but I wanted to mention it before I forgot."

Jacob pulled his keys from the front pocket of his tight black jeans and unlocked the door with a quick twist of his wrist. "You gonna be okay alone tonight?"

"Alone? Where are you going?" Evaine stepped inside, hanging her bag and jacket before bending down to unlace her boots and kick them off as Jacob tossed his keys in the bowl next to the door and flashed her a slight smile. "I have a date tonight, Princess."

"You do! With who?" Her socks were next, and she balled them up and shoved them into her boots before setting them in their usual spot.

"A boy I met at the coffee shop. Mmm. He's hot too. Taller than Gage, all muscle and broody. Yummy." That sinful grin from earlier spread across his face, and Evaine couldn't help but giggle. "Maybe you'll get lucky."

"From your mouth to God's ears, Princess." Jacob threw up his hands as he crossed their open living room, and when he reached his bedroom door, he turned. "It's been like three days already." Then headed inside.

Evaine shook her head. *Whatta dork!* He could have any boy he wanted, and most of the time, it was easier for him to find a date than it was for her; before she met Gage, anyway.

All she wanted to do was curl up on the couch and enjoy the food coma overtaking her. *Too bad.* There was a stupid paper to write, so she grabbed her messenger bag from the hook with a sigh and trudged across the room to the dining table.

At least these seats are comfy, unlike the hard wooden ones in the library that made her feel like she was ninety years old. When she finished pulling everything out and sat down, Jacob came out of his room and kissed her head as he walked by. "Love you, Princess. Don't work too hard, huh?"

"I'll try not to." She smiled. "Love the eyeliner."

"Thank you." He ruffled her hair before going to grab his jacket and keys. "Getting the swoops even was a bitch. I've got a new appreciation for your abilities."

"Practice makes perfect. Have fun," Evaine said.

"I intend to." Jacob grinned before slipping out the door and remembering to lock it for once.

It took some effort, but eventually, Evaine focused and fell into a groove. When there was a knock on the door, it jolted her. "Just a minute." She threw her pen down on her pad and climbed to her feet, crossing to the door and pushing on her toes as she peeked through the peephole and was surprised to see a delivery guy with an arm full of red roses. When she opened the door, he asked, "Evaine Maire?"

Evaine nodded. "Yes."

"Well then, these are for you." The man smiled and cleared his throat when she didn't reach for the offered flowers.

"Who are they from?"

She let him shove the vase into her hands as he said, "No clue, Miss, but I'm sure there's a card." He tipped his cap and turned for the elevator without looking back.

"Thank you," Evaine said, as he pushed the down button, and closed her apartment door, locking it. The vase was heavy, so she set it down on the counter in the kitchen before looking for a card among the red, white, and green. There wasn't one. "Huh?" The glass bottom rubbed on the marble counter as she turned the vase around. The twenty-four long stem roses surrounded by white sprigs of baby's breath and green ferns were beautiful, and Evaine sniffed them with a smile. *They smell lovely, too.*

It wasn't unusual for Gage to surprise her with sweet, unexpected things, but this was extravagant, not that she didn't love being spoiled. *Now, I'll have to figure out a way to thank him.* Evaine set the flowers in the middle of the dining room table, their scent wafting through the room as she finished her work. Gage wouldn't be home until three-thirty. She'd have to do her best to stay awake and groaned when she glanced at the clock. *Only six more hours.* "Ugh, shit."

The jingle of keys and click of the door jostled Evaine from her dream, and it took her a minute to keep her tired, burning eyes open, blinking a few times to clear the blur of sleep from them before she pushed her upper body off the table and glanced at the door.

"Hey there, Princess." Jacob crossed the room and ran a cool hand down her sheer-shirted back, making her shiver. "Did we fall asleep?"

Evaine smiled, wiping the drool from her mouth with the back of her hand before giving him a tired nod. "You're home early." Sleep edged her raspy voice and made her clear her dry throat with a cough.

"Early?" Jacob plopped into the chair next to her with a shrug. "It's three, Baby."

"Oh, shit." Evaine ran her hand through her mess of hair, "I must have fallen asleep," and then rubbed her eyes with her balled-up hands. "How was your date?"

"He was a hottie for sure!" Jacob's smile widened as he side-eyed her with a smirk. "And we made out a little, but." He pulled the collar of his T-shirt to the side and flashed a quick view of the purple hickey at the base of his neck, chuckling. "He certainly liked to use his teeth. Maybe a little too much."

Evaine furrowed her brow in confusion. "But I thought you like it when they used their teeth?"

"That's on my cock, Princess. I'm not a fifteen-year-old boy and could do without the hickeys, for fucksakes. What, do you think I am that kinda tramp?"

Evaine giggled. "A tramp? Never crossed my mind."

Jacob's eyes settled on the expensive vase of roses in the center of the table. "Flowers, huh?" He grinned like sin. "Did you finally let Gage stick it in your ass?"

"Ew, Jerk!" She tried to smack his arm, but he dodged, though she still landed a glancing blow to his bicep.

"Come on now, My Little Psychopath, we've talked about the abuse. You need to learn to keep your hands to yourself." He leaned away, rubbing the spot with his hand. "Besides, don't pretend like you don't like it."

Evaine chewed the end of her Merlot-colored index fingernail and grinned like the Cheshire Cat, baring her straight white teeth. "Still, ew!"

Jacob laughed and kissed the top of her head. "Whatever. Deny all you like; I know the truth." When he glanced at the clock, he groaned. "Ugh! It's time for bed. I've got class in 5 hours."

"Night, Jay."

Jacob ruffled his hand across the top of her head, making her hair an even bigger mess. "Night, Princess."

After watching him cross to his room and close the door, Evaine gathered her school stuff into her bag and hung it on the hook with her jacket before heading into the kitchen for a glass of water. She'd emptied most of it before she heard the jingle of keys outside the front door and downed the rest before setting the glass in the sink and meeting Gage as he slipped inside. He smiled. "Hey, Baby."

"Hey yourself." Evaine pushed on her toes and kissed his jawline.

His large hands wrapped around her waist, pulling her flush against his lean body until she felt every hard line. "I'm surprised you're still up." Cool hands wandered down her hips and hooked the back of her thighs to lift her, and she wrapped her legs around his waist as he easily lifted her. Face to face, he kissed her. "It's a pleasant surprise for sure."

The soft, quick kiss made her pulse bump just a little, and she draped her arms over Gage's shoulders, her fingers playing with the long strands of hair. "Thank you for the flowers," she said in the same silky tone and kissed him again.

A black eyebrow hitched in confusion as Gage jerked his head back. "What flowers?"

Confused, Evaine tilted her head at the dining room table. "The roses." Gage continued to look at her like she had two heads. Finally, she huffed, pointing at the flowers. "Those freaking flowers!"

As easily as he'd picked her up, he let her slide back down his body and strode to the table. "I didn't get you any flowers, Baby." Gage rifled through the twenty-four long stems, his eyes narrowing as he turned back to her. "Who are they from?"

The agitation in his tone was something she rarely heard; he was usually so level-headed and mellow about most everything. Her breath hitched, and tension spread along her shoulders as she closed the distance between them. "There was no card, so I thought they were from you." Evaine's gaze flicked from the flowers to Gage as she waited for him to say something helpful, but there was only an edge of anger in his eyes when he said, "That's two hundred dollars worth of roses from someone. Who would just buy you two hundred dollars worth of roses outta nowhere?"

Anger surged, her hands landing on her hips as she glared at him. "What are you trying to say?"

Gage chewed his lip ring for a second. "Seems you have a secret admirer, huh?" The thin silver bracelets on his wrist jingled together when he pointed at the flowers. "What were you doing to make them this interested in you, Baby?"

The way he said Baby made Evaine cross her arms over her chest and raise her voice in frustration. "Didn't you know I started stripping between classes for extra cash? Must have been one of my regulars."

"Don't be an asshole, Evie!"

"You're the asshole!" Evaine huffed when his jaw ticked. "You know that, right?"

Annoyed, Gage barked, "Really? The flowers aren't from my secret admirer, are they, Evie?" Anger swirled in his eyes as he spat her name, and she flinched even though she had nothing to be ashamed about. Disbelief and frustration chewed at the back of her brain, mixing with just a hint of fear. Evaine loved him more than anything and would never cheat, and it hurt that he didn't realize it. She also wanted to smack him upside the head for being so stupid.

As he stared, jealousy darkened his mint-green eyes to almost the same emerald as hers. Despite her rational mind saying no, it made her insides jelly, and her sad tone held a touch of lust. "I didn't do anything, Gage. I don't know who the freaking flowers are from." Her hands shook as she scooped the heavy vase from the table and pinned it against her chest.

When she headed to the kitchen, Gage crossed his arms. "Where are you going?"

"To throw them out!" She stomped across the open rooms. Water splashed from the vase onto her shirt, the coolness seeping through her tank top.

His tone softened. "Wait, Evie."

"Wait, nothing! I don't want them!" Evaine glared at him as she dumped the roses up-end over the trash can, water splashing the wall, floor, and the tops of her bare feet as she dropped the vase in the black-lined can with a loud thud. "I don't give a fuck who sent them. I don't fucking want them!" Her words came out louder than she intended, and her tone sounded unhinged even to her ears as she slammed her hands on her hips and fought to keep the stupid tears from falling.

A smirk ticked up the side of Gage's full mouth as he watched her meltdown. He was in front of her with a few enormous strides, his muscles flexing under his shirt. His strong hands slid over hers, grabbing her waist and setting her up on the counter, the hard marble jolting her spine, the cold from the stone seeping into her ass cheeks as he slid between her parted thighs. "Don't cry, Baby." His lips brushed her temple, his hands gripping the sides of her face to pull her gaze to his.

Jacob's door swung open with a whoosh, and he shoved his head out with a huff. "What the fuck is going on out here?" His tone was sleepy and annoyed.

"Nothin', Man. Sorry for the noise," Gage tossed over his shoulder without breaking their eye contact.

"Everything's fine. Go back to bed, Jay," Evaine assured him.

"Just keep it down, huh?" His voice was hoarse with sleep. "And no crazy kitchen sex. I cook on those fucking counters, you deviants."

The moment they heard the soft click of the door, Gage's lips were on hers, his tongue delving between them to infiltrate her mouth. He tasted like whiskey and smelled like stale cigarettes, but she wouldn't change a thing and moaned, kissing him back just as desperately. After a couple of minutes, he broke the kiss. "I'm sorry, Baby," he said against her lips, nipping at the bottom one, his half-lidded eyes flicking up to capture hers. "You forgive me for overreacting and being such an asshole?"

The bratty part of her wanted to give him a black eye to mar his perfect face. *Even Steven!* But the frown curling down the corners of his full mouth washed away any thoughts of revenge. She was never very good at staying mad at him and wanted his lips so badly she could taste them, her tongue unconsciously darting out to wet her own. "I would never cheat on you. You know that, right?"

Gage glanced at her lap before meeting her eyes and nodded. "Hence, why I'm an asshole." His usual sarcasm, combined with a hint of a smirk, dampened her thighs as his hands ran up her back.

Lust and exasperation collided inside when his nails skimmed her skin. "Gods! You drive me crazy!"

He kissed the sensitive spot under her right ear, his tongue flicking out to taste her flesh as her hands wrapped around his shoulders and her fingers twined in the long strands of hair at the back of his neck.

"Is that a yes?" He asked, trailing kisses along the column of her neck. She cocked her chin up to give him better access, closing her eyes and enjoying his mouth. Gage gripped her hips and pulled her flush against him. "It's a fucking yes," came out in a low, breathy moan, and she felt him smile against her skin, his hot breath skating over it while he worked his way along the edge of her jaw.

When Evaine's hands gripped the hem of his long-sleeve T-shirt and tugged, Gage gave her enough time to pull it over his head before his mouth was back on her neck and his fingers were working the buttons on the front of her shirt. Her hand slithered along the ridge of his collarbone and down his chest over Death's black and gray image inked there, with her smirking smile and fluff of black hair. Tight muscles fluttered under her tentative touch as he gave up on the buttons and yanked her shirt off her shoulder, nipping at the exposed skin.

His heated body felt good under Evaine's hand as she snaked it up his back and dug her nails into his shoulder blade, grinding against his cock through his leather pants.

With ease, he scooped her off the counter, his fingers biting into her ass as he carried her to their room. She wrapped her legs around his waist and crossed her ankles at the small of his back. Her arms around his neck, she kissed his jaw, cheek, and mouth before letting go long enough to turn the knob.

Gage kicked the door shut with his combat boot, letting her slide down his body in a way that made her aware of every ridge and plain, and watched her like a predator as he bent down to unzip and remove his combat boots.

Evaine loved when his eyes darkened with need but broke contact long enough to pull her shirts over her head and disregard them in a pile on the floor. She wore his favorite bra and panties; his tongue darted out and ran over the silver ring in the middle of his lip like he could eat her alive, making butterflies tickle her insides with anticipation.

When he straightened up, Gage reached for her. "Come here, Baby."

The simple words made all the heat in her limbs pool in the crux of her body, and things throb low in her belly. Evaine took his hand, humming softly as his heated body encircled her, her nails grazing over his back muscles and around his sides to his belt buckle.

He flinched and mumbled, "That tickles," before stealing a kiss. Evaine grinned against his mouth. "I know."

The silver metal studs of his belt felt warm from his kicked-up body temperature, her fingers adeptly maneuvering the buckle and then the button and zipper until she could slip her hand inside and stroke him. He was rigid and hot, and she loved how her touch made his cock jerk when her thumb grazed the head. Gage quickly freed her from her bra as she fondled him.

The desire to see him stripped down overwhelmed her. "Take these off." Evaine pulled on the open zipper, making him smirk as he bent to flick his tongue along her nipple before sucking it into his mouth. Hands at her waist worked to peel her leggings and panties off. Once he got them to her knees, she pushed them to the floor, the cool air making goosebumps prickle her naked skin as she ticked up the demand. "I said, take them off!"

Her impatient, spoiled brat tone made him chuckle around her nipple, and he bit hard enough to make her squeak before standing up with another smirk. "Yes, Ma'am." His words were a breathy sigh as he shoved the leather down his hips and pulled each leg off before discarding them.

Everything about Gage was beautiful. The way his hair fell in his face and his dark, lust-filled eyes. He chewed his lip ring as he watched her take him in, his cut arms and ridged abs, and her favorite part, the V of muscles pointing right down to his sizable cock.

The cock she wanted to taste so bad her mouth watered.

Evaine forced him down on the edge of the bed, his hands roaming up her legs, his fingers brushing the insides of her thighs on their way to the damp spot between. With unwavering determination, she wrapped her hands around his wrists, her finger catching on the rough row of scars that ran across them. He'd been a cutter in high school, his way of dealing with stress. But to her, the imperfections just made him that much more perfect.

"No touching." She pulled his hands free and kissed each of his scarred wrists before dropping to her knees between his spread legs, his cock jutting at her, demanding attention. Evaine enjoyed the ragged hisses as she licked the tip, her tongue swirling around the head like a lollipop before engulfing him with her mouth. It took some effort to take him all in, but the groan that rattled through him made it all worthwhile. His skin tasted like musk, with a hint of the citrus soap he used and the bitter smoke that permeated everything after working all night.

"Uh, Baby," he groaned, fisting his hands in her hair, and instantly, she wanted to make him come in her mouth and consume him, sliding her tongue along the pulsing vein on the underside of his shaft. He groaned louder when she upped the suction and picked up her pace, bobbing her head in his lap.

Within minutes, she felt the tension building in his body and him twitch as he inched closer to the release she intended to give him, his fingers wrapping in her hair and yanking the roots almost painfully. Unable to ignore her own building need, Evaine slipped her hand between her thighs, her fingers dipping into the wet heat and teasing sensitive flesh as they worked at the same pace as her mouth, sliding in and out.

Gage fisted her hair as he pulled her off his cock with a pop that almost made her giggle, if not for the fact her eyes were watering from the sting creeping across her skull and revving up her need. He jerked her body up with ease, his free hand covering the one between her thighs, his fingers joining hers. "Let me help you with that." Mischief glimmered in his eyes, and a jolt of excitement spread up her naked body, her thighs clenching around his talented fingers.

With the hold on her hair, he contorted her body, giving him access to her aching pussy and allowing him to clamp his mouth over her nipple. She squeaked, sucking in a quick breath as the friction became too much. Heat crept up her chest, flushing her face, and that heavy feeling of tension built low in her belly.

"Gage," she sighed, unable to control the gentle thrust of her hips as he fucked her with his skilled fingers.

In response, he nipped her flesh and growled, "I like it when you beg, Baby," around her nipple. His warm breath tickled the sensitive skin before his tongue smoothed over it. He slipped another finger inside, thrusting harder -- deeper, pulling a groan from her as she edged close to satisfaction. Her body teetered on the precipice, so close that she whined out a spoiled breathy, "NO!" when he pulled his hand from between her thighs and gripped the back of her knee to jerk her across his lap by her fire-red hair.

Despite disappointment at the loss of his touch, Evaine scrambled to keep up with his demands, fumbling as her trembling legs protested against the change of position. Gage cupped her ass, moving her exactly where he wanted her, which was on his cock. He rewarded her with a growl as she enveloped his length, burying him to the hilt before languishing her way to the tip again. Her body quivered around his rigidness as she tortured him with languid movements until his fingers un-twined from her hair to grip her hips, digging in as he guided her thrusts. He kicked up her pace and drove up into her harder, faster.

Evaine threw back her head with a breathy moan, letting him have his way with her body. Her fingers latched on to the long hair at the base of his neck. He made her feel small and out of control, and she relished it. Tension twitched in his shoulders, his hard thrusts turning more erratic and animalistic. Evaine gripped him tighter, chasing her satisfaction, his name falling from her lips in a panting opus to just how good he was at making her come. Her body bowed, her insides clenching around him as she found release. Stars burst behind her closed eyes, her mind splintering.

"Fuck, shit," he growled against the curve of her neck, biting at her throat as he punished her with a few quick, deep thrusts and spent himself inside her.

Evaine enjoyed the comfortable silence ticking by as they drifted back to reality. Gage's long fingers played with the loose curls stuck to the side of her sweaty face and neck, his heavy breathing sending warm breath across her neck and chest.

"I love you," she mumbled when she could find words.

Gage hugged her, kissing her collarbone. "I love you too, Baby." His lips traced the protruding bone. "Sorry about earlier. I just." He paused. "I overreacted."

Evaine ran her hand over his mussed purple hair, resting her cheek against the side of his face. "I kinda like it when you get all jealous."

Gage chuckled. "I'll keep that in mind."

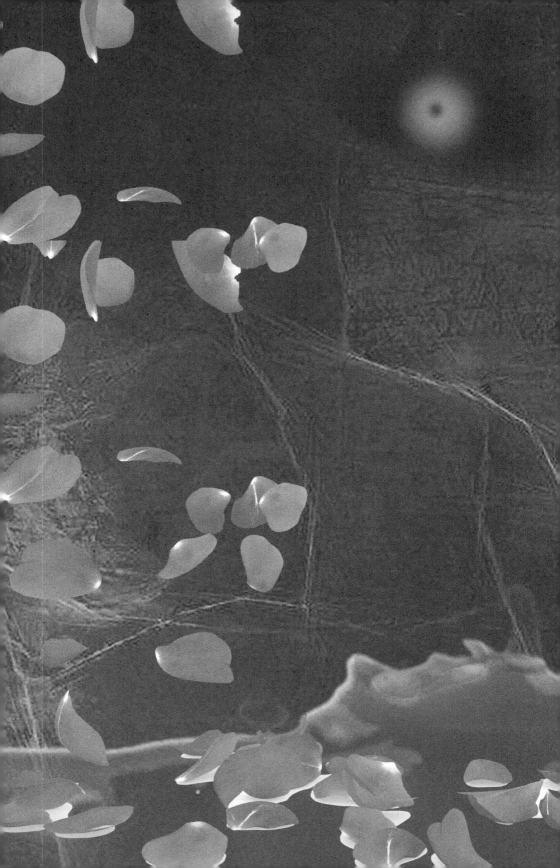

Chapter
Four

Four

Sunday Dinner & Bowler Hats

Her parents' house was too far away to walk. When the boys were with her, they always took the subway, but when she was alone, she wasn't overly comfortable on the subway, especially after dark. The underground tunnels made her feel trapped.

Tonight, she took a taxi down to the business district, flagging one down quickly. The driver was an older man who spoke broken English. Evaine didn't recognize his accent, but she appreciated the upbeat music he played during the ride and smiled when he glanced up through the rear-view mirror before shifting her gaze to the bustling streets as they eased by at a consistent pace.

Evaine's insides churned with excitement and dread as she worried her bottom lip. She always looked forward to seeing her dad and could even admit the idea of seeing her mother was okay, but something gnawed at her gut and jangled her nerves. Daddy always told her to listen to her gut, and right now, it said something wasn't right. Being followed and watched made her uncomfortable, and the unexplained flowers certainly put her on edge. She didn't like any of it.

As they turned onto her parents' street, Evaine stuck it away to deal with later because she needed to put her best foot forward for her father tonight.

Which meant pasting on a smile, laughing at cheesy jokes, and listening to her father ramble on about how proud he was of her or how awesome he was for building his business from nothing.

"Here you are, Miss." The driver pulled to the curb and jolted her from her thoughts. "That will be eleven-fifty."

Evaine shoved a twenty through the window into his waiting palm, "Thanks. Keep the change, and have a good night," before climbing from the cab.

After yesterday's conversation with her dad, Evaine dug into the back of her closet to find something presentable for tonight's family dinner. She settled on a knee-length black pencil skirt and a conservative, somewhat professional-looking silk blouse almost the same shade of purple as Gage's hair. She opted for thick black tights and dressier patent-leather platform Mary Janes, her fire-engine curls flowing down her back and framing her face. And finished the outfit with reasonable earrings and a necklace to match. Overall, she looked respectable.

Daddy will be pleased.

With her smile, she smoothed her straight skirt and headed for the lobby of the towering glass building.

To say her parents were wealthy was like saying Bill Gates did okay most days. Her father was from old money that spanned generations, not to mention he was one of the wealthiest mucky-mucks on Wall Street. Something to do with corporate finance. All Evaine knew was that he wore nice suits and sat in an office behind a computer all day. She never cared much because she lived a charmed life and didn't need to.

Evaine had many fond memories of growing up in this building and playing games with Jay when they were in middle school. When she crossed the threshold into the well-lit lobby, she heard a friendly voice echo across the open space, "Evening, Miss Maire."

"Hello, Markus. How have you been?" She smiled at the man as she crossed to the elevator.

"Good, good. Thanks for asking."

Evaine hit the button before facing the older man at the desk. "And your daughter? How's Amy?"

Markus lit up at the mention of his daughter, his broad smile gleaming from across the room. "She's wonderful. Just got engaged last month."

The elevator dinged as the doors opened.

"That's great to hear. Please send her my best." Evaine stepped into the car and swiped her keycard before pressing the penthouse button. The doors closed with a soft whoosh, and her stomach tugged down as the elevator shot up. Evaine didn't like elevators or tight spaces, and the feeling of falling made her incredibly uncomfortable. And this was the worst elevator she'd ever ridden, except maybe when Daddy took her to the Sears Tower. *That elevator sucked too! And fuck those glass floors!* She'd thrown quite a tantrum that day, and her mother needed at least three gin and tonics to get through the outing.

Evaine grabbed the bar to keep from bumping her hip on the wall when the elevator jolted to a stop, and the doors opened to the extravagant foyer. She swiped her key card on the pad next to the wide double doors, and they popped open with a soft click before she stepped inside.

"Daddy, Mom! I'm here!" She pulled her jacket off and hung it in the entry closet.

"Evie." Gwen's heels clicked across the marble floor as she came to hug her daughter, her gold bracelets jingling in Evaine's ear. Her strong floral perfume burned Evaine's nose and made her eyes water until her mother stepped back, inspecting her before flashing a half-smile that didn't reach her emerald-green eyes. "So good to see you. How're your classes going?" Gwen smoothed her shoulder-length carrot-orange hair, Evaine's natural color.

"Good. I'm just about done with my last assignment. All I have to do is get it into Word. I'll do that after class tomorrow while the boys are gone. That laptop Daddy bought me is too heavy to lug to class."

"Wonderful, Dear. Come sit down." Her mother's voice edged with disinterest as she crossed to the formal living room, her gray dress pants swishing in the silence. Her heels click-clacked, and her bracelets jingled like a warning signal, reminding Evaine of all the times her mother had almost caught her and Jacob doing something they weren't supposed to do. It was amazing how many times that click-clack and jingle saved their little asses from punishment.

Not surprised by her mother's tone, Evaine sighed, nostalgic for her youth. Even as a child, she never kept her mother's attention for long because Gwen didn't have the patience. Her father always made time for her, listening to silly stories and drinking imaginary tea. Those were Evaine's favorite childhood memories.

Instead of following her mother, Evaine headed for the bar and wasted no time mixing vodka with anything she could find in the small fridge under the black metal bar. *Grapefruit! Awesome!* "Would you like a drink, Mother?" she asked, to be polite.

Gwen smoothed the front of her pants as she glanced over the back of the couch. "Why don't you whip me up a gin and tonic, Sweetheart? Light on the Gin, though, please. You definitely inherited your father's heavy hand for mixing drinks."

Evaine ignored the critical tone and sharp words. "Coming right up."

"I thought I heard your voice, Princess." Her dad rounded the corner from his office as she finished at the bar and caught her in a hug before she could pick up the drinks. He smelled like cigar smoke and some outdoorsy scent, like pine. She nuzzled into him as he squeezed her, inhaling deeply. "Hi, Daddy."

Like her mother, he stepped back and surveyed her outfit, his lips ticking down in a slight frown when he reached Evaine's footwear choice. He expected her in the same boring black heels her mother wore, so of course, he disapproved of them.

Not happening, Daddy, no matter how much I love you!

He smiled when she caught his eyes. "You look beautiful, Evie."

Evaine wouldn't have spotted the lie if she didn't know him so well, but she let it slide, leaning up to kiss his cheek before grabbing the drinks. "Thank you, Daddy." She handed her mother her glass as she passed, her dad settling next to her mother on the couch. When she sat in one of the black wing chairs on the other side of the glass and metal coffee table, he asked, "So, how are the boys?"

She took a large sip of her drink, licking the tart juice from her lips. "They're good. Jacob got an A on his final performance piece, and Gage pulled off a B+ for his art history final." Evaine unconsciously scrunched her nose, making her dad grin.

"Just a B+? Maybe he isn't good enough for our little girl, after all." Chandler slid his arm along the back of the couch as Gwen sipped from the tall, frosted glass.

"He's plenty good enough." The alcohol warmed Evaine from her throat to her empty stomach as she took two large pulls from her drink and thought about how good he was last night. "Trust me."

Her father liked to joke and always found ways to give the boys a hard time. "Well, I guess we'll just have to keep an eye on him for now. Just a B+, really?"

Evaine clasped her hands in her lap, flashing her sweetest smile. "If I can live with a B+, you can too."

"You'd never settle for a B+," her mother said.

"Of course, she wouldn't; she's my daughter." Chandler chuckled as the housekeeper came around the corner and whispered in her mother's ear.

"Oh, excellent, Maria. Thank you."

"Everything on track, Gwen?" Chandler asked his wife.

"Yes, yes. Everything is fine. Maria was just informing me that Markus called from downstairs." She looked at her watch. "Seems your guest is a little early. He's sending him up as we speak."

As if on cue, the doorbell chimed, and Chandler's face lit up. "And there he is!" He pushed from the couch and rounded it on his way to the door. "Now, remember, this is a great opportunity for our company. He has quite a few ventures that could make us a ton of money if we invest with him."

Gwen waved him along like she'd done this a million times, which is probably exactly how many times she has done this dog and pony show. Truly, Evaine loved her parents, but she never wanted to become them. She was sure they loved each other but couldn't ignore that they seemed to be in a rut for the last ten years.

"Tristan! So glad you made it."

Before Evaine saw their guest, she heard his heavy British accent. "Good evening, Mr. Maire. It was easy enough to navigate."

"Glad to hear it. Let me take your coat," Chandler said as Mr. Basile handed him his long, black trench coat, and he hurriedly hung it next to Evaine's in the hall closet. When he stepped back, he gave her a glimpse of the man in the doorway. A charcoal gray bowler hat sat atop his well-trimmed chocolate hair, and he wore a well-tailored matching pin-striped suit, as if he'd just stepped out of some classic British drama, and shiny pointed dress shoes.

Evaine had to admit he wore them with a dashing style that made her think more men should dress like him. The hat was good, too, though it wasn't likely that Gage or Jay could pull off a bowler hat. But maybe with the proper suits. *Who am I kidding?* She'd never get either of those boys in suits, short of her funeral, and quickly concluded they would look silly in bowler hats, chuckling as her parents fawned over their guest.

"So nice to meet you. Mr. Basile," Gwen said when their guest turned his attention to her.

Tristan gave her a sharp nod and a genuine smile as he reached for her hand and bent to kiss her fingers. When his eyes flicked up and locked with her mother's, Evaine saw the flush of red that traveled up her neck and across her cheeks, as if his mere touch warmed her skin. Tristan was an attractive man, and she really couldn't slight her mother. But he couldn't be more than a few years older than her and looked too young to be as affluent as her father indicated. She wondered if Tristan had inherited his money. Either way, he was much too young for her mother to be fawning over.

"The pleasure is mine. Lovely to finally meet you. Chandler has talked a lot about you." When he glanced over at Evaine, his hazel eyes seemed to drink her in from head to toe. Her breath hitched in her throat and her face flushed. "Both of you." His dark eyes sparkled with an edge of mischief like Jacob's did when he was up to no good, and she smiled from across the room and earned a wink that made her giggle like a schoolgirl. Although Jacob would have done something similar, this guy wasn't your typical twenty-something.

As Tristan dropped her mother's hand, Chandler said, "Could I offer you a drink before dinner?"

"Whiskey neat would be ideal."

"Come join us in the living room, Mr. Basile, while Chandler pours your drink. This is our daughter, Evaine," her mother said as they drew closer.

That was her queue to turn on the charm, so she pushed from her seat and shook his hand. "Nice to meet you, Mr. Basile, was it?"

His hazel eyes locked with hers, a smile turning the corners of his thin lips. "Yes, Basile, but you can call me Tristan." He smiled wider, flashing his straight white teeth as he reached for her outstretched hand. "In fact, I insist you call me Tristan, My Dear." His canines were a little longer than the rest of his even teeth, and his fingers colder than hers. Which was saying something, considering. When he drew hers to his lips, she resisted the urge to pull them from his hand.

"Nice to meet you then, Tristan. My father tells me you are in town for business." *Gods!* She sounded like an idiot or, worse, her mother. Suddenly, she despised her father for making her deal with this stupid shit and wondered why she was still part of this dog and pony show. *I'm an adult, damn it! He was sorely mistaken if* her dad thought she could entice Tristan into investing with him.

I sure as hell hope not! She'd tolerate this little charade but drew the line there.

"Some business, some pleasure." His voice was rich and swirled around her as he pinned her with hazel eyes, lulling the urge to escape his touch. Instead, she wanted to swim in the greenish-brown pools as the tension melted away and her body relaxed. "What kind of pleasure?" rolled off her tongue in a whisper, like they were long-time friends or even lovers.

Tristan rewarded her with a smirk and rubbed his fingers over hers. "Perhaps we can discuss that at length after our meal." His seductive tone sent heat spreading up Evaine's chest and neck, her cheeks flushing bright red as his gaze captivated her until Daddy rescued her by rounding the bar and handing Tristan a half-full crystal tumbler of whiskey.

"Tristan, your drink." Chandler seemed oblivious of the encounter and cupped the younger man on the shoulder like they were old friends.

Relief washed over Evaine when he dropped her hand to take the glass. With his mesmerizing gaze focused squarely on her father, Evaine settled into the black wing chair and tried to tamp down the electricity strumming through her.

"Please, have a seat." Chandler motioned to the chair next to Evaine.

"Of course." Tristan moved silently and was sitting before she had a chance to look up from her drink.

Who is this guy?

Chandler took a sip of whiskey. "So, let me tell you a little about our newest venture. I think it would be something you'd definitely be interested in."

After a few more minutes of her dad droning on about something she had no interest in, Evaine was ecstatic to see Maria come around the corner and clasp her hands behind her back. "Dinner is served."

When Gwen said, "Very good, thank you," Maria gave a slight nod and then headed back the way she came.

"Well, let's continue this conversation in the dining room, shall we?" Gwen popped out of her seat with way more enthusiasm than Evaine had seen from her in years. As she passed, she held her hand out. "Come along, Dear."

Evaine smoothed her skirt before taking her mother's hand and allowed Gwen to lead her around the couch and into the large doorway. Chandler and Tristan followed close behind, her father still discussing some revitalization project.

They decorated the dining room in the same modern style as the rest of the house. Her parents had a thing for black and white and shiny silver. The top of the table was glass with sleek metal legs wrapped under each end, reminding Evaine of the smooth chrome hand bars of the purple bike she had in elementary school. A large vase of white lilies sat in the center of the enormous table, and ten chairs made from the same sleek metal, with smooth black leather seats, around it. Even though the table was probably older than her, it was in pristine condition because they didn't use it very much when she was growing up, opting instead to use the smaller table in the kitchen.

Chandler sat at the head of the table with Gwen on his left, which put Evaine on his right. When she reached the chair, Tristan was already pulling it out.

"Thank you," she said as he helped her tuck in.

"Most welcome." He tipped his square chin with a slight nod before smoothing his jacket and sitting next to her.

Though Tristan looked close to her age, his accent and how he spoke made him seem much older and more worldly. He piqued her curiosity, and without thinking, she said, "Daddy told me you and I are close to the same age. Is that true?"

Tristan hitched a sleek eyebrow. "I just turned twenty-three a few weeks ago."

"I'm turning twenty-one on the twenty-seventh." Evaine smiled.

"Twenty-one is a fun age." Tristan straightened his silver cuff link. "Hopefully, you have something good planned."

"Hanging with my best friend. We are going to Eucharist."

"Hmm." Tristan grinned. "That's interesting. My firm just bought that building. We hope to renovate the basement and expand the maximum capacity of the building. We are working closely with the tenet, but it should be profitable for everyone."

Yeah, not your typical twenty-three-year-old.

"So you live in the States?" Evaine asked without missing a beat. *Curiosity killed the cat, right?*

Tristan chuckled. "I have a home here, but I don't spend much time there. London is home for this old chap." He sipped his whiskey as Maria and Stanley brought the covered plates from the kitchen.

"London was quite nice when we visited, despite the rain. But Paris! It's so pretty in the springtime." Her lashes brushed her cheeks as she glanced at her lap. "My parents took me there when I graduated from high school. I haven't had the chance to get back, but I'd like to one day. Maybe after I get my degree."

Tristan cocked his head away from her. "Yes, I understand you will graduate soon." His hazel eyes made her squirm in her seat as Marie set a covered plate in front of him. "Your father has mentioned you want to be a writer."

"One more week, and I'm done. I'm looking forward to it, to be honest." Evaine side-eyed her father as Maria set the other plate in front of her. "I'm sure Daddy will push me to get a master's." Evaine sipped her vodka and grapefruit.

"Of course, I will." Chandler chuckled as Stanley set the covered plate down in front of him.

Steam wafted as Stanley lifted the lid on the silver-domed plate in front of Gwen before following Maria from the room.

"I'm giving you fair warning, Daddy. I'm going to hold out as long as I can."

Tristan lifted the lid from his plate and set it aside, inhaling the steam rising from his meal. Chandler loved Fillet Mignon, so it was no surprise that a medallion of rare meat sat on the black plate with a baked potato and steamed broccoli.

Man, I'm hungry! She followed Tristan's lead, revealing her delicious plate of food, her mouth watering as she grabbed her napkin and unfolded it in her lap.

"It's important to take some time to live a little, Evaine. All work and no play make for a very dull time." He already had his knife and fork in hand, cutting into the bloody meat.

"Trust me, Tristan, she does plenty of playing. In fact, she has her annual Halloween party coming up in the next two weeks. Right, Dear?" Gwen asked as she picked up her steak knife.

Mouth full of broccoli, Evaine nodded, chewing before she swallowed it. "Next week, after finals. It's gotten so large we had to find a bigger venue. It's always fun, and I'm super excited."

"See, now that's the right kind of fun." Tristan grinned as he bit into the meat, red juices bleeding onto his thin lip as his canine punctured it.

"That reminds me, Evie. Tristan mentioned he has an employment opportunity. I thought you might be interested. What was it again, Tristan?" Chandler forked a sizeable chunk of beef into his mouth.

Tristan wiped his with the napkin and pulled a long sip from his tumbler. "I am searching for a personal assistant while here in the States. It is a full-time job. Monday through Friday and may require a weekend day from time to time as needed for business. But of course, I would compensate you well for your private time." He paused. "It would also require traveling with me on business when needed."

After graduating, Evaine planned to finish one of the many half-written books she'd been working on for the last few years. With school behind her, she could focus on finally getting something published.

"Sounds like a wonderful opportunity, Dear. You really should consider it." Gwen shot Evaine a loaded look and filled her mouth with steamed broccoli.

Ugh! Why does she always put me on the spot? Evaine wiped the corner of her mouth and smiled at Tristan. "It sounds like a wonderful opportunity, for sure. I'm just not sure what I want to do when I finish school."

"I agree with your mother on this one, Princess. You should really consider the opportunity. Tristan is a prominent businessman, and it wouldn't hurt to have the extra experience to put on your resume."

Tristan sipped his whiskey as her parents pushed her in the direction they thought was best, smiling when her father glanced at him, his canines peeking from under his lip.

After a tick, his eyes caught hers. "How about you come to my office and check it out? You could spend a few hours with me to see exactly what it entails before deciding. How does next Monday, the twenty-eighth, sound?"

Evaine felt her parents' eyes on her, her father's especially, boring into the back of her head. Her first instinct was to decline. But looking at the gentlemen beside her, she found it impossible. As a nagging urge tugged her, she met his smile with one of her own. "That sounds great."

"Wonderful!" He sounded pleased and fished a hand into his jacket pocket before handing her a smooth, white business card. "Here is the address. I'll expect you promptly at four p.m." His lips turned up in a grin almost as wicked as her best friends. "I do my best work after dark."

Evaine giggled, setting the card on the table next to the plate.

Once she'd agreed to visit Tristan, the rest of dinner passed silently as everyone cleared their plates. Tristan favored the steak over the potato and broccoli left untouched but only ate a few bites. Evaine cleared her plate and finished her drink, fidgeting with the edge of Tristan's business card as her father finished his meal and tossed his napkin on his plate.

"Delicious as always, Maria. Stanley outdid himself." Chandler complimented and then turned his attention to his guest as Maria cleared his plate. "Tristan, I have a bottle of Glenmorangie in my office that you must try." When her father stood, he kissed the top of her head and then said, "Come join me for a glass," to Tristan

"Sounds wonderful." Tristan stood and reached out his hand.

Evaine hesitated a tick but gave him her fingers and was surprised when he helped her to her feet like a gentleman and leaned down to brush his lips along her knuckles. The simple touch sent a shiver down her spine as his cool breath tickled her skin. "It was very nice to meet you, Evaine. I look forward to our meeting next week. I implore you to have a wonderful birthday, My Dear."

She had to clear her throat to find her words. "You as well. I will do my best." Evaine smiled. "I'll see you next week."

"Night, Evie," her father shot over his shoulder before heading through the door to his office.

"Love you, Daddy."

Once her father and Tristan were behind closed doors, Evaine's mother stood from the table, leaving her mostly uneaten meal for Maria to clear. "I'm glad you could join us tonight, Dear."

"Me too." It wasn't quite a lie, but it wasn't the truth. "But I need to get back to studying for my exams."

"Of course, Dear." Gwen led Evaine out of the dining room and across the living room to the door. "I wanted to remind you we are spending our anniversary in Italy again this year and planning to leave on the first."

"I figured."

With a frown, her mother said,. "Your father wants to attend your party, so we pushed it a day." Frustration edged her voice like she'd lost that argument, making Evaine wonder why it was so important for them to leave early. Or maybe her mother just didn't like it when Daddy made her a priority. It was gone so quickly that Evaine thought she imagined it as her mother opened the closet and handed Evaine her jacket.

"Make sure you take a cab, not the subway."

Evaine slipped into her long velvet jacket. "I was planning to take a cab."

Her mother nodded and opened the front door. "Good night, Dear."

"Good night, Mother." Evaine kissed her cheek and headed for the elevator.

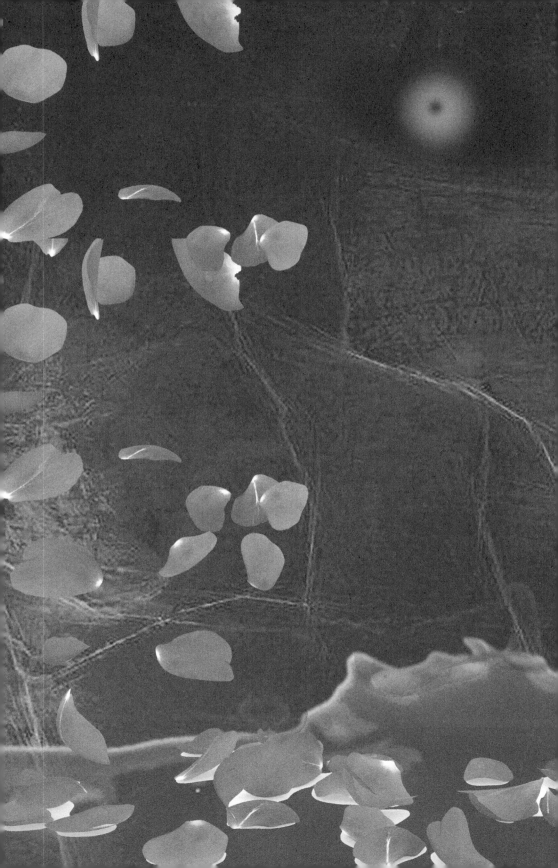

Chapter *Five*

Five

Dread & Diamonds

E vaine turned in her paper three days ago and finished her last final yesterday. Now that the research books were finally returned to the library, everything was finished. An enormous weight lifted off her shoulders as she walked off campus for the last time, accomplishment and pride washing over her as she crossed the street and headed toward Central Park. She was supposed to meet Jacob there at eleven. If she hurried, she wouldn't be too late and picked up the pace.

They'd agreed to meet at the Alice in Wonderland statue at the far end of the park. This was about the time Evaine wished they'd chosen something closer, like Haddlestone Arch. It would've saved her legs a lot of pain. But even her protesting muscles couldn't dampen her fantastic mood.

I'm done!

She was proud of graduating with honors in the top five percent of her class and smiled as she jogged along the path, trying to make up time. Jacob would wait for her, but he'd also complain about it, like the prissy bitch he was.

Even with alternating between jogging and brisk walking, it took her fifteen more minutes to get to the statue, which was her favorite one in the park. The madness and mayhem of the Alice story drew her. She loved the darker undertones of the queen and the hatter and wanted to write a haunting and exquisitely dark version of it.

I'll have time to do that now!

Jacob sat on the bench to the right of Alice and her friends, and when Evaine saw him, she jogged up and dropped next to him. "Before you bitch, recognize that I jogged my ass just for you! Do you see this sweat?" She pointed at her glistening forehead before wiping the back of her hand across it.

He flipped his long hair back off his shoulder, cocking his head and smirking, his sea-green eyes hidden behind wide black sunglasses. "Well, that was very sweet of you, considering." He pulled up his sleeve enough to look down at the heavy silver watch wrapped in a thick leather band around his wrist. "You're only twenty minutes late." His tone was sharp and flippant.

"You can't be mean to me today, Jerk!" she huffed, pointing at her chest over her snug-fitting, black-and-green striped hoodie. "Birthday girl, damn it!"

He put his hands up in surrender. "Okay, okay. Going right to the, it's my birthday card, huh? Cheap move, Princess."

Like he wouldn't do the same thing!

When he leaned in to kiss Evaine's cheek, she pivoted her head to catch the corner of his mouth and grinned. "Where do you think I learned it from?"

Jacob chuckled, then forced a solemn face as he side-eyed her. "I hate you sometimes." His delivery was as deadpan as he could manage without cracking his serious veneer.

"I know, but I really don't care. I just want the celebratory cream puff you promised me!"

"Yeah, yeah." He pushed from the bench, mumbling, "You're a fucking cream puff," as he smoothed the front of his Siouxsie and the Banshees shirt, her heavily lined eyes staring out from his chest under her fluff of black hair.

It was a chilly day, but the sun was bright, and Evaine shielded her eyes with her hand to look at him. "Wasn't that your last boyfriend's pet name for you?"

A grin spread across his face as he reached down and pulled her to her feet. "Don't you know it? There's no shame in my game, Baby."

Evaine loved how his hand enveloped hers as they walked toward the side gate. The park always reminded her of all the crazy adventures they'd had when they were younger, not to mention the trouble they got into for wandering off. Ms. Lebowitz got so angry when they disappeared, especially when they came back covered in dirt from head to toe.

Landuree's was just a couple of blocks, and she could already taste their amazing vanilla pastry creme. "Don't let me forget to grab an eclair for Gage. Otherwise, I'll never hear the end of it."

When the light changed, Jacob nodded and pulled her across the busy street. "He was sleeping when I left."

"Yeah, well, I kinda kept him up a little too late last night." Her pulse bumped at the thought of him naked in their bed, all mussed and worn out.

Jacob glanced over his shoulder and said, "You're such a dirty girl," loud enough to make the older couple walking next to her look over with distaste. All she could do was shrug her shoulders and wave at them with an innocent smile.

After two blocks, they reached the small pastry shop, the green and white fabric of the building's awning snapping in the gust that whipped around them before they stepped inside the warm shop that was almost empty, which meant they could get their treats and sit down at one of the small white tables to enjoy their coffee. Well, Jacob had coffee. Evaine opted for Landuree's legendary hot cocoa. It was her favorite. She took a big bite of her cream puff and washed it down with chocolaty goodness. "Oh, my gods," she groaned as the creamy sweetness danced on her tongue.

"That good, huh?" Jacob stirred his coffee.

Evaine nodded with her mouth full and then swallowed the bite. "We really need to come here more often."

"I'm not sure either of our asses needs more cream puffs." Jacob took a small sip of his coffee, his sharp nose wrinkling as he swallowed.

Evaine pointed her powdered-sugar covered fingers at his untouched Praline Millefeuille. "Are you going to eat that?"

Jacob kicked up his well-groomed eyebrow and side-eyed it like it would bite him, his nose wrinkling. "Nah, my stomach's been off the last few days, and I'd rather not risk it since we'll be celebrating, like a bunch of heathens tonight."

"You're not allowed to be sick on my birthday." Evaine pushed her bottom lip out in a pout before frowning. "Seriously though, I'm sorry you're not feeling well. Maybe it's the flu or something."

"Probably is, this time of year." Jacob took a small sip of his coffee as he watched her shove the other half of her puff into her wide-open mouth.

"Your mother would be so proud." He blew on the steaming hot liquid. "Such a lady."

Evaine shot him the finger before trying to dust the powder off her black legging but only made it worse, white dots turning to streaks as she groaned with annoyance.

"I can't take you anywhere, can I, Princess?" He handed her his extra napkin.

A muffled "Birthday" was all she managed with her mouth full. They had rules about birthdays, and he was breaking them.

He shot her a droll look and then nodded before taking another sip of coffee and watching her chew.

Once she finished her cocoa, Jacob shoved his coffee away and jutted his chin at the pristine praline pastry he'd been ignoring. "Why don't you take that home for Gage? I'm sure he'll eat it."

After adding his un-eaten pastry to her glossy pink to-go box, they took a taxi home.

It was just after twelve-thirty when Jacob unlocked the door to their apartment.

"What time's dinner with your parents?" He tossed his keys and sunglasses in the bowl next to the door while Evaine dropped the shiny pink box from Landuree's on the kitchen counter before she headed toward her bedroom. "It's an early dinner, so we have to be there at four." She slipped inside and gently closed the door.

Gage's soft snores filled the quiet room, his long, lean body sprawled out. One of his toned legs peeked from under the black sheet and heavy purple comforter; the black and gray Giger's Alien Queen inked on his calf, glaring at her. He had one hand thrown over his eyes, and the other stretched across her side of the bed. Gage looked so peaceful and perfect she didn't want to wake him. But he wasn't the only one tired from last night. Evaine yawned as she sat on the edge of the bed to untie her black converse all-stars, lining them up at the foot before standing up to unzip her fitted hoodie and strip it off. Her powder-streaked leggings were next, and she kicked them into the same pile.

Evaine tried not to wake Gage as she climbed into bed but had to move his arm enough to settle against his side. The heat coming off his naked body made her hum with appreciation, and he stirred when she rested her head on his chest and laid her chilled leg over his, pulling her closer like he always did. "Hey, Baby. What time is it?" His voice was rough with too little sleep, and she loved the raspy edge.

"Around twelve-thirty." She kissed his chest. "I didn't mean to wake you."

"It's okay," Gage mumbled, still groggy, and rolled onto his side, wrapping his arms around Evaine and tucking her against him. He kissed the top of her head. "Happy Birthday," came out slurred and partly under his breath, but it didn't matter; it still made her smile. She didn't think he could get much more amazing if he tried, as she closed her eyes and snuggled into his warmth. "Thanks." Her body relaxed as sleep crept over it, and Gage's soft snores lulled her toward the edge of dreams.

In that wonderful dream-like space where she wasn't awake but not sleeping, Evaine felt warm fingers roam down her bare stomach, rousing her. They slid along her side and over her hip, tracing the line of satin material as they crossed under her belly button, full lips grazing the shell of her ear. She moaned softly, forcing her tired eyes open a crack.

A very awake Gage smiled, "Hey, Sleepyhead," his hand slithering under the band of her panties, long fingers caressing the sensitive crease of her thigh and working their way lower. A muffled "Mmm" stuck in her throat as she stretched like a napping cat who had her belly rubbed. Her eyes struggled to stay open, but her body lit up when he dipped two fingers inside her. Lust thrummed up her spine, a heaviness building low in her belly as she ran her fingers over the ridge of his cheek before her thumb toyed with the silver ring in his bottom lip. He kissed the end of her finger. "Morning," she said before dropping her eyes to watch his hand work between her thighs, the effort pulling another moan from her dry throat.

"You like that, Birthday Girl?" Gage leaned on his elbow and smirked, looking quite satisfied with himself before capturing her lips in a soft kiss. His fingers stroked her wet slit, sliding in and out at an excruciatingly slow pace. When his thumb teased her clit, she sucked in a quivering breath, her body arching as he hit just the right spot. Tension coiled with the promise of sweet torture creeping over her.

"Yes." She barely formed the word before he stole her mouth again, his tongue invading. Her hands laced into his hair, pulling the long strands at the back as she returned the kiss with the same brutality. He rewarded her with a low growl that ignited the tension further, like tossing gasoline on a lit fire. Her body combusted as he picked up the pace. His fingers moved faster -- harder, making her shamelessly pant his name and grind against him as he fucked her.

Gage's lips skimmed up her jaw to her ear, where he whispered, "Say it again," which liquefied her insides even more if that was possible. Her hips bucked to meet the downward thrust of his fingers, his name tumbling from her as she did as she was told.

When he shifted against her, his cock nudged her hip, and all she wanted was to touch him, make him gasp and moan, to torture him in the same way he relentlessly made her suffer. But when she reached for him, he pulled away from her ear and shook his head, the corner of his mouth quirking up. "Nope, no touching." Evaine blew out a frustrated huff and dropped her hand.

Pleased, the jerk chuckled. "That's my good little birthday girl." His thumb brushed back and forth over the swollen, needy flesh between her thighs, making her fist up the sheets and beg him.

"Are you gonna come, Baby?" *Still smug.*

Evaine met his mint-green eyes and nodded, pulling her bottom lip between her teeth. A humming moan was all she could manage; her body strung so tight it felt like it was about to snap. His fingers slowed. "I wanna hear you say it, Evie." He rocked his hips again, his silky cock stroking against her.

"Gods," she hissed, gripping the wrist between her thighs and digging her nails into his scarred flesh. "Yes." Goosebumps burst over her skin as his tongue ran up the curve of her ear, his warm breath tickling it when he said, "That wasn't so hard, was it?"

The crux of her thighs throbbed, her insides clenching with the need for him to continue, to bring her the reprieve she needed so badly. Instead, he slowed his pace, his fingers torturing her with slow thrusts and tentative flicks. The flex of his wrist as she rode his cruel fingers harder strung her tighter and made her pant, but it wasn't enough to take her over.

Not above begging, she panted a breathy, "Fuck, Gage, please," as she dug her nails deeper into his skin.

"Oh, yeah, there it is- the magic word." There was humor in his voice, his fingers thrusting deep inside of her and hooking into the spot he knew would push her over the edge.

"Oh, gods!" Tension snapped, her body bowing, her thighs clenching around their hands. Evaine pitched over the edge. Trembling, her body writhed.

When she finally opened her eyes, Gage's sparkled with smugness. "Happy Birthday, Baby." He kissed her softly before laying back on his pillow.

"Mmm. Thanks."

Long bangs fell into Gage's eyes as he turned his head. "Did you enjoy your gift?"

"It was nice," she mumbled as she worked to slow her breathing, her hand snaking out to run along the deep V of his pelvis on its way to his cock. When Gage picked up her wrist and moved her hand as her fingers wrapped around him, she frowned.

He shook his head before dropping it. "I have another gift for you, and that isn't it."

She watched his back flex as he climbed out of bed, his exquisite ass and thighs making her push out a pout as he crossed to the dresser. "Why not?"

His hair hung in his eyes as he glanced over his shoulder, his tongue darting out to toy with the ring in his lip as he smirked. "Really, Baby, I'll fuck you until you're screaming my name if that's what you want." His large hand scooped up a brightly wrapped gift the perfect size of a book, and Evaine's excitement ticked up a notch. "But I wanna give you this first. Are you gonna be able to control yourself?"

She sat up. "Don't be an ass."

Gage settled in next to her, sprawling his long body out before handing her the gift.

Interest flickered. "What is it?"

His bracelets jingled as he shoved his hand behind his head, his bent elbow resting against the black leather-covered headboard as he smiled. "Open it and see."

As a child, Evaine always loved her birthday. So much that she talked her parents into having two parties, one on the day and her Halloween party. It gave her two chances to celebrate and get gifts, not that she went without much, considering how badly Daddy spoiled her. Those were impressive, but something about Gage's gifts made her little black heart melt. He always knew exactly what she wanted.

Her fingertips worked the edge of the neatly wrapped box, ripping away the sparkling purple paper. "Is it a book?" she asked when she shook it. "It's heavy enough to be a book."

Gage shook his head, laughing at her excitement. "Open the damn thing and see."

Evaine set it on top of her thighs and removed the lid before pulling back the black tissue paper wrapped around it. "I knew it was a book!" When she opened the hardcover, her excitement increased tenfold. "Oh, my gods! I can't believe you found this!" It wasn't just any book; it was one of her favorite books, Lost Souls by Poppy Z. Brite.

"It's a signed, first edition."

She set the book down and leaned in to kiss him. "It's freaking amazing is what it is!" And then she kissed him harder.

When she broke the embrace, he licked his lips. "I'm glad you like it."

"I love it. Thank you, Gage. If you thought I wanted to fuck you a few minutes ago, you won't believe how much I want to now!" She grinned and crawled over him with an easy shift of her lithe body, settling atop his half-erect cock.

"Why don't you remind me?" Gage's large hands skimmed her hips before slithering along her sides and under the swell of her breast to the front of her bra. But just as they found the clasp, there was a hard rap on the door.

"Evie, you might wanna come out here and see this shit." Jacob's tone was serious enough it stopped Gage in his tracks.

"I'm kinda busy, Jay. Can it wait?" she asked over her shoulder, her fire-red hair tickling her face as she shifted.

"No, Princess. I don't think it can wait. I mean. Well. Nah, I think you wanna come out here now."

Gage cocked a dark eyebrow. "You better find out what he wants."

She squeaked when he lifted her off him and set her feet on the floor, grabbing her robe from the hook on the bathroom door as she passed and wrapping it around her half-naked body as she stomped toward the door. "It better be fucking important, or I'm going to choke his ass."

Gage laughed, grabbing his boxers and climbing into them.

"Yeah, I'm gonna kill him," she huffed as she watched him dress, his hand running through his purple hair before following her.

"What's so-" The words died on her tongue as her eyes landed on the five vases of long stem roses on their dining room table. Dread churned in her gut, and she fisted her hands at her sides, trying to control the wave of nausea lodged in her throat.

"What the hell is this?" Gage stepped around Evaine and rifled through the flowers.

"Don't know, Man." Jacob shrugged

"No card," Gage said with an edge of frustration.

"Of course not," Evaine snapped sharply. "Just like last time."

Jacob pointed at the rectangle jewelry box sitting between the vases. "There's that."

Anger churned in Gage's eyes, but she appreciated that he was trying to keep his cool. He jutted his chin toward the package, his fists flexing much like hers had moments ago. "I'd like to know exactly who I'm going to have to kill. Maybe they were stupid enough to sign that card. Open it."

"I don't care who sent it." She closed the distance between them, gripping his forearm. "It's all going in the trash."

He pulled her hand into his, lacing their fingers together. "Just open it, Baby, or I will."

"Fine." Evaine pulled her hand free and snatched the small box with the card taped to the bottom off the table. The hinge creaked as she forced the velvet cover rectangle open and stared at the expensive bracelet tucked inside. It was a beautiful antique-looking piece with intricate swirls of silver and diamonds along the bands connected to a larger, more intricate diamond-shaped face. A large, deep green stone sat in the center of the face with two smaller but still prominent diamonds framing it.

"Holy shit," Evaine mumbled, eyeing the thing in disbelief, and felt the heat coming off Gage's chest when he stepped behind her and growled, "What the fuck?"

Evaine snapped the lid shut and tossed the box back on the table. "It doesn't matter. I'm not keeping it."

Gage picked up the card and shoved it into her hand. "Open it."

His tone was lethal, dark, something she'd never heard, and made her hands shake as she fumbled with the lip of the envelope, acid eating her insides.

Unlike Gage, Evaine didn't care who it was from. When she finally freed the card, she read it and swore, "For fucksakes!"

Unable to stand to look at the neat cursive writing for a moment longer, she threw the card back on the table. Gage snatched it up. "Nearly as beautiful as your emerald eyes. Birthday Wishes." He flipped it around, "No fucking signature," then discarded it with an angry flick of his wrist and glared at her.

Under his hard stare, heat flushed her chest and face, and she glanced at Jacob to save her. But he just stood there, looking dumbfounded for a minute before clearing his throat. "I don't even know what to say, Evie. That's fucked up."

Evaine forced a small smile. "Tell me about it."

"You've gotta know this guy, Evaine." Gage paced behind her, his bracelets jingling as he combed his fingers through his hair repeatedly. "Think about it really hard."

Oh, shit! He used her full name; that was never good. Tension ran along her spine and up into her shoulders. "Don't you think I'd tell you if I knew?"

"It's gotta be someone you know. They know your birthday, for shitsakes."

"Alright, well, I'm gonna leave you guys to talk. I need to shower before dinner." Jacob booked it out of the living room.

"Thanks," she mouthed as he shot her one last look before closing the bathroom door and leaving her to deal with a wound-up Gage, who gripped her shoulder and caught her eyes with a serious gaze. "Really think about it, Baby. Has there been anyone at school that seemed odd or out of place? At the library when you were working on your paper?"

"No, I don't remember anyone." Evaine thought for a few minutes. "I had something odd happen in the library the other day. Someone left a single rose on the table, and it felt like they were watching me while I was working. You know that feeling when someone's eyes are on you? But I didn't see anyone when I looked around. That was right before the first vase came."

"You didn't tell me about that." He crossed his arms and narrowed his eyes.

"You weren't exactly open to discussion that night."

He frowned, his gaze flicking to the floor for a tick. "I apologized for that, Evie."

Evaine grabbed his hand and tugged it, lacing her fingers into his. "I know that, Gage. I'm just explaining, not blaming." She squeezed his fingers. "Birthday."

Gage half-smiled and nodded, "Birthday," his shoulders slumping slightly as he tugged their clasped hands. "Come here, Baby."

Evaine slipped into his arms without hesitation, wrapping hers around his waist. "What are we going to do?" she asked against his warm chest.

His arms encircled her. "I don't know yet, but I need you to be careful until we figure it out. Whoever it is, they aren't playing around, Evie. That bracelet is nothing to fucking sneeze at."

The warmth of Gage's body and his fingers combing through her mess of hair lulled her back from the edge of the panic attack threatening to take over. She closed her eyes and focused on slowing her breathing.

A few silent moments ticked by before she looked up at him. "I love you."

He smirked. "How could you not, Baby?" Even though she felt like she'd lose it, he made her smile and gave her another squeeze. "It's almost three. We need to get ready to meet your parents."

Evaine nodded and let him lead her toward their room to shower and change, trying to ignore the foreboding feeling eating at the back of her brain. She glanced back at the blood-red flowers one last time before shutting the door behind her.

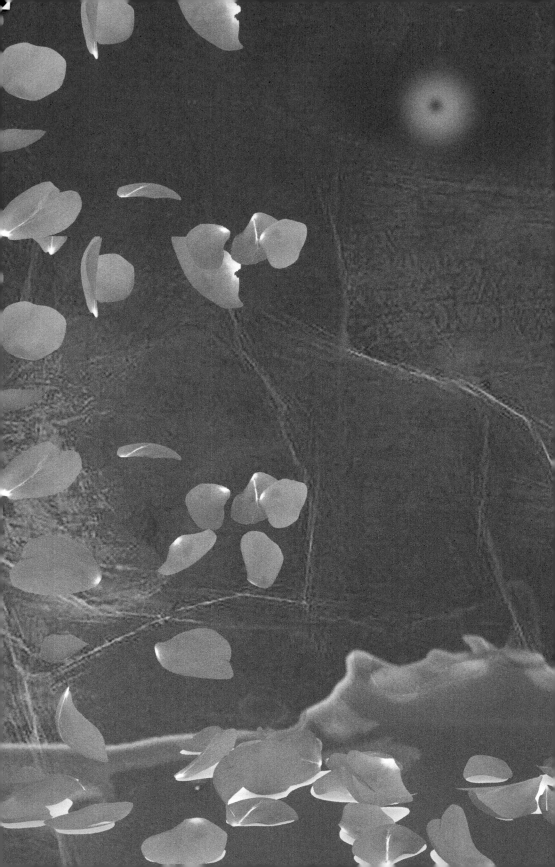

Chapter

Six

Six

Boys & Booze

Dinner with Evaine's parents went the way it always did. Her mother spent most of the meal frowning every time Jacob's voice got a little loud or his hand gestures became more than she could stand to allow in public. Evaine lost count of how many times her mother reached for Jacob's hand and pushed it to the table with a whispered, "Yes, Dear, that's wonderful," which was her go-to when she didn't know what else to say.

Daddy badgered Gage about what he planned to do now that he had graduated, and at one point, he looked like he was going to make a break for it, his light eyes flicking toward the front door. The boys were troopers and humored her when it came to her parents, and she recognized how fortunate she was to have them both, all of them.

As usual, Daddy slipped her a sizable check on the way out, even though paying for her Halloween party was supposed to be it. "Buy some clothes for your new job, Princess." Evaine didn't blame her mother when she shot him a dirty look because it was getting more expensive every year.

After dinner, Gage went straight to work for his monthly employee meeting, which mostly entailed Matt getting everyone high and reminiscing about how awesome the eighties were, which left her and Jacob alone at home for a few hours.

The first thing they did was dump the five vases of roses down the garbage chute at the end of the hallway. She wanted to throw the bracelet away, but Jacob talked her out of it because it made little sense to throw it in the trash when she could sell it and donate the money or give it to someone in need to pawn.

There were plenty of homeless people on the streets that could use the cash. She planned to take it with her tonight and find someone who needed it.

Being Birthday Girl meant she got to pick the movies, and Jacob even made her popcorn, not that she ate much because she was still full from dinner. Snuggled with her back pressed against his chest, she tucked her head under his chin, his arm resting in the curve of her hip, and they watched one of her favorites, Pretty in Pink, before moving to the Breakfast Club. Evaine enjoyed spending time with Jacob because he comforted her soul.

By the time they finished the second movie, it was time to get ready. And per the usual, Jacob took forever to figure out what he was wearing, which ended up being pretty much the same thing he wore most days, leather pants and a black Bauhaus T-shirt. Though to his credit, he had fishnets covering his bare arms and thick leather bracelets cinching his wrists. He wore his new big, stompy combat boots with large metal buckles.

Once dressed, it took him another forty minutes to put his mohawk in liberty spikes. It was certainly worth the effort because he looked hot as shit with his hair sticking up and his clean-shaven head, not to mention his heavily lined sea-green eyes.

Her date was a babe!

Evaine wanted to dance tonight, so she went for comfort more than fashion, choosing a simple pair of patent leather pants with her shiny twenty-hole Doc Martens, a sheer short-sleeve shirt, and a red satin bra. She pulled her fire-red hair into a high ponytail, the curls brushing her neck and cheeks. A thin leather collar wrapped around her throat with a small silver ring that matched the ones on her wrist. It was just tight enough to remind her it was there. An Aunk hung from a long silver chain, resting between her small breasts.

When they arrived at Eucharist, the line wrapped around the building, but there were definite benefits to having a boyfriend who worked there, like being friends with the bouncer who liked to come to the house and jam with Jacob. He waved them in without even checking their ID. Evaine showed it to him, anyway. "You only turn twenty-one once, right?" He chuckled as he wrapped the striped paper band around her wrist and sealed the ends together. "Twenty-one. Got it." Once he finished banding Jacob, he said, "Have fun, Girlie." Her cheeks felt like they were on fire from the perma-grin she'd had since they left the house, but she flashed him a big grin and thanked him.

Eucharist was in an old, abandoned church that was gutted and repurposed into a nightclub. Evaine loved the stained-glass windows; they were the best part of the whole place. Lights were mounted on the outside of the windows to make the colors sparkle and dance in time with the heavy bass that thumped from their state-of-the-art sound system, shooting fractured light around the entire club. It felt otherworldly.

Old wooden pews lined the walls, with large antique mirrors hung above them. The bar was at the back of the building, where the altar would've

been, and lined the whole wall. It took four bartenders to cover it, sometimes five on super busy nights.

Jacob held her hand as they weaved through the crowd toward the bar, a
smile curving her lips when Gage came into view. He blew his purple bangs
out of his light-green eyes, flicking his head back as he poured what looked
like vodka into a large silver tumbler, and then grabbed the gun to add a
mixer. And looked beautiful doing it.

By the time they made it to the bar, he'd just come back from giving a
customer their drink, and the way he looked at her made her insides melt.
When he stretched across the bar to give her a quick kiss, she clenched her
thighs. "Hey, Baby," he said against her lips. The sultry way he said it gave
her the urge to climb over the bar, but she slipped her hand into his mess of
hair and pulled his mouth back to hers for another kiss. When she let go,
he asked, "Kamikaze? Or, do ya wanna get crazy and try something else,
Birthday Girl?"

Evaine shrugged. "Why mess with a good thing?" Gage nodded and then
turned to Jacob, who leaned against the bar and asked, "Where's my kiss
hello?" Without missing a beat, Gage planted one on Jacob and then shot
back, "Whiskey and Coke?" Jacob licked his bottom lip and nodded in a
way that made Evaine seethe with jealousy, and she slapped his chest with
the back of her hand. "Hey, hey. I know that look, and he's off-limits. I'm
not sharing my toy with you."

"One night with me, and he'd forget your name, Evie." A wicked grin
spread across his mouth, his liberty spikes shining in the flickering lights
of the club.

Before she could respond, Gage set their drinks in front of them and
took the money Jacob put on the bar. "I've got a break in an hour. I'll find

you." He dropped off their change and then returned to the waiting mob of thirsty customers.

"Let's go find a table over there," Jacob yelled over the music, pointing toward the back corner next to the large black box on the edge of the dance floor. She sipped her drink before nodding and following him.

The smell of dry ice and thump of the music melted away all the tension in Evaine's body. Dancing always made her feel better, and after the afternoon she had, all she wanted to do was down her drink and hit the floor. The first was easy enough, but the second was a bit of a challenge, considering how packed the dance floor was. With a bit of finesse, she snuck between a few people and found an open spot where she could pick up the beat.

Jacob wasn't much of a dancer. She was lucky to get him to dance in the living room at home. It was the one thing her entirely-too-confident friend didn't like to do. So, he sat at the black high-top table drinking his whiskey and people-watching.

When she glanced up after several songs, a tall, dark, and handsome boy leaned against the wall next to Jacob, with his arms crossed over his broad chest. Evaine wondered who he was as she headed back to the bar to get another drink before joining them.

Mister Tall, Dark, and Handsome seemed to have brooding down to a science. He didn't bother to acknowledge her when she walked up, continuing to talk the Jacob, who grabbed her hand and pulled her into his side. "Raven, this is my bestie, Evaine."

Evaine smiled at the stranger when he flicked his eyes in her direction. His stormy-gray stare held a mixture of curiosity and maybe a bit of disdain as he nodded his head in lieu of an actual hello. Jacob leaned in close to her ear. "This is the boy who likes to use his teeth. I'm kinda hoping I can get him to use them on my cock tonight." She couldn't help but laugh, making Raven hike a thin black eyebrow before flicking his long black hair off his shoulder.

Oh, my! Raven was a wee bit too serious, and she wondered if he'd know what to do once Jacob had a few more drinks in him and really got mouthy and boisterous. The idea of Mr. Grump Ass putting anything in his mouth seemed unlikely.

It caught her off guard when Jacob said something that finally made him smile. His teeth were white and straight, even though his canines seemed to be longer than normal. The laugh lines that formed across his handsome face made him much more approachable than the severe expression that seemed to rule it most of the time.

Still, she wasn't sure he could handle Jacob, even on his quietest days.

Raven glanced down at his silver watch. "My sister, Skye, should be here in a few minutes with my buddy Julien."

While Jacob nodded, Evaine sipped her drink, enjoying the warmth spreading over her skin as the soothing sense of intoxication worked through her. So far, her birthday celebration hadn't been very remarkable, with Gage working and Jacob focused on Mr. Brooding. She sighed and sucked down the rest of her drink. "I'm going to get another," she told Jacob, who smiled and said, "Great! Will you grab me one too?"

She forced a half-smile, "Sure," and headed back to the bar.

"That was quick," Gage said when she handed him her empty glass.

"Jacob is all goo-goo over some stupid boy, so I'm drinking." She pouted.

"Really, Baby. The lip already? You've only been here like an hour." Gage laughed and then poured another round for her. "I'll put it on your tab." He slid the drinks across the metal-topped bar.

Two new people were with Jacob when Evaine returned to the table. A short, petite, pink-haired girl with dark eyes that looked to be about sixteen, if she was lucky. And a tall, well-built blonde with bright blue eyes that seemed to track her as she approached.

The stranger sipped his drink and tipped his chin in her direction as she came to stand next to Jacob. Evaine handed him his glass and mouthed the word, "Hello," when she felt everyone's eyes land on her. Suddenly, she felt like a poor meerkat surrounded by a pack of hungry hyenas but met each pair of eyes, unwilling to let them know how they affected her. When Jacob leaned in, his warm breath tickled her ear, making her shiver. "This is Raven's sister, Skye, and his friend Julien. We were going to play some pool upstairs. You wanna come with, Princess?" She knew there were a couple of tables up on the balcony, but she'd never gone up there and had no interest in playing pool, especially when there was thumping music and a dance floor full of writhing bodies to enjoy. Evaine wrinkled her nose, shaking her head and pointing to the dance floor.

"Figured as much." Jacob frowned, sipping his whiskey. "I'll be back in like thirty, okay? I promise."

Although the bratty part of her wanted to point out that it was, in fact, her birthday and he was supposed to do everything she wanted on her birthday, she nodded and forced a smile as she eyed the three standing off to the side. Jealousy twisted in her gut when he planted a kiss on her cheek and walked away, leaving her standing there alone.

Bastard! She downed her drink and watched him disappear into the crowd, the warm liquor spreading over her limbs.

As one song faded out, the next, faster one took its place and drew her to the dance floor, where she could work out some frustrations in the pit forming in the middle. She was a tiny thing but could throw punches and kicks with the best of them. It also helped to know the bouncer, who was twice the size of Gage across the shoulders and at least two inches taller and stood in the center of the mosh pit with his muscled arms flexing over his chest. Every so often, he would toss one of the more energetic individuals out of the circle or shove them away from Evaine before they slammed into her.

By the time the Ministry song ended, Evaine was out of breath, covered in sweat, and determined not to let her stupid friend bum her out on her birthday. She didn't need him to have fun. *No, not at all.* When she pushed through the churning crowd to the table in the corner, the tall blond was standing next to it; his cornflower eyes focused on her. Evaine forced a smile and glanced at her patent-leather-covered feet for a tick, startling when she looked up to find him right next to her.

His cool breath tickled her ear when he leaned in. "I think you may have given that gentleman a black eye."

I SO did! And she couldn't help but smile about it. "That's what he gets for finding his way in front of my fist."

Julien laughed. The genuine kind that made his shoulders shake. "Quite right, Ma Petite Rousse." His words were breathy against her ear and sent a shiver down her spine, his heavy accent wrapping around her like silk and making her want to lean into him. Evaine glanced up, catching his eyes, and found it nearly impossible to break the connection as she stood there with the stranger. "Julien, right?" She tried to find her resolve to sever it.

Julien pushed a long, loose strand of white-blonde hair behind his ear and nodded. "You really are quite beautiful," he said almost off-handedly as he reached for one of her curls, wrapping the tendril around his long finger. His nails were longer and perfectly manicured.

"Thank- thank you," Evaine stuttered out and smoothed her fingers over her sheer-covered stomach, unsure what to do with her hands. This stranger made her want to run but rooted her to the ground in the same breath. Again, she felt like helpless prey. It was insane.

"I do so love red-heads." Julien's golden rings caught the overhead lights when he pulled his hand back and flashed her a devastating smile.

"Well, umm, that's kinda funny cause so does my boyfriend." It was challenging to get the words out, but she managed. A big part of her hoped that would send him on the way, but a sliver wanted him to stay, to continue to talk in that satiny French accent that made everything sound like sex.

Julien quirked the side of his mouth, reminding her of a cat who ate a canary. "That's too bad, isn't it, Ma Rousse? Au revoir." He walked away, leaving her staring after him.

Why did it feel like she woke up in the twilight zone the last few days? Was she secreting some pheromone that attracted the crazies? She sniffed her armpit and mumbled, "Nope," before heading back to the bar for another drink. Gage was sane; she needed sane and always needed him. It didn't hurt that he made her the best drinks, too. When she downed this one without leaving the bar, he cocked an eyebrow and asked, "You okay, Baby?"

"Fine. Just had some guy hit on me."

"Where's Jay?"

Evaine crossed her arms over her chest, pushing her exposed cleavage up further, the rings on her leather cuffs jingling as they collided. "Off playing with his new friends."

Gage dropped his eyes and smirked. "I'll see if I can take my break early."

A few minutes later, an arm snaked around her stomach and made her tense until she glimpsed Morpheus from the Sandman graphic novel staring up at her, his mess of black hair and sparkling eyes inked into Gage's forearm. She relaxed and let Gage pull her against him, shivering when his warm breath tickled her ear. "I've got fifteen minutes, and I made you a promise to fuck you until you screamed my name. Wanna go to the back room so I can keep it?"

Evaine turned and slid her hands up his neck to rest at the nape, her fingers twining into the long strands, using her grip to pull his mouth to hers and kiss him. The last drink had tipped her from barely drunk to almost too buzzed, and she swayed slightly when she broke the kiss. "Just fifteen minutes? Do you think you can make me come in fifteen minutes?"

Gage slid his hand between her thighs, his long fingers stroking her through the slick patent leather. His lips brushed against hers, his tongue darting out to flick the corner of her mouth before he said, "It'll take me at least ten to peal you outta these fucking pants, so I'll bet you I can do it in five."

Even through the material, his touch ignited a smoldering lust that churned low in her belly and made her want him inside her, not that it took much. She gripped his studded leather belt and jerked him against her. "You're on."

Without hesitation, he grabbed her hand and led her toward the do. the left of the bar. It wasn't the first time she'd ended up pinned against the metal shelves with the sharp-edged cardboard biting into her lower back as Gage ravished her mouth, and she supposed it wouldn't be the last, considering she couldn't get enough of him.

"I love the way your ass looks in these pants, Baby, but fuck." He yanked at them with an urgency that made her pussy weep, her hands grasping the buckle of his leather belt as he struggled to push hers down her damp hips. Her fingers worked adeptly, and he rewarded her with a deep groan when her hand wrapped around his cock and stroked him.

He only tolerated it a couple of ticks before he gripped her forearms and jerked her forward, shoving her against the empty wall on the other side of the small closet. The cool stone felt good against her flushed face as he gripped her hips and yanked her ass to him. His rigid length pressed against her slick center, making Evaine bite her lip, her body clenching as it anticipated his cock buried inside. "Gage," she panted in a breathy plea. He curled his body along her back, wrapping two fingers into the ring at the center of her throat. "What do ya want, Baby?"

"You." She squirmed against him.

"My cock?" he growled, jerking her collar. "Say it, Evie."

"I want your fucking cock," she panted.

"That's my girl." He used her collar to keep her in place, gripping her hip with the other hand as he drove inside her, burying himself to the hilt in one hard thrust and forcing a moan from her as he shoved her against the wall.

Evaine loved the long, low growls as he punished her from behind. His cock hit just the right spot with each thrust, making her shamelessly squirm ension skyrocketed. His fingers tightened the leather ...neck, making it hard for her to breathe, her pants coming ...s that tickled her cheeks as they bounced off the wall. He ...dy like he owned it, and in some ways, he did and always would. The way he timed each savage thrust with the heavy thumping beat drove her closer to the edge and made her body hum with anticipated pleasure.

When he released his hold on her collar and slid those fingers between her damp thighs to fondle her sensitive spot, she ground against his hand, panting his name as she begged for release. It only took a few more thrusts to make them both come with his fingers roughly working her.

"Told you so," Gage said against the shell of her ear as she tried to catch her breath.

"Jerk," she panted.

Before Gage went back to work, she had to promise to stay at the bar for the rest of the night. He wasn't usually so demanding, but she understood why he felt the need to keep an eye on her and was okay with it. She didn't see Jacob for the rest of the night, and when bright overhead lights flicked on and the music stopped, she assumed he went home with Raven to get serviced.

It only took Gage twenty minutes to break down his station and count his register, and by the time they headed out of the bar, Evaine couldn't keep her eyes open. They walked a few blocks up to one of the busier streets to hail a cab, and when they reached their apartment, Evaine dug into her pocket and handed the older gentleman the emerald bracelet. He stared at her until she said, "Consider it a tip," and climbed from the back seat.

Gage's face showed his surprise when she grabbed his arm and p.
him toward the glass double doors. "I told you I didn't want it. He looked
like he could use the extra cash. There was a picture of his wife and kids on
the dash."

He smiled and kissed the side of her head. "I love you, Evie."

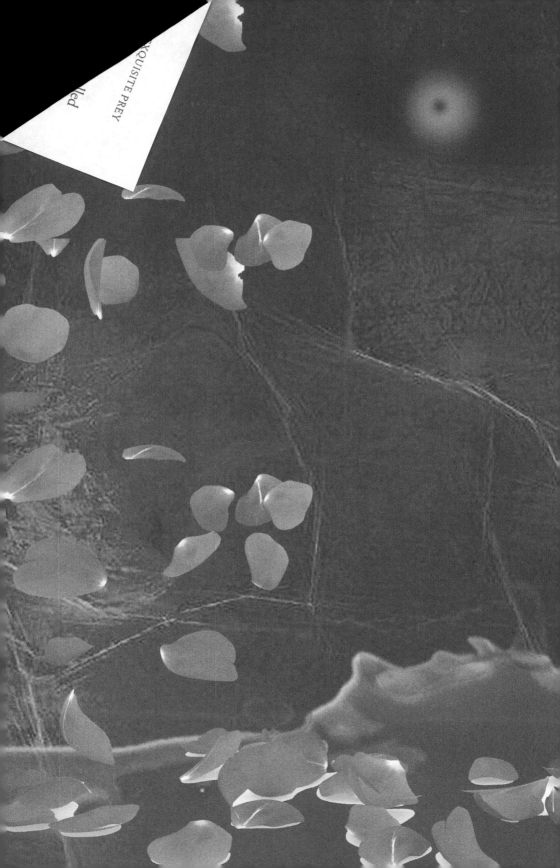

Chapter
Seven

Seven

Pinstripes & Panic

J acob didn't come home Sunday, which was surprising, considering. Evaine chalked it up to infatuation and spent the day vegging on the couch with Gage, watching bad sci-fi on cable. When they got hungry, they ordered a pizza and munched in front of the television. Gage drank a few beers; Evaine sipped red wine. All around, it was a relaxing day that they both needed.

Evaine woke up Monday afternoon to get ready for her meeting with Mr. Basile and immediately checked Jacob's room, which was still empty. Concern chewed on the back of her brain and made her nervous. This wasn't the first time he'd disappeared for days, but that didn't mean she wasn't concerned. She always felt better when she knew where Jacob was.

As she dressed, Evaine convinced herself he was getting a little dick and would be home tonight. She chose a knee-length black dress with pleats that hit her waist, making it cling to her thin form. It had a high white lace collar that brushed the underside of her chin as she fastened the antique cameo brooch, her mother brought her for Christmas when she was sixteen, in the middle of it. The pretty white silhouette sat against a black background, wrapped in scrolling silver. Evaine chose thick black tights to keep her legs warm, pulling her hair into a neat pile on top of her head and keeping her makeup light, her lips lined in dark red and her eyes with thin black lines that made them look larger, before putting her platform Mary Janes on. She kissed Gage's cheek goodbye, which earned her a gruff grunt, and headed for her meeting.

The quickest way to get to Tristan's office was by cab, and she arrived ten minutes early. When she opened the door, the reception walls were painted a stormy gray, and there was a comfortable-looking black leather couch along one wall with two matching chairs on the other. A small wooden table sat between them, the top the same deep cherry coated in shiny lacquer, like the large desk on the other side of the room.

There was an open door to the left, and Evaine could hear Mr. Basile's sharp English accent and a deeper, more roguish voice as she crossed the room. Her footfalls were silent on the plush carpet, but Mr. Basile still came out the open doorway wearing a suit similar to the one he'd worn to dinner, gray with thin white pinstripes, a light-blue dress shirt, and a blue-gray tie. He tugged at his sleeve and smiled as she approached. "I thought I heard you out here." He clapped his hands together and rubbed them against each other. "Lovely. I'm so glad you made it, Miss Maire."

His excitement was contagious, making Evaine smile. "Hello, Mr. Basile."

Tristan's eyebrows furrowed as he frowned. "Uh, uh. What did I tell you at dinner?"

Long lashes tickled Evaine's face when she glanced down before meeting his hazel eyes. With a tug on the strap of her messenger bag, she corrected herself, "Tristan."

"Much better, My Dear." Tristan grinned as he turned his slim body and gave her access to the doorway, stretching his arm out to invite her in.

"Please have a seat. I just need to walk my associate out. It will take but a few moments, and I'll be right back with you."

"Okay."

The burly man with long, copper-colored hair sitting in a chair in front of a massive wooden desk surprised Evaine. She'd never seen a Scottish Highlander up close, but this man looked exactly like she imagined one would. The front half of his hair was pulled into a ponytail at the back of his head, the rest cascading down his broad back, almost to his ass. "Hello," Evaine said when he glanced at her over his massive shoulder, his piercing green eyes focusing on her face.

"Ah, ye mus' be Evaine." His Scottish accent was so thick it was hard to understand him as he climbed to his feet and smoothed his plaid kilt, straightening the leather pouch that hung off his wide belt resting over his crotch. He smoothed the front of his brown wool jacket. "Yer just a wee bairn, are ye not?" The highlander rubbed his long beard with his massive hand; his other hooked onto the small knife hanging from his leather belt.

Under his penetrating gaze, heat flushed Evaine's cheeks. "I'm sorry, but I'm not sure what that means."

"It's his barbaric way of saying you look young," Mr. Basile said from behind her. "And he was just leaving. Were you not, Keegan?"

"Tat I was," he said to Mr. Basile before dipping his hairy chin in her direction, his long copper beard brushing his chest. "It twas a pleasure, Lass. Surely, I'll be seein' ye again."

Evaine watched him cross the room and disappear through the large doorway. *There can only be one!* She chuckled as she sat in the emptied chair, which was surprisingly cold under her, and looked around the room that was decorated with a masculine touch, a massive desk the centerpiece of the entire space.

Mr. Basile was only gone for a few minutes before he returned. "Sorry for the interruption. It was an unexpected visit."

"It's fine."

Tristan crossed the room and sat behind the imposing cherry-wood desk, that reminded Evaine of the president's desk, and leaned forward, resting his clasped hands on the blue-gray pad on top, its color matching the walls. His well-trimmed chocolate-brown hair was slicked back from his handsome face, like an old-school British gangster. At first glance, his smile seemed genuine but felt more like a mask to Evaine. "Good. Now, shall we get started then?"

Evaine nodded as her eyes were drawn to the large rows of blue-gray shelving behind him. She scanned the many leather-bound spines. He had several first-edition books from authors like Shakespeare, Vonnegut, and Poe. *At least he has good taste in authors.* Maybe she could work for him.

"As I said, this position will be full-time Monday through Friday, eleven a.m. to six p.m., and may require a small amount of travel. There could be occasions where the required travel falls on a weekend, but I will compensate you well for the time." He paused, and his silence brought her focus back to him. She cleared her throat and nodded. "Of course."

Tristan's eyes twinkled with what looked like humor. "It will mostly entail reception, scheduling, and light document work." He steepled his fingers. "I do not believe this role will pose a challenge for you. In truth, you are probably overqualified, but what I can offer you is an opportunity to step out from under your parent's wing and become the vibrant young lady that I believe you want to be."

Is that his polite way of saying time to grow up? The directness made her eye twitch, but her professional facade stayed intact. "Sounds simple enough."

He watched her over his hands a moment, making her shift in her seat with the weight of his stare. "Your father shared that you are an aspiring writer. I have a soft spot for authors." He chuckled like it was some inside joke.

"I am. My degree is in American Literature with minors in English and Media." Mr. Basile- Tristan unnerved her; maybe it was the intensity of his eyes or the tension that seemed hidden just under his polished exterior. Something about him screamed predator, making her want to get up and leave without another word. She wasn't sure what kept her planted in her seat.

"Quite impressive indeed." Tristan cleared his throat. "That said, if you agree to take this role, I would be more than happy to allow you to work on your writing while you are on the clock. Would that make it more palatable?"

Evaine couldn't see a downside to getting paid to sit at his reception desk and write. It was pretty cushy. "I would really like to finish some of my projects this year."

"Then, perhaps, we should give it a go and see if it works for both of us. What do you say, Evaine?"

His hazel eyes bore into hers, and any doubt she had dispersed under his scrutiny. Before realizing it, Evaine nodded. "Sounds like a plan, Mr.- Tristan."

"Wonderful." He leaned back in his gray leather executive chair with the same smug look Gage wore when he made her come really hard, and it made her wonder what she'd gotten herself into. "How do you feel about jumping right into it today?"

Evaine shook her head to clear the stray thoughts and nodded. "Today's fine."

"Perfect. Let's get started then." His large hands gripped the arms of his chair as he pushed to his feet and rounded his heavy desk. "I'll show you your desk, and you can take some time to settle in and fill out the mandatory paperwork. That way, you can hit the ground running tomorrow. Sound good?"

As Evaine followed Tristan out to the exterior office, she noticed his fluid movements, like a lion. He had confidence and self-assurance that Evaine didn't even think was possible, and she couldn't ignore the flex of his broad shoulders or the way his expensive, retro-looking suit was tailored to him perfectly, or his pristinely polished, pointed shoes. When they reached the desk outside his office, he pulled the chair out like a gentleman.

Who said chivalry was dead?

"Please sit," he said when she stood a couple of ticks too long.

"Thank you." She dropped into a smaller version of his executive chair, and he loomed over her as he reached for the center drawer of her new desk. His cologne was spicy and reminded her of her father's, though it had a bit more of a coppery scent to it. Or maybe that was his scent. When the drawer opened, he pointed a slim finger at the set of keys sitting in one corner. His closeness made her shift in her seat, and she could hear the smile in his voice as he said, "You will need those to open the office tomorrow."

"Keys, check." She collected them with a nod before he closed the drawer.

"Your paperwork is right here." Tristan indicated with a pointed finger and then jutted his chin toward her computer before he reached for the small piece of paper next to the keyboard and slid it across the surface to her. "And this is your username and password to log in to the system."

When he stepped back, she let out the breath she'd been unconsciously holding.

He clasped his hands in front of him and rubbed them together. "Now, settle in, and let me know if you need anything. I'm looking forward to working with you, Ms. Maire," he said, then headed back to his office.

Evaine stared at the paper for a few moments before reaching for it. *Pretty confident I'd take the job, huh?* She wasn't sure if she liked the presumption. In fact, she knew she didn't like the presumption. *You are here, so ya know?* "Cocky bastard," she mumbled and heard Tristan laugh from the other room. *Is he on the phone?* He couldn't have heard her. Heat flushed her face as she realized he might've.

After resigning herself to her new job, she spent the next couple of hours familiarizing herself with the phone system and organizing the piles of untouched paperwork in the stacked baskets on the corner of her desk. It seemed like he hadn't filed anything in months, and it took her several hours to figure out where the files went; the system used to file them and then get them all put away correctly. It was seven by the time she finished, and Tristan ushered her out of the office for the day.

Gage sat on the couch drinking his morning coffee when she returned to their apartment. Evaine toed off her shoes, lining them against the wall before throwing her jacket and bag on the hook and padding to the couch to sit next to him. When he glanced up from his cup, he asked, "How was your meeting?"

"I took the job." She snuggled into his side, his arm draping over her shoulder.

"You did?" He sounded as surprised as she'd felt when she'd agreed to it.

"Yeah, I wasn't going to, but I couldn't say no once I got there."

"Huh," Gage said around the rim of his mug.

"He said he has a soft spot for authors and that I can work on my writing while I'm on the clock."

With a black eyebrow raised, he cocked his head to the side. "Soft spot for authors? More like a soft spot for hot little redheads." Gage seemed to amuse himself and smirked. "You realize you don't need the money, right? That you could work on your writing full time without the extra pressure of a job? Or a pervy old man watching you all day."

"I know." She was as confused as he was by her decision to take the job.

Gage shrugged. "Okay, then. If that's what you wanna do, Baby. It's up to you."

His unyielding support made her insides warm and mushy, and she leaned up to kiss him. "Have I told you how awesome you are?" His eyes twinkled with something akin to mischief when he said, "Not today, and you know, I prefer it when you show me."

"Of course, you do, Jerk!" She slapped his pajama-covered thigh. "Has Jacob called?"

His leg jerked from the impact as he sipped from his mug. "Not since I've been up. He hasn't come home yet?"

"I'm not sure if it's just all the weirdness lately or what, but I'm kinda worried about him." Evaine pulled her feet up and wrapped her arms around her bent knees. "I hope he's okay."

"I'm sure he's fine, Baby. You know how he is."

"I know. Like I said, I think it's just the shit that's been happening that has me on edge."

"I don't blame you there." Gage set his empty mug on the coffee table and then pulled her into his lap. "Everything's gonna be okay."

She felt a hundred times better with his arms wrapped around her and melted into his embrace, nuzzling her face against his heated skin and kissing his chest, the muscle fluttering under her soft caress. "I know. I just wish he'd call."

"You worry too much, Baby," he said against her hair, his long fingers twining into the curls as they pulled her head back until their eyes met. "How 'bout we go to Harlem's for shakes before I go to work?"

"Shakes make everything better."

"I figured you'd say that." He kissed her one last time before heading to the shower.

They dressed and went to get an early dinner before Gage had to go to work. As usual, he had a salad and another cup of coffee while Evaine went for onion rings and a large vanilla shake. By the time she finished the frozen treat, she felt better, which had more to do with Gage's constant reminder to stop worrying about nothing.

Before they parted ways, Gage reminded her to be careful walking home and kissed her goodbye. The sun was setting, which meant she had plenty of time to walk the few blocks, and other than a brief moment where she felt like someone was watching her, it was uneventful, though the incident rattled her.

Evaine tried to stay busy at the apartment and keep the unease of being alone out of her thoughts. She hated that her *admirer* knew where she lived and felt the need to send her something so extravagant for her birthday. This kind of vulnerability was foreign to Evaine because she'd always felt safe living with her parents and then with Gage and Jacob. It was hard to process the discomfort that chewed on the edges of her psyche.

Since she was alone, she could blast whatever music she wanted without hearing either of the boys complain and opted for the eighties mixed Jacob made her a few weeks ago. Evaine danced around the kitchen, putting dishes away and cleaning the counters before moving to the living and dining rooms. Cleaning was an excellent distraction, and by the time she finished, she'd straightened both areas and swept and mopped the floors. It was well after ten when she looked at the wall clock in the kitchen.

Despite how exhausted she was from cleaning, she still couldn't relax and checked the locked door every half-hour. It pissed her off that this asshole made her uncomfortable in her own home. She was determined not to give them the satisfaction or her the stress of it.

Evaine pulled a large wine glass from the cabinet and poured the rest of the open bottle of Merlot that was in the fridge, chugging it down in a few big gulps before opening a second bottle. It took three large glasses before she relaxed, and by then, she had a nice buzz and was sleepy. Wine always made her tired, and she never understood why. She poured another glass, even though she could barely keep her eyes open and her lips felt numb. All she wanted was a hot bath and to crawl into bed, sipping her wine as she padded toward her room.

By the time she finished in the tub, her eyes were so heavy she couldn't keep them open, and she was ready to sleep. Not bothering to dry off, she wrapped the towel around her body and headed for bed. It only took minutes for her to doze off, curled up in the soft sheets and downy comforter.

At first, all the wine lulled her into a peaceful sleep, but then her dreams became plagued with scenario after scenario of terrible things happening to Jacob and Gage. The nightmares made her restless, tossing and turning as she tried to find her friends in the dark place her worried and stressed sub-conscious crafted.

Evaine was on that edge of sleep, where her body felt weightless and her conscious mind hadn't quite shaken free of the dream's hold, where she wasn't sure what was real or imagined, when she felt icy fingers running along her cheek, over her neck and collarbone, and across her nipple, tightening it into a stiff peak.

The touch chilled her bones, jolting her awake, and she half-expected to see Gage standing over her with his warm smile. Instead, a cold draft slithered across her skin, making her shiver uncontrollably. Goosebumps spread over her body as she scanned the room for intruders, her eyes landing on the wide-open window. She pulled the towel up around her and climbed from the bed to close and lock it, jerking the curtains shut before she padded across the room with a shiver and wondered how the window got open. It wasn't like they left them unlocked or ever opened them. Dread churned in her stomach at someone being in her room, and she tried not to panic as hot tears burned the corners of her eyes.

The rational part of her understood someone couldn't get into her fourth-floor apartment, especially through her window. But she had no idea how it got open, and the icy touch still tingled on her skin like it was the most real thing she'd ever felt. Evaine glanced at the glowing-red digital clock on the nightstand. It was at least two hours before Gage would be home. Two hours try not to dwell or panic.

When her eyes settled on the single red rosebud next to her alarm, Evaine mumbled, "Fuck." The top was bent and almost snapped off, likely when she and Jay shoved them down the garbage shoot. Next to the mangled rose sat a velvet-covered bracelet box. Her blood ran cold as the realization settled in. *The velvet-covered bracelet box.* A wave of nausea washed over Evaine as she picked it up, her hands shaking while prying it open. The bracelet she'd given the cab driver sat inside with a small, folded paper on top, mocking her.

"Shit!" Evaine dreaded what the note said and sucked in a shaking breath to steel herself as tears burned the rims of her eyes, threatening to tumble down her flushed face. Her fingers fumbling, she unfolded it. The handwriting was smooth and neat, the letters swirling with a flourish that reminded her of the penmanship from the past.

Despite being alone, she read it aloud, "Something so beautiful is meant to be worn, and trust me; I will know if you refuse, Evaine." She crumpled the paper and threw it on the nightstand. Somewhere between the fear and panic, anger bloomed. "What the literal fuck!" *Who is this person?* The note was a pretty direct threat. It scared the shit out of her and made her want to punch someone in the face at the same time. Determined to stop the fear that threatened to overtake her, she took a deep breath, counted to ten in her head, and blew it out slowly, trying to control her thumping heart.

For years, Evaine became convinced hiding was the only thing that kept her safe. When she was five, all she wanted to do was hide her head under the covers so the monster under the bed wouldn't steal her away, and sixteen years later, she felt the same way. "Son of a bitch. I really hate my life sometimes!"

Evaine dropped the towel and crawled back into the cocoon of her bed, pulling the covers up around her naked body, but resisting the urge to bring them up over her head. She laid there, continuing to focus on slowing her breathing. Every minute ticked by painfully slow as the tension and fear overwhelmed her. If someone wanted to get in, she couldn't stop them. Terror clawed at her brain, and she wanted Gage to come home. When she heard the bedroom doorknob turn, it took everything to keep her from hiding under her bed.

"Gage?" She hated the tremor in her voice.

"Hey, Baby. Why are you awake?" The door clicked shut behind him, and Evaine could breathe again. "Are you okay? You sound off."

She pulled the blanket under her chin, fisting it tight. "I couldn't sleep." She wasn't quite ready to explain why yet. His weight shifted the bed as he sat on the edge to take off his combat boots and then pulled his T-shirt over his head. She could barely make out his pale silhouette as he asked, "Why not?"

"Bad dreams." She settled for a half-truth, still unable to share more and make it real.

Gage stripped his pants off before circling the bed and crawling in next to her. His warmth made her body immediately relax, the tension unwinding in her neck and shoulders. When she tucked in against him, his arms wrapped around her, pulling her closer. "It's just your overactive worrying. Now you're stressing in your sleep." He gave a low chuckle. "I'm sure he's fine."

Evaine closed her eyes. "Mmm. Hmm." The adrenaline that kept her wide awake for the last hour slipped away, replaced by exhaustion.

He kissed the top of her head. "Get some sleep."

Chapter Eight

Tantrums & Tears

Evaine slept like a baby after Gage came home despite everything that happened and used every minute to sleep before starting her day. She quickly washed her face, brushed her teeth, and sorted her hair and makeup before deciding what to wear for the second day of her new job. After a few minutes of rummaging through her closet, she settled on simple black dress pants and a sheer short-sleeve shirt that was fun yet somewhat professional when paired with a silky black cammy. She opted for her chunky platform dress shoes that looked more masculine than feminine. They were comfortable to wear and made her feel like a tall bad-ass bitch, and she needed those extra three inches today.

A pit formed in Evaine's stomach as she debated wearing the bracelet because part of her wanted to test the psycho, and the other didn't want to take the chance. Then there was the issue of telling Gage what happened when he saw it on. Her eyes flicked up and caught him sprawled out on the bed, still sleeping like a baby, and all she wanted to do was crawl back in next to him. Unfortunately, that wasn't an option today.

Gage's soft snores made her wonder if she could sneak out and avoid dealing with it until after work. *He won't even know.* It seemed like a good enough plan as she crept around the bed and grabbed the bracelet box, leaving the broken bud and crumpled note where they lay. Despite her frustration, she fastened the delicate silver bracelet around her wrist before kissing Gage, who must not have been sleeping as soundly as she'd thought because he turned his head and caught her lips. "You leaving?"

Evaine forced a smile regardless of the swirling torrent of emotions in her gut because putting the delicate silver circlet on her wrist made her feel like a prisoner. It strangled her freedom like she wore a leather collar around her neck with a silver tag that said Slave. Still, she nodded at Gage, unwilling to expose her turmoil.

"Are you feeling better?" Dark brow furrowed, his sleepy eyes trying to focus as he reached for her bare wrist, his long fingers circling it.

"Yeah, I'm okay." Guilt washed over her as his mint-green eyes caught hers, and he asked, "You sure?"

Evaine was nearly incapable of keeping things from him because he had this way of reading her she sometimes hated. Her shoulders slumped as she pushed out a loud breath. "Damn it. I didn't want to do this now."

"Do what?"

"Something happened while you were gone last night. I didn't want to tell you about it until later."

Gage sat up and ran his hand through his mess of hair, purple strands sticking out every which way, and rubbed the sleep from his eyes. "Tell me what happened, Evaine!"

She worried her bottom lip between her teeth before showing him the bracelet. He stared at it for a few ticks, then looked at her in confusion. "What the fuck? Where did that fucking thing come from?"

Evaine shrugged, "It just showed up on my nightstand with that," and then pointed at the mangled flower and crumpled note.

His narrow, minty gaze tracked her finger. "Is that another rose?"

"Not another one, no. I'm pretty sure it's one that Jay and I threw away." Evaine sank down on the edge of the bed and furrowed her brow. "You saw me hand that cabbie the bracelet the other night, right?"

Gage gripped her wrist and brought it closer, inspecting the jewelry in more detail. "Yeah, Baby, I saw you."

"Then how did someone get in and leave it on the nightstand?" She couldn't fight the tears welling in her eyes and threatening to spill down her cheeks.

"What do you mean?" He paused, and worry tinged his tone when he asked, "Someone broke in?"

"The window was wide open. I never open the windows, so I know it was locked, Gage, but the flower and the bracelet were on the nightstand." She gulped a breath, trying to shove the panic back down. "And the note! How did it get there?"

"What note, Baby?" Anger darkened his beautiful face.

Evaine pointed at the crumpled paper. Gage eyed her for a couple of ticks before he snatched it up and smoothed it out, scanning it before throwing it on the bed and shaking his head.

The walls closed in on Evaine as she waited for him to say everything would be okay. She didn't believe it but still wanted, needed, to hear him say it. Tears streamed down her face, her body shaking uncontrollably.

Gage huffed and used her wrist to pull her into his lap, wrapping his arms around her and kissing the top of her head. "I think you need to call the police, Evie. It's essentially breaking and entering, Baby. You need to report it."

It was impossible for her to hold back the onslaught of tears. Small sobs shook her shoulders, and she hated it because she wasn't weak and didn't like feeling afraid. Evaine curled into him and nodded, her head bumping the underside of his chin.

"Okay. You call, and I'll put some pants on and meet you in the living room." He tightened his arms around her and kissed her head again.

All she wanted to do was stay in the safety of his arms, but that wasn't an option because she wouldn't allow it to knock her down. Evaine wiped the tears from her face and slid from his lap, crawling off the bed before smoothing her shirt, and then took a minute for her to steel herself before going to the kitchen to make the call.

After about ten minutes, Gage came out of the bedroom in a black Misfits T-shirt and jeans. His feet were bare, and his damp hair hung around his face. "Did you call?" he asked at the coffeemaker.

"Yeah. They're on their way." The edge of the counter bit into her back as she leaned against it with her arms crossed over her chest.

"Good. At least we can get a report filed." Gage filled the filter with grounds and then added water before shoving the pot under the drip. "I think you should call Mr. Basile and tell him you're not coming in today."

"It's my second day, Gage. He's gonna think I'm a flake."

"I don't really care what he thinks, Baby. Your safety is the only thing that matters right now. Plus, who knows how long it will take the police to finish once they actually get here, not to mention I'm not letting you out of my sight." He snaked his fingers through one of her empty belt loops and pulled her closer, kissing her lips. "Call him, please."

Evaine huffed against his mouth. *Like I could say no, right?* "Fine." Before dialing the number, she grabbed the cordless and stomped to her messenger bag to dig Tristan's card from the front pocket. It rang four times, and she thought he wouldn't answer, but then there was a smooth, very British "Ello" on the other end of the line.

"Mr. Basile?" she asked, to be sure.

"Evaine? Is everything okay, My Dear?" he said instead of answering her question.

She paused to choose her words, blowing out a breath to steady her tone. "I just wanted to let you know I will be late today. I'm sorry, but we had a break-in last night, and I'm waiting for the police to come and take my statement."

"A break-in? Are you okay?" His smooth tone held an edge of concern.

"We are. It was just a little unnerving."

"I imagine. Take as much time as you need, Evaine. In fact, take the entire day, and think nothing of it."

"Thank you, Mr. Basile." Relief washed over her with his understanding and patience. "I really appreciate it."

"Tristan, My Dear."

"Tristan. Thank you."

A few minutes after she hung up, there was a sharp rap on the door. When Gage padded over barefoot to open it, there were two uniform police standing in the hallway.

"Someone called about a break-in?" The taller one with the mustache asked.

"Yeah, we did." Gage stepped back to allow them through and closed the door behind them. "This is my girlfriend, Evaine. She was home alone last night when someone broke in."

Both men eyed her, but the shorter one asked her, "Can you tell us what happened, Miss?"

The police took about thirty minutes to take her statement, asking multiple questions as she explained. They wanted to see the room and inspect her nightstand, as well as check her window and dust for fingerprints on all the surfaces. The officers said they wouldn't know if they found anything until they were back at the precinct but didn't seem concerned because nothing was taken and no one was harmed. Even with the note, they brushed it off as some sort of prank, which frustrated her.

After they left, Evaine sat next to Gage on the couch and curled her feet under her, resting her head on his shoulder. "That was a waste of time."

"Kinda, but at least there's a report filed in case something else happens." Gage watched her fidget with the silver bracelet for a few ticks before reaching for her wrist, his warm fingers efficiently working the clasp as he slid it off. "I don't want you wearing this thing; I don't give a fuck what that fucking note says." And shoved it in his pocket.

She could see the anger bubbling under his calm surface, and it unnerved her more than anything else because it wasn't a good sign if Gage was concerned; nothing ever rattled him.

"I'm gonna take a few days off to be here with you." Gage shrugged. "Matt won't like it, but too bad for him."

"I don't want you to lose your job, Gage. I'll be fine."

His large hand cupped her face, pulling her mouth to his as he kissed her. "We're not debating this, Evie. I'm not leaving you alone until I know you're safe. This bastard was in our house while you were asleep alone. This could've been so much worse, Baby, and I'm not gonna give him another opportunity."

Evaine half-smiled, appreciating the concern in his tone, even though his words rattled her more than she'd like to admit. He wasn't wrong; it could've been so much worse. "Okay." She lifted his arm so she could cuddle into his side.

"Good." Gage rested his chin on the top of her head.

She and Gage sat there a while before they heard a key in the door, and Evaine was on her feet, stomping across the room before Jacob even got through it, crossing her arms. "Where the fuck have you been?"

Jacob smiled despite the stern glare she threw his way. "Hey, Princess. You miss me?" His tone was light, like he'd just gone out for coffee and not been missing in action for the last two days.

She scowled. "Where have you been?"

He threw his keys in the bowl by the door and closed the distance between them, kissing her lightly before shrugging. "Raven's place," like it was a given.

"You don't know how to call to tell someone you're alive, Jerk?"

Jacob's shoulders dropped. "I know, I'm sorry. We got distracted. I meant to call, really, I did."

"Not good enough, Jay. She's been worried sick." Gage said from the couch.

Jacob chuckled and grabbed her hand, leading her into the room. "I know, Man," he said as they approached the couch and then glanced back. "I know you're pissed."

"Beyond pissed." She dropped onto the couch next to Gage and crossed her arms over her chest. "How dare you come home and act like it isn't a big deal? I was worried."

Jacob sat on the edge of the coffee table across from her, his knees pressing into the cushion on each side of her legs. "I know, Evie. I said I was sorry." He leaned forward, his elbows resting on the tops of his thighs, his hands clasped between his spread legs, his fingers tapping her knees as he stared at the floor for a couple of ticks.

Dread gnawed at her guts. "What is it?" She'd been able to read him like an open book since they were eleven years old. This was his concerned face, and she didn't like it.

Jacob glanced up and shot her a small smile. "We need to talk, Evie."

"About what?" she snapped, unable to keep the annoyance from her tone.

"Well, see. Umm. Rave and I talked last night and- Shit, Evie, don't look at me like that." He ran a hand through his long black mohawk before wringing his fingers together again.

"Just spit it out, Jay." Evaine wasn't in the mood to give him an inch. Anger and frustration battered her insides like she knew whatever he was going to say would break her fragile control and hurt her wounded heart.

"I'm gonna be moving in with him. I'm packing up my stuff tonight and should have everything moved before the party on Thursday."

Tears threatened to spill from her burning eyes for the second time today, and it made her even more pissed off at Jacob because he caused them. "You can't just leave!"

"Evie." Gage tried to smooth her edge with his word and a touch on her arm, but it didn't help control the smoldering anger inside, and she shrugged his hand off. "How can you just leave me with everything that's going on?" Evaine yelled at Jacob, who jerked his head back in surprise.

Gage was there again, with that soothing tone that usually calmed her. "He doesn't know, Evie." She turned her fiery glare on him long enough to spit out. "Of course, he doesn't know! He hasn't fucking been here!"

Then she was on her feet, pointing her finger in Jacob's face. "Have you, Asshole?" As she glared at his confused expression, a tear broke and ran down her cheek. She wiped it with the back of her hand, sniffing hard to keep the snot threatening to run from her nose in check. "Ya know what? Do whatever the fuck you want!" As she turned to walk away, Jacob grabbed her wrist and pulled her back.

"I get you're upset, Princess. I'm sorry about that, but how about you tell me what the fuck is going on?"

"You're leaving me!" Her voice cracked in that way that made her feel too vulnerable, too weak, and she didn't like it. All she wanted was to curl up in her bed and sleep until her world returned to normal, until all this shit was over.

Jacob sighed before pulling her against him and wrapping his arms around her. "I'm not leaving you. I'll always be here for you."

Evaine struggled to get free, but his arms were like steel bands holding her tight against his chest, so she gave up and spat, "That sounds like bullshit to me," at him in frustration.

Jacob glanced behind her, looking to Gage for an explanation.

He sighed and stood up, his hand brushing down her back. "Whoever sent her the bracelet and flowers was in the house last night." When Jacob's grip loosened, she pulled away and buried her face in Gage's chest, wrapping her arms around his waist. He was the only thing keeping her somewhat sane, her life preserver.

Gage continued to stroke her back as he explained things to Jacob. "She gave the bracelet to the cabbie that brought us home on Saturday night, but it showed up on her nightstand last night with a broken rosebud and a note about how it was too beautiful not to be worn and how they'd know if she didn't wear it."

"That's fucked up," was all Jacob said.

"Kinda." Gage kissed the side of her head before sitting on the couch and pulling her into his lap. Evaine curled into him, tucking her feet under his warm thigh, wrapping her arms around his shoulders, and burying her face in his neck. "It's okay, Baby."

Evaine struggled to pull herself together, but the seams wouldn't line up. Jacob leaving unraveled the last of her resolve and made it impossible for her to keep the tears and panic from forcing to the surface and taking over. Her body shook as she felt Jacob sit down next to Gage and hug her back, his cheek resting against the sharp blade of her shoulder.

"I'm sorry I wasn't here, Evie. You know I'd never leave you." His fingers trailed circles along her lower back. "Tell me what you need me to do."

"Stay," Evaine whispered against Gage's pulse.

"He can't stay, Baby. It isn't fair to ask him to do that."

She sobbed harder.

"Anything else, Evie. I'll do anything else you need. Just tell me." Jacob's tone was clouded with a sadness she wasn't used to hearing from her vibrant best friend and made her feel guilty for asking him to stay because, deep down, she loved him and wanted to see him happy. He was just moving out, not leaving the planet, and if her rational brain had been functioning on any level, she would've been somewhat okay with it, not to say she still wouldn't be sad, but certainly not hysterical.

"I hate this," she said against Gage's collarbone.

He stroked her back, his tone soothing. "I know, Baby. It's going to be okay."

Evaine hated the pity in his words, hated that she was falling apart like some weakling, and sucked in a deep breath, trying to force control back into her limbs. As she tried to stifle the tears and shove the panic back into the deepest part of her gut, she wiped her hand across her nose and then cleared the tears from her cheeks. "I'm okay." When Gage looked down at her with a brow furrowed with concern, she said, "I'll be okay."

He cocked a half-smile and kissed her forehead. "I gotta call Matt. I'm gonna give you guys a coupla minutes to talk." Before slipping from under her and grabbing the phone from the dining room table to head into their room.

After a couple of ticks, Jacob mumbled, "I'm sorry, Evie," against her back.

As she turned to face him, she blew out a harsh, shaking breath. "I'm the one who owes you an apology. I'm sorry too." Her heart hurt at the idea of him leaving, but she couldn't try to stop him.

Jacob smirked, "My Little Drama Queen. What would I do without you?" and kissed her cheek before pulling her into him. "You know I'm here if you need me. No matter when, what time, you pick up that phone and fucking call me, Evie, and I'll be here. That asshole shows up again, and I'll help Gage kill him."

Evaine laughed, enjoying the familiar scent of him as she worked to keep her breathing in check and her panic tamped down. "You're just going to be waiting by the phone?"

"No, Silly. I finally broke down and bought a cell phone. I might need a man-purse to carry the damn thing in, but at least you'll be able to reach me whenever you need to. This won't change things, Evie. We'll still have girl's night and Sunday dinners and Harlem's. You're not gonna get rid of me that easy, Baby." He kissed her temple and squeezed her shoulders.

The words sounded pretty and were all the right ones, but something told her things would never be the same. "I love you, Jay," she mumbled into his soft black T-shirt.

"I love you too, Evie."

By the time Gage came back into the room, Evaine had pulled herself back together and was listening to Jacob tell her about the apartment Raven shared with his sister and Julien.

"Matt is not a happy camper." Gage set the phone on the coffee table and sat beside her.

"What did he say?"

"In summary?" A black eyebrow hitched up under his hair as it hung in his eyes. Evaine nodded before he continued. "Come to work or lose your job, Asshole. Exact words. He's such a dickhead sometimes."

"I don't want you to get fired, Gage. I'll be okay by myself."

Steeled determination flickered in Gage's eyes when he caught hers again. "I'm not leaving you alone all night. It's not happening."

"What if I stay with you tonight, Evie? I've gotta pack my stuff, anyway. And then tomorrow night you come and hang with me at my new place. Rave, and I will keep you company."

Jacob's staying felt like the right thing to do. She enjoyed his company and didn't want to be alone, as much as she hated to admit it. When she glanced up at Gage, a slight nod told her he agreed. "You don't think Raven will mind?"

"Nah, I don't think they'd mind at all. There are always people coming and going."

"I'd feel better if you did that until we know things have settled down." Gage ran his hand through his mess of hair. "Let me call the dick back and let him know."

Once Gage sorted things with Matt, he crashed on the couch with his head in her lap and was asleep in minutes, and she found herself watching the steady rise and fall of his breathing, a pang of guilt stabbing her chest because it was her fault he wasn't getting any sleep. Her fingers lazily shifted through his hair; most of it was still damp, but the ends were starting to dry. He looked so peaceful, and she smiled despite all the crap. "I'm a pretty lucky girl," she said, stroking his cheek, and he rewarded her with a soft groan as he nuzzled into her touch. This time, it was affection that stabbed at her.

"Hey," Jacob said from the doorway of his room, making her jump as he broke her from her thoughts. She glanced up. "Hmm?"

"I'm gonna need to run and get boxes for some of this shit. You wanna go with?"

"Sure. Maybe we can grab some lunch while we're out, too." Evaine did her best not to wake Gage as she slid off the couch and followed Jacob to the door.

"Sounds like a plan."

Between the two of them, they got all the moving supplies and lunch out of the cab, into the lobby, and onto the elevator in one go. Although Evaine had to kick the tape gun across the carpeted floor when the sharp edge tore the bag on the way up to their apartment. The moment they reached the door, Jacob dropped the boxes he'd been wrestling, and they hit the floor with a thwack as he dug his keys from his pocket. "Fuckin' things."

"This is why people hire movers. Just wait until we're carrying all these boxes back down full of your crap." Evaine thought about it for a second. "Maybe Raven will help you with that cause I'm not."

Jacob shook his head as he shoved his key into the lock. "Such a bitch."

"Hey, you're leaving me. You're lucky I'm helping you at all."

The door unlocked with a soft click, and Jacob pushed it open before scooping up the boxes and carrying them inside. Rather than picking up the gun, Evaine kicked it over the threshold after him and then used the same foot to close the door as she struggled with the bags she carried.

"What the hell?" Gage asked as he rounded the corner from the kitchen.

Jacob dropped the boxes at his feet with a mischievous smile. "What, what? We went to get moving boxes, Sleeping Beauty."

Evaine slipped by Jacob, her hands full of takeout bags, and pushed up on her toes to kiss the side of Gage's mouth. "And lunch."

"Smells good." Gage kissed her back as she passed him on her way to the kitchen.

Chapter
Nine

Nine

Boxes & Bad Dreams

After lunch, Gage set up his easel and started a new painting. Evaine loved to watch him work. The way he bit his bottom lip as he concentrated on details or hummed along to the music while blocking in the colors. Unfortunately, she'd only watched him for a few minutes before Jacob dragged her into his room to help him pack.

It was a good thing it was the middle of the day and most of the neighbors were at work because the heavy thump of the industrial music rattled the walls as Jacob sang along with the fierce German as he rifled through his closet and tossed some things in a garbage bag and others into a box. Evaine bounced to the beat in front of his tall black dresser, pulling a pile of black T-shirts out and dropping them into a box before going for the next stack because Jacob's wardrobe was pretty much the same as hers, with minimal color involved.

"I don't think I'm gonna keep these."

Evaine glanced at Jacob, who was holding up a pair of beat-up leather ten-hole Doc Martens with rainbow laces. "I think you've had those since middle school. I'd be surprised if they even fit you. Plus, the treads've gotta be worn out by now."

A dark, perfect eyebrow kicked up like she was daft. "I don't wear them." He wrinkled his sharp nose. "They were my first pair, and I haven't had the heart to part with them. But I think it's time to pitch 'em." With a frown, he shoved them in the big black garbage bag, and the moment Jacob let go of them, Evaine started to count in her head.

At about fifteen seconds, regret spread across his face, and by thirty, he was chewing on his thumbnail, doubt seeping through him. Sixty seconds, and he was utterly wavering and pulling them back out. "Well, on the other hand, maybe I should keep them a little longer." That wicked grin spread across his face as he shoved them into the box.

Evaine laughed. "You're so indecisive sometimes."

Hand on his hip, his brow furrowed as he scoffed, "Look who's talking."

"That's so not true!" Evaine folded another black concert shirt and set it on the growing pile in the box.

Jacob cocked his head, tossing his long black hair back, so both sides of his shaved head peeked from under it. "Right, so it didn't take you two years to decide on a major?"

"That was different! It wasn't indecisiveness; it was parental pressure." Another pile of shirts dropped into the box with a swoosh. "I had to get over my mother's idea of what was best for me and decisively decide for myself."

Jacob chuckled and pitched his beat-up red chucks, almost the same color as her hair, into the box with an exaggerated nod. "Decisively decide. For sure, Princess!"

Sadness washed over her at the thought of not having Jacob around every day. Of course, he had to live his life, but part of her wanted to protect and keep him close and didn't like how quickly he was moving with Raven.

When he turned to toss his platform, patent leather boots with all the big silver buckles into the box, she caught his sea-green eyes and softly asked, "Are you sure you're ready to make this move, Jay?"

His gaze dropped to the floor before meeting hers, and his face told her the answer before he spoke. "I love that you worry about me, Evie, but I need to do this."

She couldn't help but ask, "Why? Why so fast?"

Jacob paused for a tick. "Sometimes, you just know. Sometimes the path is so clearly laid out before you. Look at you and Gage; you just know, right?"

Evaine nodded reluctantly, not because she wasn't sure, but because she didn't want to admit it and strengthen his argument.

"Right, so you have to believe me when I tell you I know. It's never been like that, Evie. Ever. You're the only person I've ever loved. So, I have to chase this."

Damn! She hated the passion and conviction in his words and that he used the L-word because she knew there was no way she could change his mind. The sparkle in his eyes didn't help, either. He was smitten with this boy. *Doesn't he deserve to be happy?* She couldn't change things, no matter how much she wanted, and forced a smile as she nodded. "I get it."

The grin that spread across Jacob's face told her he appreciated her words as he stepped around the boxes and kissed her. "Thank you, Princess."

They spent another couple of hours packing up his closet, emptying his nightstands, and boxing up his music collection, including his vinyl, sheet music, and different cords. With every box they filled, his room became emptier, and the corner of Evaine's heart belonging to him ached worse. Around eight, Gage came in and kissed her goodbye. "Remember to check the locks on the windows and double-lock the door, Baby." He turned to Jacob. "I appreciate you keepin' an eye on her, Man."

"Think nothin' of it," Jacob said from his spot on the floor.

It only took them another two hours to get everything else packed. The walls were empty; Jacob's favorite band posters rolled into a neat tub to protect them, and Evaine leaned against the door frame, sipping a glass of wine she'd brought from the kitchen. Jacob sat on the bed, sipping the other, and glanced around before taking another swig. "I think we're done, Princess."

"Looks that way." Despite her efforts to be happy for him, it still tugged at her heart, and though she wanted to support him, she needed time to come to grips with the change and forced a smile in place as she asked in a playful tone, "Now, when are you gonna move this shit outta my house?"

"Oh, now I'm on a deadline, huh? Talk about flip-flopping."

"Best to just rip the band-aid right off." Her tone stayed light and playful, but she chugged her wine in two gulps. "I'm gonna get another glass."

"I need a refill, too." Jacob pushed from the bed with ease, stretching his arms over his head and yawning, his movements reminding her of a large feline as she took his glass and headed back to the kitchen. Jacob trailed behind her to the living room and turned down the music before dropping onto the couch. "Do you wanna order pizza for dinner?"

"I never say no to pizza. As long as it's Caprio's and not Vinnie's."

"Ah, come on now. We got Brady's for lunch cause that's what you wanted. You can't make me eat Caprio's too. That's just torture."

"You'll live." She sat down next to him, curling her bare feet under her and handing him a full glass. A frown creased his beautiful face before he took a large pull from it. "No, I really won't."

Gods! She didn't want things to change and would miss the small things, like fighting over dinner or what movie they were going to watch while they ate. Unable to say no, Evaine crossed her arms over her chest and balanced the bottom of her wine glass in the crease of her elbow. "Fine, but you call and order then. In fact, you can pay, too."

"Fine, I will," he shot back.

Evaine mocked him as he reached for the cordless, sticking her tongue out at the back of his head as he dialed the number to Vinnie's, and then giggled when he shot a dirty look over his shoulder and rolled his eyes. "I can see you, Bitch!"

Once they ordered the pizza, they drained their wine glasses a second time, and a welcomed fuzziness edged into Evaine's mind as the alcohol eased her sadness and worry about the future. Her belly felt warm, and her limbs languid because everything was better with wine, lots of wine. *Or vodka; I like vodka too.* Evaine nudged Jacob's leg with her toes, unwilling to get up again. "It's your turn to fill them."

One more glass, and she'd have a pleasant buzz. Two or three more, and she'd sleep like a baby, which would be utter bliss. Jacob shot her a side-eyed glance before snatching her glass from her. "I swear," he mumbled as he headed for the kitchen. "So damn demanding, bossing me around like the hired help. Bitch!"

Evaine shifted on the couch, adjusting the pillows so she could comfortably lay her head against the arm. "Don't be such a whiner."

An unexpected knock at the door made Evaine jump as Jacob said, "I'll get it," from the kitchen.

"Check the peeper."

He glanced over his shoulder with a wide, toothy grin. "Did you just say check the peter?"

Evaine sat up and clarified, "PEEPER!" with a giggle.

The grin turned into a smirk, his green eyes sparkling. "Got it!" Jacob had to crouch to look through it. "Not the pizza guy." With a flip of the lock, he pulled the door open and peeked his head out. "Can I help you?"

Evaine rarely heard such a professional tone from his sarcastic mouth.

"Is this Evaine Maire's residence?" The very British accent asked from the hallway, making her stand up and cross to the door. The voice was familiar, but she needed to see if it was him, to be sure.

"Can I ask who you are?" Jacob's tone had a sharpened edge, and she wasn't going to lie; she loved when he was protective, a smile forming on her lips as she rested her hands on Jacob's shoulder blades and peeked over to see the man. "It's fine. He's my boss- Tristan."

Jacob stepped back, his tone loosening with her recognition. "Please come in."

Tristan held his charcoal bowler hat as he crossed the threshold, his primped chocolate hair bouncing as he surveyed the room, and then nodded a greeting in Evaine's direction. "'Ello, My Dear."

Evaine smoothed her ratty black Skinny Puppy T-shirt. "I wasn't expecting company, Mr. Basile."

"Well, of course, I was worried when you told me you'd had a break-in. We were in the area, so I decided to drop by." As always, Tristan was wearing a slim-fitted suit with a buttoned vest like a proper English gentleman with his black trench coat over it. "Good to see you have a gentleman keeping an eye on you, Evaine." Tristan's hand shot out toward Jacob. "Gage, I presume."

Evaine and Jacob laughed in sync, Jacob shaking his head as he took Tristan's hand. "I'm Jacob, her best friend. Gage is working."

"I see. Good Man!" With a sharp nod, Tristan's eyes caught Jacob's and held them for a long moment. When Tristan released the handshake, Jacob's hand fell to his side limply before Tristan closed the distance between them in one stride and took her hand, squeezing it. "I wanted to check on you. Make sure all is well. Terrible to think someone broke in. What did the police say? Was it an isolated incident, or have they had other break-ins in the neighborhood?"

His concern startled Evaine and made her feel uncomfortable. If she was a hundred percent honest, it was because she barely knew this man. So why would he come across town to check on her? He was her employer, nothing more. When Evaine tried to pull her hand from his, Tristan tightened his grip. She cleared her throat to find her words. "They didn't seem worried at all. In fact, it felt like a waste of time to even have them out."

"Unfortunate to hear, My Dear." He eyed her for a tick. "Have you informed your father?"

Again, his concern rattled her, her eyes flicking to her bare feet for a moment before meeting his worried gaze again. "Not yet. I don't want to worry them."

Gaze shifting from concerned to stern, he said, "You need to tell them, Evaine. They would want to know."

She found it impossible to disagree, glancing at Jacob for support, who shrugged his shoulders like he wasn't listening. *Big help!* A familiar glaze of boredom in his sea-green eyes.

With a squeeze of her fingers, Tristan caught her eyes, making her feel like a small child being corrected by her teacher. "You're probably right," she mumbled, heat spreading up her chest and cheeks as Tristan's dark eyes bore into hers. The connection was unwavering, even though she attempted to fight it.

"Why don't you show me where they broke in, My Dear? I'd like to take a look around." The warmth of his gaze lulled her, making the edges of her vision feel fuzzier than they had a few moments ago, and compelled her to do precisely as he requested. "They came in the bedroom window." She crossed the room with Tristan in tow and ushered him through her bedroom door. It didn't matter that he was essentially a stranger or that she was inviting him into the private space she shared with Gage. All that mattered was fulfilling his request. Evaine watched Tristan inspect the window. Something in her brain flickered with concern when he leaned in and sniffed the open curtains, but it washed away when he stepped to her and was so close that she could feel his cool breath on her face. "Thank you for indulging my curiosity, My Dear." His thumb brushed along her bottom lip, making her jerk her head back. When he said, "I wouldn't want anything to happen to such a precious jewel, would I?" her body relaxed as his words lulled her into a sense of safety, making her lean into him.

Evaine didn't flinch when he stole a kiss from her numb lips but relaxed even further when he said, "Everything's fine, My Dear. Why don't you show me out now?"

"Okay." Evaine felt hollow, like everything was far off and fuzzy, as she walked him back to the door.

When they approached Jacob, he was leaning against the doorway to the kitchen with his arms crossed over his chest, and she vaguely wondered if the wine was getting to both of them. They hadn't eaten in hours, but that shouldn't make her feel so dazed. Besides, Jacob could drink her under the table most nights, so it made no sense.

Tristan jutted his chin in Jacob's direction and said, "Excellent, Son," which seemed to jolt him from his reverie.

"Everything good?" Jacob asked Evaine, who stared at him as confusion clouded her ability to remember what happened.

"Just fine," Tristan said to them both.

"Everything's fine." Evaine nodded her head in agreement, a smile curling her lips.

Tristan reached out and squeezed Evaine's hand. "That's right, My Dear," he said before turning his attention to Jacob. "And you'll be staying with her tonight?"

Jacob narrowed his eyes and gave Tristan a quick nod.

"Good, good. That puts my worries to rest." He smiled over his shoulder at Evaine. "Do not hesitate to call if you need anything, Ms. Maire, and do try to have a safe evening, young lady. Keep this door locked." Tristan turned the knob and was out the door, closing it with a soft click.

With two giant steps, Jacob flipped the deadbolt and locked the bottom lock, testing the knob before he turned and rested his back against the door. "That was weird, wasn't it?"

Evaine nodded, her brows furrowing. "Was it?" She couldn't shake the fuzziness chewing at the edges of her brain. It dulled her ability to process the last few minutes and made her feel like she was floating in a calm sea without a care in the world. "I'm not sure."

Jacob hung there with the same distant look in his eyes for a few minutes before he drew a long breath through his nose and blew it out of his mouth.

"Odd." He shrugged and then jumped at the resounding knock on the door.

"What the hell?" Evaine squeaked as he turned and looked through the peephole. The last few minutes were a vague blur that she couldn't wrap her head around.

Jacob glanced at her over his shoulder, a strange relief written across his face. "It's the pizza guy."

Evaine left Jacob to deal with the pizza guy while she collected plates from the cabinets and refilled their wine glasses, which required opening another bottle. By the time she carried everything to the living room, Jacob had set the pizza box on the coffee table and plopped down on the couch.

"Look at that beautiful pie!" Jacob tossed the lid open, the smile spreading across his face making the fact that Evaine had to eat crappy pizza worth it. As long as he was happy, she'd suffer.

Gooey cheese stretched and snapped as she pulled a slice from the box. "Caprio's is better." Her encounter with Tristan was all but forgotten.

"That's blasphemy."

After another glass of wine and a full belly, Evaine was tired and, with some effort, forced herself from her comfy spot curled next to Jacob on the couch. With a kiss on his head, she ruffled his long black hair. "I need a shower and sleep."

His half-open eyes flicked up. "Make sure you check your window locks, Baby. Gage will kill me if anything happens to your cute little ass. And well, you know, I like you a little too."

"Okay. Night, Jay." Evaine shuffled across the room toward her door.

"Sweet dreams, Princess."

The first thing she did when she walked into her room was check the locks on her windows and pull the curtain closed with a flick of her wrist, and then she stripped off her clothes and headed for the bathroom. One of the Rammstein songs from earlier was stuck in her head, and she hummed it as she turned on the facet and messed with the temperature controls. Gage had a wildly different idea about a hot shower, which meant she had to adjust the knobs to get the right level of heat.

While waiting for the water to warm, she put her hair up, washed her face, and brushed her teeth. By the time she finished, steam wafted around the room and condensation clung to the mirror, which meant the water would be perfect. Hot enough to cook her flesh, just the way she liked it. A satisfied sigh slipped past her lips when she stepped into the scalding water and let it penetrate her tired muscles, the punishing stream a hard pulse beating them into submission.

As she thought about the visit with Tristan earlier, she didn't remember many of the details and thought it must've been all the wine. Still, she appreciated his concern and that he took the time to come and check on her. He was a kind man, and she'd have to remember to invite him to her Halloween party tomorrow to say thank you. Though she wasn't sure, something told her he'd enjoy it.

Evaine washed her body and rinsed before turning the water off and toweling dry, the heat of the bathroom making her woozy. Cool air wafted over her when she opened the door and made her skin tingle as she padded to the bed and climbed in. Her body was still flush and heated from the scalding shower; she pulled the blankets up enough to cover her nakedness. Even though she was alone, she wasn't comfortable being exposed, considering recent events.

151

With a glance at the alarm clock, she realized it was still a couple of hours until Gage got home and knew she would feel better when he was lying next to her. It never bothered her to be alone in the past, and it annoyed her it did now because she didn't like her world being disheveled by some stupid asshole. Evaine yawned and curled on her side, tucking her hands under her warm cheek as she closed her heavy eyes and allowed her mind to drift toward sleep, which seemed to come easy enough.

Though it may have come easy, her dreams were another thing.

At first, they were dark and frightening as Evaine chased Jacob through a maze, never being able to catch up with him as they twisted and turned through the labyrinth. But then her dream shifted to something much different, and a tall, shrouded figure replaced Jacob and pursued her through the same frightening maze. No matter how fast she ran, she couldn't escape as the shadowy figure hunted her like prey, always right at her back, never relenting.

The dream was so vivid that she felt her heart pounding as her body screamed from its effort to outpace him. Sweat ran down her face, and wet dirt squished through her toes as she ran as fast as possible. When she tripped over the uneven ground, the momentum sent her flying. Despite her efforts to soften the impact by putting her hands out, she slammed into the ground with a hard thunk that reverberated up her arms and jarred her shoulders, mud splashing her face and getting into her mouth.

A sadistic laugh echoed around her as the figure lunged and straddled her waist, pushing her chest back into the thick, wet mud with a large hand in the middle of her back. He gripped her hair with the other and pulled her head at a harsh angle.

"You're hurting me," Evaine whimpered, hating the weakness in her voice and squirming to get free.

"Oh, Evie, I have not even begun to hurt you yet, Baby." Goosebumps prickled her damp skin with the sardonic way he said Baby, panic running over her like a freight train. *This dream is way too real!* Evaine tried to will herself to wake but failed miserably. The creature shifted his weight and shoved a knee into the middle of her back, making her groan as he pinned her to the wet ground and freed his hand to grip her chin. Long, icy fingers bit into her face as the stranger wrenched her neck at a sharp angle, making her squeal with pain.

"I do so love the way you whimper and squeal. I think I will enjoy making you beg, or even better, whimper with pleasure. The sweet little noises you make when you come are enough to drive a man mad." Sharp canines ran along the column of her neck. "Such a delectable little treat."

"Let me go!" Evaine flinched as she fought his hold with every ounce of determination she could muster. His body was solid and immovable, and her efforts earned her another sadistic laugh before he whispered, "Soon, you will bleed for me, Evie." Cool breath skated over her thumping pulse as he nipped at the tender flesh. "Until then, I bid you goodnight, My Exquisite Little Prey."

When he released her, Evaine jolted awake, sitting straight-up, and clutched her heaving chest as she struggled to catch her breath. The vivid memory of the stranger's touch made her skin crawl. Evaine felt violated and reached for the lamp on her nightstand, scanning the room when the soft light flooded it.

The curtains were still closed, and she was alone. Relief washed over her as she blew out a heavy breath and flopped back against her pillow, staring at the ceiling as the dream played over in her head. *I'm losing my freaking mind!*

Evaine listened to her pounding heartbeat and tried to convince herself it was just a dream, her overactive imagination processing Jacob's move. There was no doubt she felt vulnerable with him leaving and maybe a little lost. Her subconscious was trying to work through all the emotions and crazy stuff going on and decided to stick it all in one pot and stir.

That must be it. Despite the reasonable explanation, she still couldn't bring herself to turn off the light. Instead, she curled into a ball and pulled the covers around her until the jingle of the doorknob jolted her awake.

Gage smiled in the doorway as his mint-green eyes settled on her. "Were you waiting up for me?" He reached for the back of his shirt and yanked it over his head in one smooth motion, like some sort of god, his corded muscles flexing as he dropped it in the basket and shook his purple mess of hair out, running his fingers through it.

"Of course I was." Evaine lied like a freaking rug.

Anticipation fluttered low in her belly as he sucked his lip ring into his mouth and chewed on it. Gage cocked his head and was a thing of beauty when he asked, "Were you thinking about how good it's gonna feel when I make you come?" A cocky smirk on his mouth made Evaine clench her thighs, heat pooling between them.

Her nightmares dissipated as his fingers worked the button of his low-hung leather pants and then moved to the zipper. His body was all lean, corded muscle, and the sight of him left her with nothing but the need to have him inside her.

Evaine let go of the blanket clutched to her chest and leaned against the soft leather headboard, the coolness of the air tightening her nipples as goosebumps prickled her skin. When she kicked the sheets off and let her knees drop open, giving him a shameless view of her slick slit, Gage's eyes tracked her like a predator's. Her fingers traced down her collarbone, teasingly over her nipple, and across her flat stomach, dipping into the slit as her eyes fluttered half-closed and stroked in and out, her thumb grazing the sensitive nerves. "Mmmm. Hmmm," she purred.

His cock was already hard as he slid his pants down and stepped out of them, and Evaine licked her lips, saliva pooling in her mouth at the sight of him, stiff and thick. Her fingers picked up the pace as he crawled across the bed and settled between her open legs, his knees under him. Her insides clenched around her fingers, anticipating his touch. A moan tumbled from her parted lips when he butterflied soft kisses on the inside of one thigh and then the other, her hips lifting to meet his touch as tension built low in her belly.

Gage sat back on his feet and twined his fingers into her hair, jerking the strands and earning a whimper before dragging her into his lap and pulling her mouth to his. When her lips parted, he pushed his tongue inside and devoured the moan that tried to escape, and when he broke the kiss, he kept her lips against his, whispering, "I do like to watch you touch yourself, Baby, but right now, I wanna fuck you." And used his free hand to hoist her up by her ass and settle her over his cock.

Evaine gasped as Gage penetrated her with one hard thrust, her arms curling around his shoulders as she rode him. His hands gripped both hips, forcing her to keep a fast pace, his thrusts driving him deep inside her. Her body clenched around him as the tension built, his growl-like grunts growing louder as he fucked her.

She loved the way he used her and made her feel both helpless and ravished in a way that was always safe. He never pushed her too far and was always mindful of her needs. *Oh, Gods!* He could abuse her body like no one else. Strung tight, she arched her back and drove her hips down, trying to chase the release her body begged for.

It only took a few hard thrusts, his hands driving her up and down, for them both to find it.

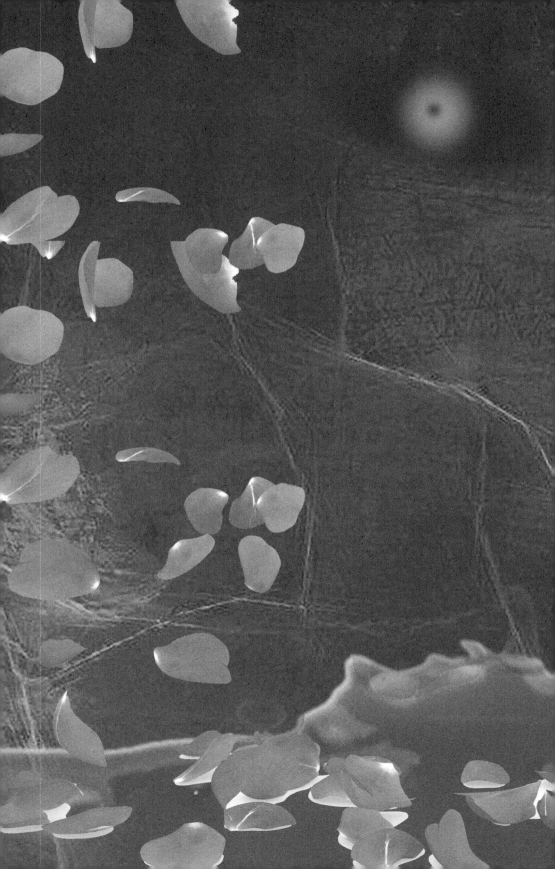

Chapter
Ten

Ten

Blood & Roses

Evaine got a good night's sleep for the first time in the last few days and was up before her alarm. The ache in her thighs made her smile because it wasn't the first time things got a little rough with Gage. She enjoyed it when they did and was pretty sure being manhandled was the reason she slept so well. It would be a perfect day if she could focus on her work and get it done.

She looked forward to getting to the office to get started, so it didn't take her long to shower, brush her teeth, and pull her hair up into a tight bun. Then she threw on light makeup, eyeliner and lipstick, and got dressed in a comfy pair of black pants and a soft, warm royal purple sweater. Instead of heels, she wore her ten-hole Docs because they were comfortable and kept her feet warm, especially with the thick socks she wore because they were a little too big.

As Evaine kissed Gage on the cheek, he was dead to the world, and his snores echoed off the high ceiling, making her giggle before she headed to the kitchen to grab a glass of water. Jacob sat at the kitchen bar drinking coffee and propped his head up with a hand against his heavily pierced ear, his long hair hanging in his tired eyes. He shoved it back, "Morning, Princess," and gave her his best kissy-face.

"Morning." She stretched over the counter to give him a chased peck on the lips, and he smiled half-heartedly when she let her body slide back down and asked, "Off to work?"

Evaine nodded as he sipped his coffee. "Why do you look so tired?"

A frown marred his handsome face, and he shrugged. "I fell asleep on the couch and woke up with a kink in my neck."

"Poor baby."

Her fake sympathy made Jacob smirk. "I'm gonna try to have all this stuff moved today. Raven is busy, so I said fuck it and hired a mover because you know I'm not gonna do it by myself." He grinned like the Cheshire Cat. "I'm too pretty for manual labor!"

"You really are, Sweetie." Evaine took a glass from the cabinet and then stuck it in the water dispenser on the fridge before downing it in a few gulps. "It's probably best, anyway; otherwise, you might hurt yourself."

Jacob guffawed in his seat. "I'll have you know I'm completely capable of doing it if I was so inclined."

With a swipe of her hand across her mouth, Evaine smirked over her shoulder before setting the glass next to the sink. "We might have to agree to disagree on this one, Sweetie."

Jacob side-eyed her, his jaw set in a hard line, "Bitch," and brought his mug to his lips.

His drama made her laugh as she smoothed the front of her sweater and adjusted the waist of her pants. "Don't sulk too much, Princess."

Coffee went up his nose. Jacob snorted and covered his mouth as he choked.

"Be careful not to hurt yourself." Evaine smiled sweetly and then changed the subject when he flicked her off. "So touchy this morning."

"Weren't you leaving?" Jacob asked in his best bitchy tone.

Evaine stuck her tongue out before marching out of the kitchen. "Yes." She grabbed her velvet jacket from the hook and slipped it on before reaching for her messenger bag. "You still have time to hang out tonight?" The strap slid over her head and settled on her shoulder, and she adjusted the bag at her hip as Jacob rounded the corner with a grin.

"Of course I do." He handed her a folded piece of paper. "Here's the address to Julien's place. Just come right from work, and we'll get dinner together."

Evaine cocked her head, confused. "Julien's? I thought it was Raven's place." She liked Jacob moving in with Julien and his crew even less and wanted to ask him to stay, but she couldn't bring herself to stop him if he thought this was right.

Don't be selfish. Don't be selfish. DON'T be selfish, she chanted in her head.

"Nah. Julien has a huge freaking apartment with like five or six bedrooms. He isn't even charging me rent right now, which is pretty awesome, Evie. They both are. I know you'll like them once you get to know them." Jacob grimaced. "Though Rave's sister, Skye- Well, I'll wait for you to meet her."

"Great. I can't wait." Evaine kissed his cheek and headed out the door.

"Bye, Princess."

At the office, Evaine had worked on her novel for two hours without interruption and was mid-thought when the door opened. "I'll be right with you," she said without looking up. It took her a couple of ticks to finish the paragraph she was working on, and she smiled as she stood. "Sorry for the delay. Ca- Can I help you?" Her words caught in her throat when her eyes landed on the waiting delivery man, who held two large vases of long-stem roses, black, not red. Her stomach roiled with dread and anxiety as he strode to her desk and set the vases on the edge before glancing at the clipboard. "Evaine Maire?"

"Yes," tumbled out of her mouth as she shook her head.

"Are you sure?" he asked with a smirk.

Evaine nodded. "Yes."

"Great. If you could just sign here, please." He handed her the clipboard and chucked a thumb over his shoulder toward the door. "I have two more in the van downstairs."

Evaine hesitated before taking the board. "I don't want them."

The deliveryman cocked his head and looked at her like she was the first person to refuse flowers, ever, his eyebrows hitching under the bill of his baseball cap. "Excuse me?"

She fidgeted with the paper clipped to the board, biting her bottom lip before summoning her voice. "I don't want them. Please take them back."

"I'm sorry, Ms. I can't just take them back."

Nausea overtook her as she glanced at the two vases on her desk, the black roses clashing with the green and white foliage. What she wanted to do was pitch them across the room, but instead, she huffed, "Fine! I'll keep these." And then signed on the line before handing the board back. "But I don't want the ones downstairs."

"What do you want me to do with them?"

"I don't care. Leave them in the lobby if you have to. Just don't bring them up here, please." Evaine struggled to control the agitation in her voice, but from the look on the poor man's face, she wasn't doing a good job. The delivery man nodded and backed up a few steps. "Okay. I'll do that." And then he tipped his hat before hightailing it out the door. "You have a good day, Miss."

Evaine was surprised when she found a card tucked into one bouquet and stared at it for a minute before plucking the small white envelope from the greenery, another wave of dread flooding her and making her fingers shake as she worked to open the envelope and remove the card. Adrenaline surged, flushing her body with an icy wave. The card had the same elegant penmanship in black ink, two neat lines.

There are always consequences for disobedience, Evie. Remember, I warned you.

It slipped from her trembling hand and landed face down on the desk as Evaine tried to dampen the panic that spread through her. This was a direct threat from a crazy person over the bracelet Gage took. Somehow, they knew she wasn't wearing it and weren't happy. Evaine struggled to wrap her head around what was happening and the fact that she had a full-fledged stalker. For a minute, she contemplated calling the police, though it wasn't likely they would be much help, and chewed on the skin around her thumb before picking up the card and rereading it. "What the fuck?"

As she laid it face down, Tristan strolled into the office. "Good afternoon, Love." His tone was light, and he smiled as he pulled off his jacket and hat and hung them on the coat rack by the door.

"Good afternoon, Tristan." The quiver in her voice annoyed her because she hated the helplessness that bombarded her every time this happened. And now, it was interfering with her work, which was super frustrating. When he turned his attention to her, Tristan's face drooped into a frown, and she wondered just how terrified she looked as he crossed the room in two strides. "What's all this?"

"I guess sending flowers to me at home isn't enough anymore because now they've started sending them to the office, too." Anger seeped into her words and was a strange comfort. In some ways, it grounded her and made her feel empowered, and she held on to it for dear life because crying in front of her boss wasn't an option.

Tristan frowned before rounding the desk and grabbing her elbow. "Everything will be okay, My Dear. Sit down."

Evaine didn't bulk as he guided her into the seat and clasped her hands in her lap to keep them from shaking. "I just don't understand why." Tears threatened to break from the rims of her burning eyes, and she struggled to keep them at bay, sucking in a breath to calm down.

NO CRYING!

One of Tristan's cool hands slid up and down her back, the other reaching for the card on the desk. "May I?" he asked and picked it up when Evaine gave him a slight nod. The muscles in his jaws ticked as he read, his eyes narrowing with anger. "What an arse." He cleared his throat and caught her eye. "I see why you are so upset. This is a serious concern, My Dear. You need to be extra cautious."

His look made her feel like she was in more danger than she realized, and she swallowed hard before asking, "Do you think I should call the police?"

"It probably isn't a bad idea. Just to be on the safe side. Perhaps we need to find you some protection."

She cringed at the thought of a bodyguard following her. "I don't think that's necessary."

"Well, at the least, we need to report this incident. I'll handle it for you. But in the meantime, what would you like me to do with them?"

"Would you just get rid of them, please?" She felt weak asking him, but she couldn't do it. Her legs felt like rubber, and her hands shook.

"As you wish, My Dear." Tristan grabbed her phone and dialed an unknown number, smiling as the line rang. When the person on the other end answered, he said, "Yes. This is Mr. Basile, on the fifth floor. I need someone up here now." Then he nodded twice. "Yes, yes. Thank you." And hung up the phone. "They'll be right up, My Dear, and we will get this taken care of." His cool hand rubbed her shoulder. "Why don't you take a brief break? Go to the lady's room and freshen up. I've got this."

Appreciative of his kindness, Evaine smiled. "Thank you. I will." Her legs protested as she stood up, but she forced them to carry her out of the office into the small restroom across the hall and went straight into the first stall, locking the door before her body dropped onto the toilet like lead, and tears streamed ran down her face.

Once she started crying, she couldn't stop. Evaine wiped her face as the tears rolled down her cheeks and dripped off the edge of her chin. Clear snot ran out of her nose, causing her to sniffle and grab a wad of toilet paper to wipe it away. Though she sobbed quietly, her weakness and frustration echoed in the large tiled space. She fought the urge to vomit up the water she'd had for breakfast, counting down from twenty and breathing in slow, deep breaths. *Gods, I hate crying!* It was the worst, especially losing it over this. But this threat rattled her to the core because she feared this person would escalate things and do something because she refused their demand.

After about twenty minutes, Evaine pulled herself back together, cleaned up her face, and headed back to the office. Despite her red and runny nose, she couldn't hide in the bathroom all afternoon and was relieved that the roses were gone when she got back to her desk.

Tristan must've been listening for her because he came out of his office as she settled into her chair. "I talked with the building security, and they will keep an eye out for anything odd. I also instructed them to stop all deliveries to verify the destination. That way, they can deal with unwanted gifts before they get to you. They have contacted the authorities and will bring them up to the office when they arrive. I am happy to accompany you while you talk to them." He glanced at his pocket watch. "But I have a four o'clock appointment this afternoon that I cannot reschedule."

"I appreciate it, but I've dealt with them before, so I can handle it." Her forced smile probably wasn't very reassuring, but he gave her a curt nod, anyway. "Of course, My dear."

"Thank you," she breathed. "I'm going to get some work done before they get here."

"Very good." Tristan nodded and then strolled back into his office, closing the door.

The note hung over Evaine like an executioner's ax as she struggled to concentrate.

After a few quiet minutes, Tristan's distinct timbre seeped through his closed door. She couldn't understand what he was saying, but it was pretty clear he wasn't happy and was giving someone hell, which differed from the kindness he showed her.

Another thirty minutes passed, and Evaine was back in the groove when two gentlemen walked through the office door. One was tall and well dressed, the creases of his suit pressed to perfection, and the other was a bit more rumpled and disheveled. It was easy to guess he was the officer, and the other worked for the building.

"Ms. Maire?" the tall one asked.

Evaine nodded before pushing to her feet and rounding the desk.

"This is Detective Jones. He has a few questions for you."

The less put-together detective smiled and shoved his hand toward her. She hesitated for a moment and then shook it. "It should only take a few minutes of your time."

"I'll leave you to it," the security officer said.

Detective Jones nodded at him. "You have my card if anything else comes up."

"I do." The well-dressed man left the office, closing the door behind him.

Evaine stood there before offering the detective a seat on the plush couch and sitting in one of the chairs next to it. Detective Jones asked her several of the same questions the uniforms had, taking notes and explaining that the flowers and card were evidence. He said they would check with the florist, though there wasn't much they could do unless they got lucky and found fingerprints because Evaine didn't know the stalker, which limited them. The detective advised her to be diligent and cautious and take the threat seriously, making the panic rise again. As they wrapped up the conversation, he handed her a card and told her to call with any new information before seeing himself out the door.

After the meeting, Evaine felt shell-shocked but focused on her work to take her mind off it because there was no way she would allow this crazy asshole to get any further under her skin. It was already bad enough that she'd lost it once today. *Can you say compartmentalize?* It was her new favorite word, and she worked diligently at her computer for an hour before Tristan swung his door open and marched out. "Evie, do you know where the plans are for the condominiums? The ones on the waterfront?"

Evaine set her pen down and looked at him. He seemed tense, but there was a controlled tone to his questions, like he was trying not to upset her. She hated the pity and sighed as she pushed to her feet. "I'm not sure I know what you're looking for, Tristan. I haven't seen any plans. What's the file name? Maybe I can find it for you that way?"

Tristan tugged the bottom of his vest and then ran a hand through his chocolate hair, messing the neat quaff before scrubbing it across his stubbled chin. "Watercrest is the name of the project. Would you please see if you can find it? I need it for the meeting at four."

"Absolutely." A large row of filing cabinets sat against the wall behind Evaine's desk, and it only took her a couple of ticks to find what he needed. When she rapped on his door, Tristan bid her inside with a very British sounding, "Enter."

"Here are the plans you asked for." She set them on the corner of his desk.

His white smile flashed as Tristan glanced up. "You are a lifesaver, My Dear. Thank you. The meeting will go much smoother with these." And then he leaned back in his chair and scanned her from head to toe. "Did you speak with the detective?"

Evaine nodded, wondering if he was this kind to everyone or if it was just her.

He quirked an eyebrow. "And are you feeling better?"

"Yes, much."

"I still think you should consider some sort of security, Evaine. It isn't safe to ignore this mad man's threats. In fact, I would go so far as to say it will be to your detriment if you do."

"I understand. I promise I'll be careful."

The intensity of his stare made her feel like a small child being scolded, and when he frowned, she wanted to crawl in a hole. "Very well then."

"Thank you." Her eyes drifted to the floor before catching his hazel ones. After everything he'd done over the last few days, Evaine felt compelled to invite him to her party.

As if he could read her mind, he sat forward and asked, "Was there something else, Love?"

"I thought that maybe you'd like to come to my annual Halloween party. It's at the Plaza hotel in the ballroom. This year it starts at eight. I'd really love it if you joined us. My parents will be there, too."

A genuine smile broke across Tristan's face, wrinkling the corners of his eyes as he crossed his arms over his chest and leaned back, seeming to contemplate it for a few ticks. Evaine thought he'd decline, but he said, "That would be lovely."

Like the universe hadn't made her day crappy enough, it chose this moment for the loud chime of her cellphone to echo through the office. "Great." Evaine kicked a thumb back at the doorway. "I should probably go answer that."

"Why don't you do that, My Dear?"

She wondered how she got so lucky to be employed by this understanding man as she rushed out the door and to her desk, digging her phone out of her messenger bag. When she pushed the green phone button, she said, "Hello, Daddy."

"Princess. How are you?" His tone was light, his mood jovial.

"I'm working, Daddy."

"Oh, right, right. I forgot you started the new job with Tristan. How is it going?"

"It's going well. I've been able to get a lot of writing done during the slow periods, which are many, considering. What's going on with you?" Her new superpower was compartmentalizing. It didn't even feel like lying.

"Well, Princess, I have some good and bad news."

"Bad first," Evaine said without hesitating.

"I figured you'd say that. Bad news; we aren't going to make it to your party on Thursday."

"Why not? I thought you weren't leaving for Italy until Friday?" The news didn't disappoint her, but it did make her curious.

"We had an opportunity come to light that I couldn't pass up. We are leaving tonight and will be gone for an extra week. I'm sorry to miss it, but it's unavoidable at this point, Princess. Will you forgive me for this one?"

Evaine giggled. "I'm sure I will survive without you and mother. I'm a big girl."

"You'll always be my little princess, Evie. No matter how grown you are. Just remember that. Best I let you go before Tristan gets upset, huh? We'll see you when we get back from our trip. We can plan Sunday dinner with the boys. Okay, Princess."

"Okay, Daddy. Have a safe trip. I love you."

"Love you too, Evie."

The next couple of hours went by uneventfully, with Tristan working in his office and Evaine at her desk. The quiet normalness of it was a balm on her frazzled nerves, but when three-thirty rolled around, Tristan emerged from his office and said, "I need you to come with me to this meeting, Evaine. It may run a little late, but I can have my driver drop you off at home after." And the balm was gone that quickly because something told her he was trying to keep her close for her protection. Appreciation and anger warred inside her. She was determined not to let the freak make her too afraid to live her life. Maybe she was hard-headed and stubborn, but she wouldn't have it.

Her hesitation spurred him, his tone sharpening. "It is not up for debate, My Dear. It is part of your job description." Before heading to the rack in the corner to collect his coat and hat. "Now, please collect the plans from my desk and let us be on our way."

Evaine couldn't do anything except nod before scrambling to comply with his order. Something about his tone made it impossible for her to resist, and she followed him into the elevator and down to the parking garage to the waiting car.

Once they were moving through the traffic in the plush Town Car, Tristan's tension seemed to ease when he glanced over and said, "I can see the wheels turning in your head, Evaine. I would warn you when it comes to this individual. He seems to be quite unstable and unhinged. It's imperative that you are cautious." Her hand rested on the leather seat between them; he gripped it and tugged her fingers to bring her attention to his eyes.

She nodded dutifully. "I understand."

His gaze penetrated her as he smiled and leaned in to kiss her fingers, his cool breath skating over them. "My only goal is to keep you safe." Mesmerized by his tone, his hazel eyes bored into hers, making her head hazy. "Do you understand, My Dear?" Cool lips brushed over her knuckles, and a shiver ran down her spine. When she nodded, he said, "Good, good. Because it will require a bold move to protect you," which made her feel anything but.

Still, his gaze lulled her into a place where she heard his words, but they were far away, not quite making sense. Or maybe it was more that she didn't care because there was only his voice and tone. Drawn like a moth to a flame, she leaned closer, the leather groaning as she shifted into him. A small smile curled his thin lips, and a flash of canine made something in the back of her brain hitch. But when he rubbed her fingers and said, "That's my good girl," it was replaced by a numbness that soothed her battered soul like the best drugs she'd ever had.

With his free hand, Tristan tipped her chin back, exposing the curve of her neck. "Just sit still for me, Love." He closed the distance between them, brushing his nose along her pulse before kissing the spot, and Evaine's body shivered with the intimate contact and could do little else as a slight prick pinched her neck. His lips closed over her heated skin as he wrapped his arms around her and pinned her to his body, drinking deeper and making her head spin with each suctioning pull. Lust injected into her bloodstream and caused her thighs to clench as slickness pooled between them with a throbbing ache that forced a soft moan from her open lips. With each almost reverently, slow draw, need flooded her body and made it tremble, and her insides clenched, longing for attention. Comfort wrapped her mind in a lull, like the warm embrace of a dose of ecstasy.

Tristan groaned, the vibration of his lips tickling the sensitive skin on her neck, and swiped his tongue over the wounds before placing one last kiss on her flesh and focusing on her face. His eyes were wholly black when he smiled and licked the traces of her lifeblood from his lips. "You really do taste sublime, My Dear."

A strange mixture of desire and satisfaction slithered across her skin. Her mind was too far gone from Tristan's thrall to do anything other than rest her head on his chest. Tristan shifted her against him, his hand wrapping a red curl around his finger as he whispered against the top of her head, "Now, Love. We had a very uneventful ride to our meeting. Did we not?"

The last few minutes fluttered from her memory like a fragment of a dream just outside her reach as she nodded against his chest.

"Say it, Evie," he said, like he was soothing a small child.

"We had a very uneventful ride to our meeting." Her words were hollow and far away, and her voice didn't sound like it was coming from her.

"That's my girl." His cool hand stroked her hair before tilting her head back to kiss her forehead. "Now, sit back and relax, My Dear. We are almost there."

As if her body couldn't imagine ignoring his order, she shifted back into her seat, her hands dropping into her lap as she sat there in a daze until Tristan snapped her out of it by saying, "We are here, Love."

"That was quick."

Tristan smirked. "I think you may have dozed off, My Dear. I dare say I'm not surprised, considering the day you've had."

When the door opened, Tristan slid from the car and held a hand out to help her. She took it without hesitation and climbed to her feet, ensuring she had the plans before letting the driver close the door. They were in another covered parking garage and sped to the elevator. As the doors opened, Tristan held out a hand and waited for her to step in before following and pushing the button for the twelfth floor. Evaine's stomach roiled when the car lurched, her head spinning as she reached for the bar. Tristan's hand on her shoulder steadied her until the wave passed. "Are you feeling okay, My Dear?" He let go of her when she nodded and said, "Yes. I'm fine."

The heavy metal doors slid open when they reached their floor, and Evaine followed Tristan out and down the hall to a set of large glass doors. "The plans, please," he said before proceeding through them when Evaine handed him what he asked for and followed him.

They certainly spared no expense in decorating the large office suite. Between the plush leather furniture and multiple pieces of well-known artwork hung on every wall. Most of which likely belonged in a museum and would make Gage freak if he saw any of the paintings in person.

A petite young lady sat at the desk and smiled as they approached. "Mr. Basile. Would you like me to take your coat?"

"No, thank you, Moira. If you could inform Ansel that I have arrived, that would be splendid."

"As you wish." She dipped her chin at him as a sign of respect and headed around the corner.

When she was gone, Tristan turned to Evaine. "Please have a seat, Love. This should not take me long, and then we will see you home safely."

The hazy feeling still permeated her mind, and she nodded obediently before following his direction without hesitation, folding her hands in her lap as she settled into the large maroon leather chair. It only took a couple of minutes before Miora returned to her desk and waved Tristan through. "He's ready for you now. Mr. Basile," she said before sitting behind it.

It was tough to determine how long she sat there, but it seemed to take forever. Evaine's stomach grumbled with hunger, which wasn't a surprise, considering all she'd had was water. Still, it was embarrassing when the girl behind the desk glanced in her direction, and Evaine mouthed a soft "Sorry" and tried rubbing it into submission.

When Tristan emerged with a smug smile from the office, Evaine assumed things went well.

"Come along, Love." He strolled toward the elevator doors. The Town Car waited for them in the garage, and Tristan guided her inside before joining. "Where are we heading, My Dear?"

Evaine had to rummage through her bag to find the paper Jacob gave her, and Tristan smirked as he waited patiently, rolling the partition down once she was ready to provide the destination.

Chapter *Eleven*

Angels & Ravens

W hen they pulled up to the curb, Tristan flashed her a quick smile. "Be safe, My Dear. And remember what I told you about taking this threat seriously. I will do my best to protect you, but you must also remain cautious and be mindful of who you trust."

"I appreciate your help. I'll do my best. Good night, Tristan." Evaine slipped out of the open door.

Julien's building was a beautiful white stone with hints of French architecture and sat right across the road from Central Park, a prime location that carried a steep price tag and made Evaine wonder precisely what Julien did for a living. Anxiety fluttered in her gut as she bounced up the stairs to the large wooden door to ring the bell.

A sing-song voice greeted Evaine through the speaker. "May I help you?"

"Hi. My name is Evaine, and I'm here to see Jacob Michaels." It seemed too formal to use his full name, and she felt funny saying it aloud. Silence ticked for a couple of moments on the other end before the door unlocked with a click. "Come on up, Evie," the young girl said like they'd been friends forever.

At the top of the massive, carpeted stairs stood a petite girl at least three inches shorter than Evaine, which was saying something since she was barely five-three. The girl was wafer-thin with big dark eyes that reminded Evaine of those scary porcelain dolls and pigtails curled into messy buns on top of her head. She wore a black dress with a white collar, which reminded Evaine of something Wednesday Addams would wear, black tights and chunky Mary Janes that looked almost exactly like the pair in Evaine's closet.

Skye danced in place with one arm folded behind her back, twisting her body from side to side with a pent-up excitement while waving her other hand. She didn't look a day over sixteen, but Evaine knew she was at least eighteen because she was with them at Eucharist. An edge of something in her black eyes made her seem like she'd seen a lot of shit in her brief life, and maybe she hadn't quite recovered from the trauma of it all. Evaine understood what Jacob meant immediately.

"Evie! We've been expecting you. The boys will be very excited that you're finally here." Skye gripped the edges of her dress and crossed her thin legs, curtsying like a little lady, ducking her head before meeting Evaine's eyes. "I'm Skye." When she popped back up, she bounced down the stairs and met Evaine halfway.

"Nice to meet you, Skye." Despite the oddness of the girl, Evaine forced a smile because part of her felt sorry for the innocent girl.

At the top of the stairs, antique paintings and tapestries decorated the large open foyer. A small round table sat in the center, painted white with gold filigree, and a huge antique vase with fresh flowers sat smack in the middle, the floral scent wafting through the space, making Evaine wrinkle her nose as she glanced around. "Where's Jacob?"

"He's upstairs, Silly." Skye stepped closer and grazed the side of Evaine's face with her hand, making her jerk her head. "You're Pretty." Unaffected by the look Evaine shot her, Skye grabbed her hand and laced their fingers together as she headed toward the large archway. Her grip was like steel, and a wide childlike smile curled her mouth as she glanced back over her shoulder and said, "Come along," when Evaine hesitated for a tick. She led Evaine through the enormous, formal living room and up a wrought-iron spiral staircase tucked in the far corner of the room.

"Wow." Evaine's mouth dropped as the large, deep-cherry bookcases on the second floor came into view.

"Ta-" Skye hesitated and started again. "Julien likes to read. He has a lot of books. Most of them are boring, but there's a small section of graphic novels. I like the ones with the pictures. They're my very favorite."

Evaine wasn't sure what to make of Skye, although the more time she spent with her, the more she seemed harmless. So she let Skye lead the way, hoping they'd find Jacob. On the other side of the library, Skye dragged her through another large archway and said, "Jacob, your friend is finally here," as they entered the room.

Relief washed over Evaine when Skye's icy fingers released their hold, and she watched as Skye bounced beside her, humming an upbeat tone, as Jacob jumped up from the couch and walked over. When he said, "Thanks," Skye smiled like he was the best piece of candy in the world, and it sent a shiver of dread down Evaine's spine, though it didn't seem to faze Jacob as he wrapped Evaine in a hug and kissed her. "Hey, Princess." The smile he flashed her quelled her anxiety, and she squeezed his fingers as he took her hand and led her to the oversized leather sofa in the middle of the family room.

Large picture windows gave them a beautiful view of the park, and the trees were a fantastic mix of reds, browns, and oranges. "That's one hell of a view," Evaine said, following him.

"I know, right?" Jacob said over his shoulder.

Raven sat on the far end of the sofa, dressed in black from head to toe, his stormy-gray eyes tracking her and Jacob. His long straight hair was smooth and neat, tucked between his back and the leather cushion. His lean, muscled body relaxed, though it seemed he could spring into action at a moment's notice, like a big cat waiting for its prey.

"Rave, you've met Evie, right?" Jacob asked as they approached.

Raven's lips seemed to curl in a minute scowl, but it happened so fast that Evaine thought she might have imagined it as a smile spread across his handsome face. "I've had the pleasure. How are you, Evaine?" He tipped his chin and stretched his arm along the top of the sofa, his hand draping over Jacob's shoulder when he dropped in next to him and tugged at her. Evaine fell into the soft leather and brushed a stray fire-red curl from her eyes. "I'm good. Thanks."

Jacob snuggled into Raven's side like they'd been together for years, not just days, his hand rubbing the top of Raven's leather-clad thigh. It made Evaine miss Gage, not to mention a little jealous because that was her Jacob. It wasn't rational, but the part of her heart that belonged to him stabbed at her.

"Jay said you're having some issues at your apartment. That's too bad." Raven's smooth voice wrapped around her, lulling her into a relaxed state that made her slouch back against the cushion. "This city really isn't safe. You need to be careful out there, especially when you're alone at night."

"She'll be fine; she's careful. And we aren't leaving her alone. So, nothing to worry about there." Jacob reassuringly squeezed her hand and then glared at Raven. "Enough of that gloom and doom." Before he focused on her again. "Now, what do you want to do for dinner, Princess? You pick."

"I love it when I get to pick," Evaine smirked.

Jacob side-eyed her and then jerked her hand. "No Caprio's!"

"But you said anywhere. That's not fair!"

Raven watched the two bicker with minimal interest, his stormy eyes glancing between them like he was watching a re-run he'd seen a million times and couldn't care less.

"Maybe we should let Raven decide," Evaine said when his bored eyes landed on her for the fifth time.

"I'm not joining you," he said, unamused.

Jacob shooed him with a wave of his hand. "He's too busy to join us for dinner, so I guess we're eating at the disgusting shithole, Caprio's."

Evaine, content with her win, grinned, suddenly starving, which wasn't surprising, considering she hadn't eaten since yesterday.

"Ah, I see our guest has arrived," Julien said from across the room.

Evaine's breath hitched as she looked at the man standing in the doorway, who smiled when she caught his cornflower-blue eyes. She didn't remember him being so attractive the last time they met, but as he strolled across the room in his black dress pants, which looked tailored to fit him, his freshly polished dress shoes that tapped on the marble floor, and a maroon dress shirt, he looked like lucifer reincarnate. Like the true light-bringer, and when his long hair, pulled back in a loose ponytail at the nape of his neck, caught the overhead lights, there were strands so light they were almost white mixed with warm, deep gold and dusty brown. A few unruly wisps framed his smooth, clean-shaven face and made him seem more approachable, despite the regal beauty he had as he moved across the room. When he stopped in front of her, Evaine pulled her bottom lip between her teeth, heat seeping into her blood and making her thighs clench because he exuded a confident sexiness that made Evaine wander to inappropriate things, like what he would look like naked.

He smirked and bowed his head like he'd read her mind, and heat flushed her porcelain skin when he reached for her hand, his cool breath skating over her fingers before his lips brushed them in a chaste kiss. As she stared into his blue eyes, he reminded her of a fallen angel too beautiful that it was painful to look at him. Evaine stumbled over her words, her heart picking up a beat. "Hel- Hello."

"It's a pleasure to see you again. Any friend of Jacob's is welcome in our home." His eyes twinkled. "But you, Evie, you are welcome to stay with us for as long as you like." Julien kissed her fingers again, and her insides clenched at the intention behind his words, guilt bubbling to the surface before she forced it down. "Thank you. That's very kind of you."

"May I?" Julien gestured to the empty cushion beside her and waited for her to nod and say, "Sure," before sitting down. He still held her hand and squeezed her fingers. "We just want to make sure you are safe, Ma Petite Rousse. It would be terrible if something happened to you." That heavy French accent laced his voice, making everything sound a hundred times hotter, and Evaine sucked in a breath as she struggled to keep from squirming in her seat because of the throbbing between her legs.

What the fuck is wrong with me? This is wrong on so many levels! Gage would be so pissed!

Evaine couldn't explain the overwhelming attraction; all she knew was that everything else dropped away when his eyes focused on her, and she wanted to do bad, very bad, things to him. She shoved it down and swallowed. "I appreciate the concern, but I'll be fine."

"I'm sure you will." Finally letting go of her hand, Julien leaned against the arm of the sofa and stretched his body, his hand sliding along the back of the couch. His well-manicured finger reached up to toy with one of her loose curls, his gold rings catching the light. "Your hair really is the perfect shade, like blood," he sort of purred, and a shiver slithered down her spine as he fondled the tendril for a couple of ticks longer before dropping it and glancing at Jacob. "Jay, why don't you get our guest a glass of wine? She looks like she could use a drink." His penetrating gaze fell on her again. "Wouldn't you like some wine before dinner, Evie?"

Her name sounded like sex on wheels as it slipped from between his lips coated in his accent, and all she could manage was a negligible nod as she stared into his eyes.

As Jacob bounced from the sofa, he was clueless about the effect Julien had on her. "One glass of Merlot coming right up, Princess."

Julien seemed to mumble something to Raven, but it was so soft she didn't hear it. When Raven chuckled from the other end of the sofa and said, "If you say so," she was sure he had, and Raven's dark smile made her feel like a mouse caught between two cats. Her body tightened with an edge of tension that dissipated the instant Julien's fingers slid over hers. "Everything will be fine," he reassured her, like he knew exactly what she was thinking. "You are safe with us, Ma Petite Rousse. We will protect you." His touch soothed the concern chewing at the back of her brain.

When Jacob came back into the room with her wine, Evaine fought the urge to grab the glass and chug it. Instead, she waited for him to hand it to her and took a couple of small sips before setting it on one of the stone coasters on the coffee table.

"Better?" Julien pulled her hand into his lap and stroked it.

"Yes, thanks."

"Very good, then. Raven and I have a matter that requires our attention." Julien smiled and kissed her hand. "It was wonderful to see you again, and I hope you enjoy your meal, Ma Petite." Then he was on his feet, with Raven following him out.

"I told you they were awesome," Jacob grinned.

"Yeah, awesome." Evaine grabbed her wine and chugged it before setting her empty glass on the coffee table as Jacob popped to his feet and reached for her hand. "Let me show you my new room." Jacob pulled her off the couch and led her in the opposite direction through a doorway, jerking her down a hallway to the last room on the right. His grin was like sin when he opened the door and stepped inside.

His unmade bed sat in the middle under the window, his dresser against the opposite wall. There were boxes stacked everywhere, and his big black amp and instrument cases were shoved in one corner. It looked like he'd moved everything today as planned, and the idea of going home to his empty room made Evaine's heart hurt.

Her face must have given her away because he squeezed her hand and pulled her into his muscled arms. "You know I love you, right, Princess?" The intensity of his hug made it hard for her to keep everything shoved down, and tears rolled down her cheeks as she nodded against his chest, her body shaking with the sobs she struggled to keep at bay.

Jacob kissed the top of her head and then pulled back enough to ask, "What are all the tears about?"

Evaine wiped her face with her sleeve and sniffled like the dignified lady she was, her nose running again. "I'm trying to be supportive, Jay; I really am. But it's just been such a shit few days, and I hate the idea of you leaving, not to mention the fact that I'm so emotional about it. I hate that some asshole has decided that I need a target on my back. And I fucking hate that said asshole thinks he can fuck with me!" With each declaration, her voice got angrier, and by the time she was done, the words were echoed off his empty walls.

"Did something new happen? Cause not for nothing, Baby, but you seem extra wound up about things since yesterday."

Evaine sighed, her shoulders dropping as she worked to get her emotions under control. "The dick sent black roses to the office today with a note that said. *There are always consequences for disobedience. Remember, I warned you.* It was a blatant threat, Jay. Like they sent a detective and took the note as evidence, and they're checking with the florist to see if they can track down who purchased them."

Jacob frowned.

"I'm sure they won't find anything, and of course, they can't do shit because I don't have a clue who the fucker is. And he's fucking lucky cause I might just fucking kill him if I ever figure it out."

"I'm so sorry this is happening to you, Evie. But I'm glad you reported that shit."

"Tristan made me. He's a good guy."

"I'm glad he's looking out for you. I'd be super fucking broken if anything happened to my Princess."

Evaine forced a smile, wiping her eyes on her wet sleeve before sucking in a deep breath and blowing out. "Enough of this drama. I want the damn dinner that you promised me. I'm starving."

When he unwrapped from her, she could see the worry in his eyes but appreciated his light banter when he said, "It's fucking gross, but whatever my Princess wants."

They didn't see anyone when they left the house and took a cab to Caprio's, where there was a thirty-minute wait to get seating. They opted to sit at the small bar, which made it easier to order drinks. Something Evaine took full advantage of, and by the third sea breeze, she relaxed and was laughing at Jacob's story about the hot mover who asked for his number.

It was a good thing they decided on a medium pizza because she wolfed two pieces down and nibbled on a third as Jacob finished the rest. The boy was svelte and fit but could pack the food away like nobody's business.

"I thought you didn't like their pizza," she said with a mouth full of cheese and bread.

He shrugged and smirked. "I'm choking it down for you, Baby."

"I bet you say that to all the boys." Evaine took a sip of her drink.

Jacob snapped his teeth, "Only the ones with enormous cocks," before taking a bite of crust.

"Speaking of big cocks, do you want to go to Eucharist tonight?"

"We can totally do that, but only if you can talk him into finally showing me that infamous tool. I mean, now that I'm not living with him, the chances of catching a glimpse have dropped dramatically. I feel like I've missed out."

"You can look, but there won't be any touching."

"Fair enough." Jacob grinned.

After dinner, they swung by Evaine's so she could shower and change into something more appropriate for the club. The buzz from the restaurant was wearing off by the time she was dressed in her black latex ruffled miniskirt that barely covered her ass cheeks with a matching latex bra and fishnet shirt. She chose her favorite garter with black thigh-highs and platform stompy boots with a row of metal buckles down the sides. She might not feel like betty-bad ass these days, but she fucking looked the part. Her fire-red curls wrapped into two high pigtails with a bow on each, her eyes painted black and her lips blood red. She was ready to kick some ass, or at the very least, look hot shaking her ass. And right now, she wanted to unwind and have fun.

"Damn, Baby, you look hottie-tottie tonight!" Jacob said when she finally came out of her room.

Evaine spun in place to give him the full effect and then grinned. "I do, don't I?"

"Let's do a shot before we go." Jacob beelined straight for the shot glasses in the kitchen cabinet next to the sink and then grabbed the chilled bottle of vodka from the freezer and poured two generous shots, handing one to her as she walked into the kitchen. He tinked his glass against hers. "Cheers, Princess." And downed it in two gulps, hissing in a way that made her smirk.

"Cheers." Evaine chugged hers in three, a shiver running along her spine as the burn spread down her throat in the same direction. She shook her head and made an ack sound before slamming the glass on the counter.

"Puts hair on your chest." Jacob clapped her on the back and, when the burning subsided, talked her into two more for the road before putting the bottle away. "We need to swing by Julien's, so I can change my shirt."

After a quick pit stop, they headed across town to Eucharist. The doors must have just opened because the line was still down the sidewalk and around the corner. Once again, Evaine was grateful that Gage worked at their favorite club because she didn't have to stand in line and freeze her mostly exposed ass off in the cold.

When they stepped into the main room, the thump of the loud music and the smell of dry ice immediately calmed Evaine. The dance floor was still pretty sparse, and after a bit of begging, Evaine got a buzzed Jacob on the floor and took full advantage of the room. It felt good to dance with him, and it helped her push away all the awful stuff and relax. By the time they finished three songs in a row, they were sweating and breathless.

It took Evaine a minute to spot her purple-haired boy at the bar because he wasn't in his usual spot in the middle but off to the right instead. Gage smiled when he saw her, and it melted her insides. When he leaned over the bar and kissed her right below her earlobe, his warm breath tickled and made goosebumps prickle her arms as he said, "I wasn't expecting you," against her ear.

She turned and kissed his full mouth, sucking the ring between her lips before grinning. "We were talking about big cocks, and well, I thought of you."

Gage chuckled. "That's my girl."

Jacob bumped Evaine's shoulder and gave Gage a Cheshire-like grin as he hitched his thumb in her direction. "She said, since I was moving out, I could see it."

Black brows furrowed as Gage shook his head and shrugged. "I'm on the clock, Man. I can't just show people my cock while I'm working. Unless, of course, you're going to give me a big tip."

A sinful smile spread across Jacob's mouth as he leaned in. "I've got a big tip for you, Baby. All you gotta do is ask nicely, and it's all yours."

She rarely saw Gage blush, but his cheeks lit up like Christmas, and Evaine couldn't hold back a giggle as Jacob cackled.

"What do you assholes want to drink?" Gage asked.

"The usual," Jacob said without hesitation.

Once they had their drinks, they headed to their usual spot in the corner and sipped them as they watched people mill by as the club filled up. The warmth from the alcohol spread out from Evaine's stomach, pushing the chill away, and a comfortable numbness seeped into her as she rested her back against the dark wall and tapped her foot in time with the music.

When Jacob went to get another round of drinks, one of Evaine's favorite songs came on, and she was on the dance floor forever. Sweat dripped from the wisps of hair around her face when she took a break. Jacob handed her a drink as she approached the high-top table.

After her third, the rest of the night went by in a blur of music, flashing light, dry ice, and writhing bodies. The exercise did wonders for her tension and stress, though the liquor was the biggest contributor to her loosening up. So when they announced Last Call, she was surprised by how quickly the night went, though she was sure she didn't need another drink.

Shortly after, the music was gone, and the house lights burned overhead, turning the dark, gothic sanctuary into a harsh, gritty reality. Jacob stayed with her until Gage finished cleaning up the bar and then shared a cab with them.

On the way home, they chatted about stupid stuff and joked at each other's expense, like they always did. When they arrived at her apartment, Jacob hugged her and told her he loved her before letting them slip out of the seat. It felt unnatural to watch the cab pull away with him still inside, and Evaine frowned and hugged Gage around the waist.

"You okay, Baby?" He walked them to the lobby doors.

"I guess. It's just weird."

Gage pulled her closer. "I know. It's gonna take time, that's all."

She sighed as the elevator doors opened. "I don't want it to become normal. I want him to come home."

Gage hit the button for their floor and then pulled her back and looked into her eyes. "That might not happen, Baby, so you've gotta try to make peace with it."

Evaine felt like a little girl that wanted to stomp her feet and throw a tantrum because she didn't like it when things didn't go her way. It was probably a product of her childhood, considering her dad rarely said no to her.

With a ding, the elevator opened, and Gage walked her to their door. "Did I mention that I love this skirt?" He cupped her ass cheek and pulled her on her toes to lean in and kiss her before letting go so that he could dig his keys from his pocket.

"Why do you think I wore it?" Evaine asked as he unlocked the door and shoved it open the door.

"Because you're a fucking tease?" Gage stuffed his keys back into his pocket before wrapping one arm around her waist and hoisting her onto his shoulder, giving him easy access to her exposed ass. He cracked her hard across one cheek, making her squeak as he carried her into the apartment and kicked the door shut with his boot. The second crack he landed on the same cheek stung and sent heat spreading along her skin, making her breath hitch and that heavy heat flutter low in her belly.

"Now I'm gonna show you what we do to little fucking teases," he half-growled as he headed for their room.

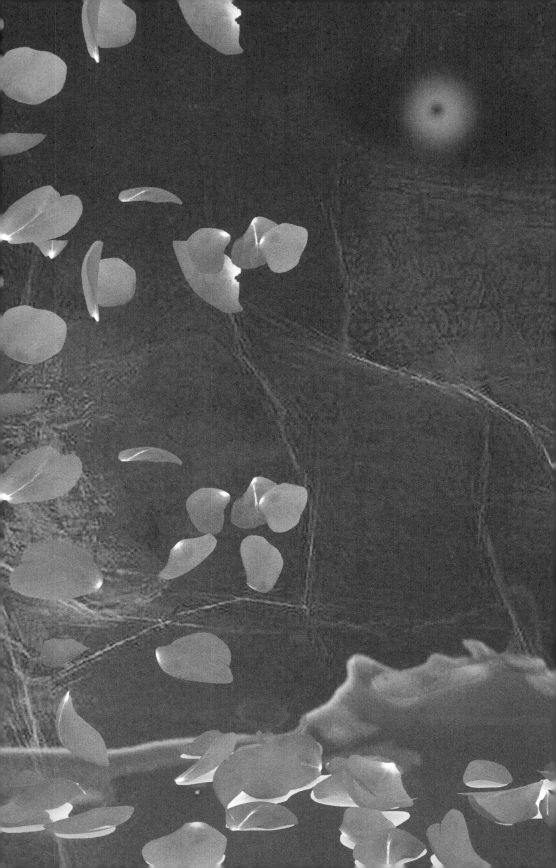

Chapter
Twelve

Eggrolls & Xanax

When the alarm went off the following day, Evaine's body felt rough from too much dancing, drinking, and fucking. Her muscles burned as she stretched before curling her naked body against Gage's warmth. He was dead to the world, softly snoring, but even in his sleep, he pulled her closer while she tried to snooze for nine more minutes.

As she drifted off, the faint ring of her cellphone chimed from the living room. It rang five times before going to voice mail, and for just a minute, Evaine contemplated getting up to check who it was because her parents were traveling and were the only ones who called on that number. But quickly decided it could wait nine minutes.

There were a couple of silent ticks before the phone rang again, jarring her from the half-sleep state she was enjoying. Evaine rolled away from Gage, cursing whoever it was as her feet hit the cold wood. Partly because her head was pounding, but mostly because everything hurt, and she wasn't ready to get up yet. She stood and headed for the bathroom with a groan because her bladder didn't care about who was trying to reach her. It needed relief now.

After using the bathroom and washing her face with a cold washcloth, Evaine padded out to the living room and dug her phone from her bag.

There were six missed calls, all from the same number, which looked familiar, but she couldn't place. Her gut swirled as she dialed into her voice mail, and the robotic woman on the line said, "You have two messages."

When Evaine hit the button for yes, and the messages played, the swirling turned into churning. "Ms. Maire. This is Justin Marcus. I've been trying to reach you and need you to call me as soon as you get this message. It is imperative that I speak with you as soon as possible. You have my number."

Evaine fought the panic creeping over her. *Why would he call me? He never calls me!* Although her parents were out of the country, there might be something in the apartment he needed. The prompt of the robotic voice jarred her from her thoughts, and she navigated to the second message, hoping he left a little more information. This time, she heard the sadness and urgency in his tone. "Evaine, please call me immediately. I need to talk to you."

Her fingers trembled, their tips chilling as adrenaline shot through her system and her body temperature fell. She sucked in a deep breath and steeled herself as she tried to calm the chaos churning inside before navigating to the redial option. Evaine put the phone to her ear as the first ring chimed and immediately heard the line connect. "Ms. Maire." It was the familiar sound of Justin, but his tone held a melancholy edge.

"Hello, Justin. I'm returning your call. You said it was urgent. Is everything okay with my parents?" When he sighed, the chill in her body spread up her arms and along her neck before shooting across her chest and clenching her heart in its icy grip. "I'm sorry to say this, Evaine, but there's been an accident."

Evaine's legs were rubber. "Are they okay?"

He paused for too long, and she knew they weren't before he said, "Unfortunately, they've both passed." She could hear the sadness in his voice as her knees buckled, and she hit the floor with a hard thud, the hand holding her phone trembling as tears streamed down her face. "Both of them?"

"Yes, Dear, they're both gone. I'm so sorry for your loss. I know this must be a difficult way for you to hear, but I wanted you to know before the news picked the story up."

Justin kept talking, but Evaine stopped listening as the phone fell to the floor with a clatter of metal on wood. Sobs racked her numb body as shock set in. Her lips were cold and tingly, and she couldn't stop the shivering that convulsed through her naked body.

She wasn't sure how many minutes passed before Gage knelt behind her and wrapped his warmth around her, his tone groggy when he asked, "What's going on, Baby? Why are you crying?" He sat down and stretched his long legs on either side before pulling her into him, and all she could manage was to sob louder and shiver harder despite his warmth.

"Baby, you gotta tell me what's going on?" His words were soft, but there was an edge of concern in his tone.

Her voice was a thready whisper when she forced out, "They're dead," before shifting to curl her feet under her and wrapping her arms around him as he shushed her, one large hand petting her head, the other rubbing circles on her back.

"Who, Evie? Who's dead?"

Evaine sucked in a shaking breath, her chest aching from the effort of saying it out loud. "My parents." The words were so soft she wasn't sure he'd heard her until he said, "Oh, fuck." And his hand gripped the back of her neck to pull her closer. "I'm so sorry, Baby." Gage kissed her head and sat with her as several minutes ticked, and she sobbed into his bare chest, her body shivering.

Finally, he scooped her up and carried her back to the bedroom, settling her onto her side and crawling in behind her before pulling the covers over them. She rolled into Gage and continued to ball until she wasn't sure she'd ever stop because the tears were unrelenting. At some point, exhaustion overwhelmed her, and she finally dozed off.

When she awoke several hours later, Gage was still at her side. His body curled into a C around her, his hand stroking her back. Pain radiated from her chest, choking her, and she sucked in a shaking breath at the thought of never seeing her dad again. The reality that she'd never hear him call her Princess again made her guts clench and roil with the urge to vomit.

They can't be gone!

"I'm gonna be sick." Evaine struggled to get up and stumbled to the bathroom. Barely making it before, the burn of bile forced its way up her throat and out her mouth with a loud gagging noise. Heat flushed her body with another wave of nausea, and she shivered before dropping to her ass next to the toilet and pulling her legs under her, her head resting on the cool porcelain, thankful for the slight relief it granted her.

After a few silent minutes, Gage came in and ran a washcloth under the cool tap before kneeling beside her and wiping her face. The coolness was sheer bliss on her heated skin and made her close her eyes with a soft moan.

"You okay?" He kissed the side of her face, and she nodded without opening her eyes. "How 'bout we get you back to bed, hmm? You can't sleep here on the floor, Baby."

Evaine let him help her up and lead her back to the bed, a small wave of sick sweeping over her as she laid down and closed her eyes. Gage tucked the blanket around her and brushed away the damp wisps of hair plastered to her forehead. "I'm gonna get you a glass of water and call Jacob to let him know what's going on, okay?"

She nodded and curled up in the fetal position.

"I'll be right back."

The next time Evaine opened her eyes, Jacob sat beside her, his hand rubbing her back. He smiled when she caught his eyes. "Hi there."

The physical pain was so bad she couldn't manage more than "Hi" in return.

His eyes shone with unshed tears as he leaned in to kiss her on the forehead. "It's going to be okay, Evie. Gage and I are here. Whatever you need to make you feel better, you just have to ask, and it's done."

Two thoughts speared through her grief-ridden brain. "Someone needs to let Tristan know what happened."

Jacob's thumb rubbed her temple. "Done."

"And the party tonight. We need to cancel the party."

"Don't even think about it, Princess. We'll take care of it."

Evaine's eyes welled with tears, and Jacob cursed under his breath before leaning in to hug her. "I'm so sorry. It's a habit. Shit, Evie. I didn't even think about it," he whispered into her hair.

Tears broke free, and she quickly wiped them away. "It's okay."

When Jacob finally broke their embrace, he shoved her unruly hair behind her ear. "I think you need to get a little more rest. I brought you something to help you sleep." And stuck his hand in his front pocket, pulling out a small baggie with a few little white pills. When she furrowed her brow, he said, "Xanax, you just need one," and then shook it out into his hand and placed it into her mouth as she opened it before handing her a glass of water from the nightstand.

Evaine took a couple of big swallows before handing it back to him. With a smile, he set it down and tucked the blanket around her. "Now get some sleep, and we will take care of the party and Tristan. Love you."

"Love you too," she mumbled as she felt his weight leave the bed and heard the soft click of the door closing.

It only took a little while for the pill to make her relax as it did its job. Evaine curled on her side and pulled the blankets over her head as she drifted into a blissful, thoughtless sleep that only came with drugs or alcohol. She appreciated Jacob for giving it to her because the last thing she wanted was to think about the loss of her family and that she was an orphan. Even though it still hurt, the meds made it seem far away and less raw.

When Evaine woke up the next time, there was a moment she believed all of it was a terrible dream, but unfortunately, her mind cleared the sleep away, the harsh reality slamming into her. Tears streamed down her face as she fought to gain control over the onslaught of emotions threatening to bury her once more.

I can't let this break me!

After several minutes, she finally talked herself into getting out of bed and showering before dressing in a T-shirt and yoga pants, her hair up in a messy, wet bun. The boys were sitting on the couch watching television, and they both looked up and gave her similar half-smiles. *Gods!* She loved them, but the pity she saw in their eyes made her cringe.

"Come here, Baby," Gage patted the cushion between them, and Evaine padded over and dropped next to him, his arm automatically wrapping around her, long fingers tugging on the wet strands that came out of her bun. Jacob scooted closer and kissed her cheek. "I'm glad to see you up." He snuggled into her other side.

Though her heart hurt, having the two of them made her feel better. She smiled before she asked Jacob, "Did you call Tristan?"

"He said to take as much time as you need," Gage answered. "He was very understanding and seemed genuinely concerned."

"After talking to Jessica, we decided to let the party go forward as usual. You'd have lost all the money anyway, so let people have a fun night, and we'll just forgo it. She agreed to handle everything and sends her condolences." Jacob explained further.

Evaine cringed when he said the word condolence. She hated funerals and dealing with everyone's sorry for your loss and you have my condolences bullshit, and dreaded having to do that for her parents. But she tried to push it down for now, and the Xanax seemed to help take the edge off because she was doing a pretty good job of ignoring the hole in her chest. "That's probably for the best, right?" She glanced at Gage for reassurance.

He nodded at her solemnly. "I hate to bring it up, but you need to know the lawyer called again while you were sleeping. He'll handle as much of the estate stuff as he can, but he said you'll need to go to the funeral home tomorrow to take care of a few details that were not addressed in your parents' arrangements and stop by his office to sign some paperwork."

Evaine nodded and crossed her arms over her chest as she snuggled against him. She had no clue how she was going to face that tomorrow.

The idea of walking into a funeral home and dealing with any of it made her stomach roil with anxiety. "Did he tell you what happened?"

"He didn't tell me much, Baby. I'm not family. He just asked me to make sure you were at Wilmington, Blount, and Jameson's tomorrow at two. That was it."

As much as she dreaded the discussion, she wanted to know precisely how her parents died. She needed to know precisely how they died because the threat against her screamed foul play, even though she couldn't imagine how someone would have gotten to them. In her mind, her dad was invincible. Guilt chewed at her when she realized she hadn't even told Gage about the flowers and note from yesterday because she'd been too distracted when they got home last night. And now, she didn't have the energy or resolve to discuss it.

The look on her face must've betrayed her thoughts because Jacob pulled her into a hug. "What can I do to help you? Do you want wine? Another Xanax? Maybe a dirty, sweaty threesome? Just tell me."

His dark sense of humor was one of the things she loved about him, and for the first time that day, she actually smiled as Gage slipped his arm around her shoulders and across her chest to pull her back against him. "I'm thinking maybe we feed her first, Jay. She hasn't eaten all day."

Jacob glanced at Gage for a tick and then asked, "Are you hungry?"

A pang of hunger gnawed on her hollowed guts and made her nod, Gage's collarbone brushing the back of her head.

"Good! We'll feed you first." Jacob winked at her. "And then have the threesome after."

"You know Gage isn't gonna give it up to you, Jay." Evaine giggled because she could picture the glare coming from the boy with his arm wrapped around her. Gage wasn't offended by Jacob's jokes or even his advances, but she knew he wasn't interested in boys.

Jacob's sea-green eyes sparkled with amusement as they flicked up to Gage. "Not even to make his Baby feel better?"

"You two are obnoxious," Gage grumbled and pulled her into his lap. "Just go get the girl some damn food before she wastes away, huh?"

"Touchy, touchy." Jacob chuckled and climbed to his feet, adjusting the buckle of his studded leather belt and straightening his black leather pants. He shoved his long hair out of his pretty face before leaning in to kiss her lips. "Chinese, sound good?"

"Mmm... Hmm," she said against his mouth.

"All right, Kitten. I will be right back with your dinner." As he passed Gage, Jacob ruffled his purple mess of hair. "Yours too, Baby."

When the front door closed, Evaine let out a heavy sigh, and Gage squeezed her with the arm still draped across her collarbones, the hand hooked around her shoulder, keeping her firmly against his chest. "I feel like this is my fault," she mumbled so softly it was barely audible. The short reprieve from the harsh reality of her parent's death slipped away with the loss of her best friend.

"Why, Baby?" Gage asked.

"I forgot to tell you about the flowers that came to the office yesterday. There were four vases of long stem black roses with a card that said there were consequences for my choices and that I would have to learn the hard way. What if my parents are dead because I refused to wear that stupid fucking bracelet?"

"First of all, that wouldn't be your fault. That would be some crazy psychopath's fault. And second, did you call the police and report the threat?"

"I did. Tristan made me report it and got the building security involved."

"Good, though I wish you would've told me last night."

"I'm sorry; it just slipped my mind."

"It's a pretty big slip, Evie." It was a mild reprimand, followed by a soft kiss on her temple.

"I know."

After a couple of ticks of silence, he said, "But at least there will be a paper trail."

"I don't expect them to find anything on the note or from the florist. So little good it's going to do me. Plus, it just seems like too much of a coincidence for them to just die in a freak accident for no good reason."

He kissed the top of her head. "Maybe it's just easier for you to accept that someone hurt them rather than a senseless accident took them from you. Either way, Baby. It's not your fault. I know you're gonna try to blame yourself, but you need to recognize that no matter what, it wasn't in your control."

Gage was right; he was always right. It was crazy how well he knew how her mind worked and could read her like an open book. It was also a double-edge sword; sometimes, she loved it, and some hated it. Tonight, she loved having him there to hold the pieces of her shattered world together because she certainly couldn't do it herself.

When Jacob returned with dinner, they sat in front of the television and ate every bit. Gage begrudgingly agreed to let her have a bit of wine, despite the meds she took with her meal. Between the three of them, the bottle was gone pretty quickly.

With a full belly and the warm tingle of wine and Xanax saturating her system, she snuggled between her best friend and boyfriend while watching bad movies on the Sci-Fi channel. It was the closest thing to perfection that she'd probably ever have again, and she loved them for it.

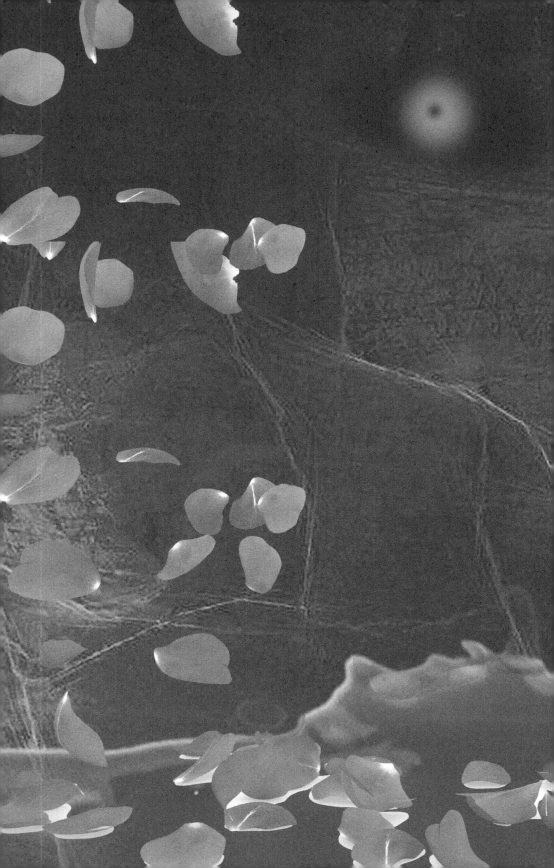

Chapter
Thirteen

Thirteen

Fear & Funeral

Dreading the entire affair of going to the funeral home made it difficult for Evaine to get out of bed the next day, but Gage was extra attentive and patient, washing her hair and body as they showered. He gently reassured her she could do this and would be right there with her for everything because she wasn't alone. Unfortunately, it did nothing to change that she felt one hundred percent alone. Nothing could fill the massive hole left by her parents' deaths. She never thought about being an orphan because, in her mind, her parents were going to live forever. Now she faced a lifetime without them, and that was excruciating to think about as she numbly allowed Gage to dry her and get her dressed. He picked a comfortable black dress and her flat, Mary Janes, and turned her toward the mirror when he finished. "Okay, Baby, you just need to put your hair up, and then we're ready to go." He kissed her temple and asked, "Can you do that for me?" Evaine stared at his reflection and nodded before reaching for her Scrunchy. With one more squeeze of her shoulders, he said, "I'm gonna go make some coffee while you finish up," before leaving her to it.

After fixing her hair, Evaine brushed her teeth and tried to hide the black bags under her emerald-green eyes, but there wasn't much she could do except apply a thick coat of foundation and powder. And thankfully, she didn't look quite so heroin-chic when she finished and glanced in the mirror one last time. "You're a bad-ass. You can handle anything!" The affirmation did little to convince her, but she had to try because making it through the next few days would be the hardest thing she'd ever done, and no matter what it took, she needed to get through it.

And when she was done, there was a wonderful stash of Xanax to make it all disappear.

When she finally found the determination to leave her bedroom, Gage sat at the counter as he sipped his coffee, his minty eyes watching with a mixture of pride and concern.

"I'm okay." She reassured them both.

"I know you are, Baby. You're a Bad-Ass, right?"

Gods! I love him! She smiled. "And don't you forget it." Then padded into the kitchen for a drink.

The rush of traffic made the ride to the funeral home painfully slow. Evaine's guts roiled the entire ride, and the minute she sat down at the large oval table in their conference room, she went on autopilot, unable to engage with the pain of the situation. Gage nudged her a few times to get her to focus on providing answers for the death certificates, like her mother's maiden name and her mother's and father's full names, which was hard enough. But when it came to talking about her dad, it was a painful struggle to keep the tears at bay because he wasn't supposed to leave her alone; she was his princess.

After finishing the paperwork, the funeral director went over all the arrangements. Thankfully, her parents planned ahead, making it easier to cruise through the details. While the kind woman talked, Evaine stared around the large room at all the urns and plaques lining the shelves, the jewelry made from ashes or colorful glass orbs, and pondered why her parents decided to be buried instead of cremated. Then she wondered how badly the bodies were injured in the accident and if they were already here or still at the medical examiner's.

"So, as you can see, your parents were very thorough in their planning. But we will need you to decide on a final outfit for each of them, and if you can provide some recent photographs of the family as well as them individually, we will create a photo collage for the service. Otherwise, Evaine, I think we're done for today. I know this must be so difficult for you."

Evaine pushed to her feet, her legs like rubber. "Outfits and photos," she mumbled as Gage's arm wrapped around her shoulder to steady her.

"It's okay, Baby. I'll take care of it if you want."

"No, I want to do it." Evaine shook her head.

Gage kissed her temple. "Whatever you need."

"Again, I am sorry for your loss, Ms. Maire. Please know our goal is to provide you and your friends and family with a soothing environment to grieve. If there's anything we can do to help, don't hesitate to ask."

"Thank you." Evaine's words sounded hollow, and she wondered how many times a day this lady had to say those very words to people who lost family members. *It must be a demanding job.* Anything to keep from thinking about her parent's bodies that could be stored in the funeral home's deep freeze, just waiting to be stuck in the ground on Monday. Her stomach roiled as she glanced up at Gage. "Can we go, please?" He nodded and used her elbow to guide her to the door and said, "Thank you, Mrs. Jasper," as they left.

"Are you sure you want to go to the apartment today?"

"I have to. The stuff needs to be dropped off before they close tonight for the service on Monday."

"I'm just asking, Baby. I'm more concerned about you than the funeral home, okay? If we need to push the service to Tuesday, we push it. So, I need you to tell me if it's too much."

"I'm okay," she lied through her perfect teeth.

Reality smacked her dead in the face like a runaway locomotive at her parents' apartment and knocked her down a few pegs. She wasn't okay or ready to do this, but she forced herself, unwilling to admit that it was too difficult to be in their home knowing they were gone.

"Mom kept a few photo albums in her office. They should be on the bookshelves there. Would you mind getting them while I pick clothes out?" She crossed the empty living room and headed down the hall to the bedroom suite. Dread ate at her insides with each step, but she wouldn't let it slow her down, determined to get through all of it, no matter how painful.

When Evaine pushed open the door to her parent's room, Maria was standing at the foot of the bed, looking at two outfits. Her eyes were sad when she glanced at Evaine, and she closed the distance between them, wrapping Evaine in a fierce hug. "Ms. Evie. I'm so sorry about your parents, Sweetheart." Maria had been good to Evaine growing up, and she hugged her back with the same enthusiasm. "Thank you, Maria."

Several minutes passed before Maria broke the embrace and pointed to the bed. "I picked out outfits for them. I thought it might make things easier for you." Evaine stepped to the edge and surveyed Maria's choices. Her mother's outfit was a white pantsuit she frequently wore to her charity functions. "She would love this choice." Evaine half-smiled when she realized Maria even thought to include her favorite jewelry pieces.

When she looked at the choice for her father, Evaine's hand ran down the lapel of the dove-gray suit. "This is almost perfect, Maria. Except, maybe if we could find the purple tie I bought him for Father's Day last year." Tears welled, and Evaine bit the ragged skin around her thumbnail, shoving the emotions back down.

"Yes, Ms. Evie. That would be perfect." Maria scurried into his closet and returned with it in moments. When she swapped it with the other, Evaine ran her hand over the soft silk. Her father hated the paisley pattern but pretended to love it, regardless. "Thank you for taking the time to do this. I really appreciate it."

A smile spread across Maria's lips. "You're are welcome, Sweetheart. It is the least I can do for them. They were always so good to us."

Evaine nodded as tears threatened to flow again. She'd done pretty well keeping them at bay so far, but being in their room was increasingly difficult.

"If you'd like, I'll have Rodney take them over to the funeral home."

"That would be a great help, Maria. It's Wilmington, Blount, and Jameson on East Twenty-First Street. Gage is getting the photographs. If he can take those as well."

"Of course, Ms. Evie." She reached for Evaine's hand, squeezing it with her small, warm fingers. "Whatever you need, Dear."

The pity in Maria's eyes made Evaine's heart ache. "Let me go get them for you." She pulled free and hurried out of the room as tears streaked her cheeks, wiping them with the back of her hand as she beelined it to her mother's office, where she found Gage flipping through one of the older photo albums. He smirked and then sucked his silver lip ring between his teeth as she walked up. "You were a cute baby, Baby."

"Of course I was." Evaine quipped, determined to keep the sadness at bay, sighing audibly with the effort. "Maria picked out clothes, and she's going to have Rodney take them with the photo albums to the funeral home before it closes today."

"That will save us some time for sure. I thought these two were the most recent, but I wanted you to look at them to make sure."

The small pile of albums encompassed a lifetime of memories. They seemed so insignificant compared to the immense lives of her parents. Evaine flipped each cover for a split second, catching glimpses of birthday parties, recitals, and family picnics in Central Park. "Shit," she mumbled as she dropped the last cover in place and scooped them into her arms, turning to leave the room. "They're good. I'll take them to Maria and meet you in the Foyer." She didn't wait for Gage's response because she didn't want to be there longer than necessary.

After a quick talk with Maria, Evaine was relieved to be back in a cab, heading to Mr. Marcus's office. Part of her never wanted to step foot back in that apartment and sell everything so she could forget they ever existed. *Compartmentalize, more like ignore completely!*

At Mr. Marcus's office, she sat across the desk and listened to him ramble about how great her father was and how much he would miss working with him. Autopilot kicked in, and she nodded and agreed without really hearing him. It was all too painful. There was no way she could talk about her dad. It devastated her to lose her mother, but her relationship with her father was so much more, and his loss hurt a hundred times worse.

Suddenly tired of it all, Evaine cut him off mid-sentence. "Mr. Marcus. I appreciate your kind words, but the reason for my visit is to find out exactly how my parents died."

Justin frowned but gave her a knowing nod. "They are still investigating the scene, but they were in a head-on collision with another car on their way to the airport last night. Thankfully, they believe it was quick for both of them."

Tears welled as she glanced over at Gage, who grabbed her trembling hand. "Really, don't sugarcoat it for her or anything," he sneered at the well dressed man across the desk. Justin's eyes narrowed, but his tone was controlled. "I respect her enough, to tell the truth, Son. It's what she deserves. It's how she will find peace in the tragedy."

"That's so fucking noble of you." Gage's tone was sharp and made Evaine squeeze his fingers as she said, "I'm okay. I asked, remember?"

"Still unnecessary, Baby," he half mumbled.

"It's okay. I'm okay," Evaine said softly to him and then focused on the lawyer again. "So, they are considering it an accident."

"Yes." Justin nodded, and then his brow furrowed. "Is there a reason they shouldn't, Evaine?"

For a tick, she considered mentioning the stalker and the note, but it made her feel foolish. *How could he get to my parents?* She couldn't wrap her head around someone going through so much trouble to torture her, so she shook her head. "No, Sir. I just want to be sure."

"Okay." He sat back. "If something changes, you will be the first to know." And paused for a moment. When she remained silent, he said, "Now. As executor of your parents' wills, I will handle all the details of transferring of assets over to you. To get it rolling, I'll need you to give me a limited power of attorney on your behalf." There was a manila folder on the edge of his desk that he flipped open, sliding a legal document in front of her. "Just sign and date on the line at the bottom. If Gage would be a witness, that would be perfect."

Evaine nodded, reaching across the desk for the pen Justin offered, her hand shaking as she scribbled her signature and then the date before sliding it to Gage to do the same. When she caught the lawyer's beady brown eyes, she wondered how much money he'd made from her parents over the years. She was never involved with her father's business but knew he was worth millions with a massive S. Something about the man made her a little wary of dealing with him, but her father trusted him, so she would too, for now.

"I'd like to sell my parents' apartment as soon as possible."

"Are you sure, Evie?" Gage asked. "You're emotional right now, Baby. You probably should wait a few weeks to make those decisions."

"It will take weeks to transfer ownership and get the documents in order. After things have wound down and we get to that point, we can discuss it again," Mr. Marcus said as he scooped up the paper in front of Gage. "Now, I'm sure this has been a difficult day, and you could probably use a little downtime." Autopilot kicked back in, and Evaine nodded and slid her hand into Gage's when he offered it, letting him guide her out.

By the time they got home, she was physically exhausted, and when Gage suggested she take a nap, she didn't argue, stripping off her clothes and climbing right into bed. She pulled the comforter over her head before Gage gave her a soft kiss and shut the door behind him.

The weekend went by in much the same manner, with Jacob and Gage taking turns making sure she ate and cuddling with her when she couldn't keep the tears away. Despite Evaine's efforts to shove her feeling down, they bombarded her at every opportunity, and she needed to take a Xanax about every six hours to keep from totally unraveling.

When Sunday evening rolled around, Jacob finally talked her into getting up for a few hours, and she sat with him in the living room, eating cream puffs and drinking cocoa from Landuree's. Then they snuggled up and watched eighties movies for the rest of the night until she fell asleep with her head in his lap, his fingers brushing the loose strands of her hair.

The next thing she knew, Gage was carrying her to bed when he came home from work, and she wrapped her arms around his neck and snuggled into the familiar scent of him, cigarettes and all. The heat of his body, his soothing tone as he lulled her back to sleep, and not to mention the Xanax she took with her cocoa made it easy to comply, and she curled into him when he tucked in next to her smelling like soap.

On Monday, the services for her parents were at two in the afternoon, and Evaine forced herself out of bed by eleven and spent an hour nursing a glass of Merlot at the kitchen counter. At Noon, Gage finally talked her into getting ready to go to the funeral home because they needed to be there early to make sure everything was prepared.

She wasn't sure what she would do without the perfect boy who helped her dress and do her hair so that she didn't look like death-warmed-over. He was patient as she put on her makeup and even made her laugh a few times, which was a miracle these last few days, and he looked handsome in his slim black suit with a black dress shirt and tie.

"You clean up nicely," Evaine said as he stood up from putting on his Doc Marten's and straightened the legs of his pants over the shined combat boots. Gage smirked and rolled his shoulders in a half-shrug, his silver bracelets jingling as he ran his fingers through his somewhat combed purple hair. "Right, who knew?"

Evaine couldn't resist the urge to close the distance between them, slipping her hands up his chest and around his neck before pulling his mouth to hers and giving him a chaste kiss. She loved he didn't ask or expect anything more, his hand brushing her back as she broke the embrace. "Me. I always knew you were perfect."

Pink flushed his cheeks, and his smirk was on the edge of sarcasm as he caught her gaze and held it, which told her he appreciated the compliment as he stole one more kiss before licking his lips. "Alright then. Let's blow this popsicle stand, huh?"

Gage took her hand and didn't let go of it until they were standing in a room full of her parents' friends and co-workers. Autopilot kicked in as they milled by her, sharing stories and giving condolences she would rather not receive. And Evaine did her best to force a smile and hold the tears at bay. She still hadn't gone up to the caskets and wasn't sure she ever wanted to, preferring to remember them happy and alive rather than laid in their soon-to-be tombs.

At some point in the service, Jacob came up and hugged her, followed closely by Julien and Raven, sharing their condolences before finding seats in the back of the large room. Evaine slid her arm around Jacob's and clung to him like he was a life-preserver that could keep her from drowning in this ocean of grief. When she caught his eyes, his smile was sad, but he mouthed, "I love you," and bumped her softly with his shoulder.

A few minutes later, Tristan arrived and offered his condolences as well, reminding her to take as much time as she needed to grieve. "There is no rush for you to come back to the office, My Dear. But if you need the distraction, you are always welcome." His smooth accent soothed the tension in her shoulders and made her relax despite the stress of the entire ordeal. This would have been a more private affair if she had had her way. It wasn't that she didn't want to honor her parents; it was more about how this felt like salt being ground into an open wound.

Even after Tristan took his seat, it felt like they stood there forever, and Evaine was thankful when Gage finally led her to a seat at the front, which she quickly decided was too close to her parent's caskets. There were several wreaths around the coffins. One was white roses with deep green foliage, another purple and white with baby's breath, which was lovely. But the one that caught Evaine's eye made her want to puke. A large arrangement of black roses with a sinister red silk banner that read Beloved in a script that reminded her of the note she'd received just a few days ago. Another wave of nausea crashed over her as the heat of anxiety flooded her body, tightening every muscle with fear.

"I'm not sure I can do this," she whispered to Gage, who squeezed her hand and said, "You can, Baby. I know it's hard, but you can." Apparently, he hadn't noticed the wreath. She jutted her chin in its direction and hissed, "Look," as softly as she could manage with her surging anxiety.

As he caught sight of the black roses, his eyes widened. "What the fuck?" he mumbled, dropping her hand and walking over to look at them, likely looking for a card or some other indication of where they came from. Evaine watched him cross to the back of the room and speak with the funeral director, who shook her head and looked wholly confused when Gage walked away from her.

He settled into his seat again and whispered, "There's no note, and no one knows where they came from." Tension tightened his shoulders as he squeezed her hand and chewed on his lip ring, his jaw muscles ticking as he stared at the offending arrangement.

Part of her wanted to get up and run and never stop running. The other, more stubborn part wondered if he was here watching and relishing the lesson he was teaching her about consequences. Because now, Evaine had little doubt her parents' deaths were an accident, which fueled her anger, making it easier for her to stay in her seat and endure whatever came next. She refused to give him the benefit of seeing her crumble, no matter what it took to keep it together. When she glanced at Jacob, he seemed just as annoyed as Gage. Evaine could feel the energy wafting from them, which fueled her determination.

Her parents' pastor spoke first. Next was Mr. Marcus, who told a few of the same anecdotes she'd heard at his office on Friday, and then offered others the opportunity to do the same. Several people took to the small podium and spoke about her mother or father, and with each one, Evaine wondered if they were the one. But it was hard to tell when they all spoke of her parents' generosity and efforts to contribute to the community, painting her parents as the kind and caring individuals she grew up with. It took every effort Evaine could muster to keep from breaking down in the middle of all these strangers, but she was determined not to.

It was well after four by the time everyone who wanted to speak finished, and there was a strange sense of relief when Gage led her from the room away from those flowers and into the Town Car that would take them to the cemetery.

Jacob joined them for the ride since Julien and Raven weren't coming. Tristan also said his goodbyes to her at the funeral home because he had a meeting across town he couldn't reschedule.

The few peaceful moments in the car did a great deal to soothe her ragged soul, and she curled into Jacob, closing her eyes as he asked, "Are you okay, Sweetheart?" against the top of her head. With a sigh, she said. "Yeah, I'm just trying to find the strength to get through the last hour of this morbid spectacle that this asshole is putting me through. I never liked funerals, and now I like them even fucking less."

"I know, Evie. You're almost done. Just hang in there a little bit longer, and then we find you a good bottle of wine on the way home."

Despite the tears threatening to break, she smiled because Jacob always got it and never gave her grief; one of the many reasons he was her dearest friend in this shit-show called life.

"That is exactly what I need. That and maybe a gun."

"How about we start with another Xanax? Hmm?" Jacob gave her another kiss on her head.

Evaine relaxed into her best friend, zoning on the blur of buildings as the Town Car weaved through the traffic. Her eyes burned from the unshed tears, and her chest felt like someone was sitting on it, but she held it together, if only by a thread.

The procession had no issues navigating the route through the city and into the Midtown Tunnel, and once they got on the expressway, it cut the time even further, especially with the police escort. The whooshing of the engine lulled her to the edge of sleep, and all she wanted to do was stay there and dream.

But soon, they pulled through the black iron gates of the Calvary Cemetery, the sprawling hills dotted with tombstones and pristine white statues, some angels and other saints. There were cherubs and even a Mother Mary. As they followed the narrow road, large mausoleums made of different shades of stone were tucked between rows of perfectly straight headstones. It reminded Evaine of a miniature city hidden among the bustling Queens neighborhood.

Jacob squeezed her hand, "We're here, Evie," making her sit up straight and nervously adjust the hem of her knee-length black dress. The back of her hand swiped under each eye, and she sniffled once before the driver opened the door to let them all out. The cold, sharp wind whipped her velvet coat around her, wisps of her hair flying across her face and into her mouth as she followed Gage off the asphalt and onto the gravel path.

Her parents were to be placed in the family mausoleum with her father's side of the family. The impressive white marble building sat under a large oak tree that looked like it had been there forever. The small iron doors were open, and a man in a gray suit stood to the side with his hands clasped in front of him.

As they approached, another attendant ushered them to the large white pavilion that sat off to the side of the tomb. The caskets were already in place near the entrance, and Evaine was grateful she wouldn't have to see the inside of the mausoleum as she took her seat in the front while others filled the rows behind them. Once everyone was seated, the pastor quoted a few lines of scripture that meant little to Evaine, but she imagined her mother requested since she was the most religious.

All she could think about was the wreath sitting next to the closed caskets and how it mocked her and her family in a way that made it hard to ignore. Guilt seeped in around the anger, squeezing her bruised and beaten heart because it was her fault they were dead. *Just because of some stupid bracelet. Seriously? How the does this shit happen? It isn't supposed to, right?*

When the graveside service finished, relief washed over Evaine. The attendant handed her two white roses and guided her to the caskets, her fingers shaking as she set each one down. The tears she'd worked so hard to keep at bay broke and ran down her cheeks. She wiped them away and curled into Gage's waiting arms. He hugged her tight and walked her back to the car with Jacob behind them. This was the last time she'd be in the presence of her parents, even if it was just their corpses at this point.

Evaine didn't remember much of the ride home besides crying into Gage's chest. True to his word, Jacob gave her a Xanax with a wine chaser as soon as they got back to her apartment, and then Gage tucked her in. It only took minutes for the day's exhaustion, the medication, and the wine to do their job.

Chapter

Fourteen

Necklaces & Evil

E vaine slept through most of the following morning. When she finally woke around eleven, she decided to be a contributing member of society rather than letting grief consume her, which would happen if she didn't force herself through this nightmare. It didn't help that she blamed herself for her parents' death, but she was determined not to let him see her break, and sadly, that ultimately got her out of bed, showered, and dressed for work.

"Where you going, Baby?" Gage asked when he came in to check on her.

"Work."

He cocked an eyebrow at her in the bathroom mirror as she finished putting her mascara on. "You sure you're up for that?"

Evaine grinned. "I've already had this discussion with my inner child and ID, and we've concluded that we can't stay in bed and wallow. It isn't good for any of us, so we are going to the office." And then shrugged. "Besides, it's a good distraction."

Gage looked more than a bit skeptical but didn't argue. "Okay."

"See! That right there is exactly why I love you so much." She turned to wrap her hands around his neck, pulling his upturned mouth to hers, his warm breath skating across her lips as he pulled back enough to say, "I love you too."

"I'll be fine," Evaine said for his benefit as much as hers and then stole another kiss before ducking around him to go find her boots. After a couple more minutes, she headed to the door, where Gage kissed the top of her head and helped her with her coat before handing her the messenger bag. "Please be careful. And call me if you need anything. I'll have the phone close."

As he walked into the kitchen, he said, "By the way, I have to work tonight because there's a show. You should see if you can hang with Jacob."

"I'll call him when I get to the office."

"Good. I'll feel better if you aren't here alone all night."

When Evaine hit the lobby, Jon, the doorman, waved her over to the desk. "Good afternoon, Ms. Maire. I have a package for you. Someone delivered it late last night, and Michael wasn't comfortable bringing it to your apartment." His smile was friendly as he handed her a small, rectangle box covered in velvet.

Evaine's hand trembled as she wrapped it around the box. "Someone delivered it last night?" Despite the dread already churning deep inside, the need to confirm his statement overwhelmed her. "You don't by chance know who delivered it, do you, Jon?"

He frowned and lowered his eyes for a tick before catching hers again. "Sorry, Ms. Maire, Michael didn't say."

"Thank you, Jon." Evaine tapped the box against the palm of her free hand and then shoved it in her bag. "Have a good day." Part of her wanted to run back upstairs and hide under her covers, but she forced the urge aside, her legs feeling like rubber as she strode across the lobby and out the door to hail a cab.

He isn't gonna stop me!

In the cab, curiosity got the better of her, and she pulled the box from her bag and forced the stiff lid open. Nestled in the black velvet was a simple silver choker with the word MINE in scrolling cursive. The audacity flipped a switch, and her dread and fear seethed into blinding anger. "Are you fucking serious?" she growled and fumbled with the small, folded note tucked inside the lid as her fingers unfolded it.

It wasn't much of a surprise to find the small, neat penmanship, the scrolled letters perfectly aligned to say, *Have you learned your lesson yet, Princess?* Evaine's stomach roiled at the pet name, and she had to fight the urge to toss the whole thing out the window. *Are you fucking kidding me?* She couldn't even fathom the balls it took to send something like this to someone you didn't know. Evaine stared at the note for a few ticks and then the shining necklace. It was pretty clear the intention was for her to wear the thing.

Fucking son of a bitch! Not in a million fucking years!

Every ounce of her raged against the idea of being someone's possession, especially someone other than Gage, and there was no way she was going to wear it.

Fuck that!

But then the rational part of her brain kicked in. *What if he hurts Gage or Jacob? What then?* That part wanted to be a good little girl and put the stupid thing on as expected. That part wanted to keep her friends from finding the same fate as her parents. And the one thing her entire being agreed on was that this individual was willing and able to kill the people she loved to get what they wanted.

"Fuck!" She pulled her bottom lip between her teeth and fingered the fancy cursive *Mine*.

As she neared Tristan's office, the pressure to decide weighed on her. By the time the cab halted at the curb, she already pulled it from the box and was toying with the clasp, despite the aversion. It only took a tick before Evaine slid the chain around her neck and clasped it.

The cabbie glanced at her in the mirror. "That will be three dollars, Miss," he said with a thick accent, and she handed him a five. "Keep the change. Thanks."

Even with the late start, she still beat Tristan to the office and worked for about an hour before he arrived. His hazel eyes surveyed her as he hung his coat and hat on the corner rack, his thin lips curling. "'Ello, Love. I didn't expect to see you today."

Without thinking, Evaine's fingers darted to the necklace that felt like it was burning a hole in the hollow of her throat, a glowing symbol of her weakness. His eyes tracked her, his head cocking before he crossed the room to the front of her desk and read the word scrawled at her throat. "Is that new?"

Evaine's cheeks flushed with embarrassment, and she dropped her hand to the desk, nodding. "It was a gift." *Not technically a lie.*

Tristan hitched an eyebrow. "From Gage?"

For the briefest moment, she wondered why he cared. But then he slid his cool fingers under her chin and forced her to meet his gaze, and it fell away with his penetrating eyes.

"Tell me, Evaine, where did you get the necklace?" There was an edge of sternness to his tone, though his words were hushed and almost a growl. The compulsion to tell him was unbearable and overrode the embarrassment. "It was a gift that my stalker left at the desk at my apartment with a note. I got it this morning."

"And what did the note say, My Dear?" His thumb dragged across her closed lips, sending a chill along her spine as she said, "Have you learned your lesson yet, Princess?"

Tristan's eyes narrowed, his jaw ticking. "And why are you wearing it?" The truth tumbled from her lips before she could contain it. "Because I'm afraid he'll hurt Gage. Or Jacob."

A frown marred his handsome face as he furrowed his brow and shook his head before his thumb settled into the dip of her chin, and he pulled her face to his as he rounded the desk to stand beside her, forcing her chin up, exposing her neck. Tristan licked his lips and used the hand gripping her chin to pull her from her seat. "You poor child."

Unable to break the gaze, she stumbled, her hands planting against his chest as she tried to steady her clumsiness. Evaine flinched when he stepped into her and ducked his head, grazing his lips against her thumping pulse. "You are such a beautiful creature, My Dear. And all I've been thinking about is your taste, sweet and fruity like a fine wine. No wonder you've enamored this stranger." His words were gruff, filled with something akin to lust but darker, hungrier, like a thirsty man that craved water. They sent a shiver down her spine, goosebumps prickling her skin. Some small, faraway part of her knew this was wrong in a million different ways. Still, the undeniable draw held her in his arms and made her placid to the idea of his advances, a soothing fog settling over her as his tongue darted out to taste her skin as she gripped the front of his blue dress shirt.

"Relax, My Dear, I won't hurt you," he purred, running a hand over her hair, and her body turned fluid, languid- compliant, melting into his embrace as his sharp teeth slid into her neck and his lips clamped onto flesh. At first, it stung, and Evaine pulled a pained breath, her body tightening, but it quickly turned into pleasure, and her insides heated as an ache built with each draw, clenching her insides with the need.

Evaine whimpered when he growled and pulled her tighter, taking more- faster, her legs turning to rubber when a wave of ecstasy washed over her. Stars flashed behind her closed eyes, and her head swam from the blood loss.

With a flick of his tongue, the throbbing in her neck disappeared, and when Tristan pulled back, he licked his lips and gently settled her back into the leather chair, dropping to one knee and gripping her chin. He forced her to focus on him as he leaned in and stole a kiss from her slack lips. "Such a precious thing you are, My Dear. Everything is going to be fine. I will make sure of it." He smiled, letting go of her face and standing. "You won't remember anything."

Evaine's eyes snapped up to his as the words passed his lips. "What was I saying?" she asked, feeling confused, and he merely smirked and crossed his arms over his chest. "You were telling me about the necklace, Love." Evaine shook the cobwebs away and gripped the blasted thing. "Right."

"Well, My Dear. As I said, I think you should report your concerns to the authorities. It's important to document it." Tristan disappeared into his office, closing the door behind him.

The rest of the afternoon, Evaine waffled between struggling to focus and crying in a bathroom stall, unable to keep the pain at bay. Her body felt tight and heavy, exhaustion and constant tears taking a toll, and her stomach wouldn't stop growling. So bad at one point, she went downstairs to the vending machines to get a soda and a bag of chips to tide her over, which didn't stop the bouts of tears but helped refuel her focus enough that she remembered to call Jacob.

When four-thirty rolled around, Tristan came out of his office and said his goodbyes before heading out. He had a stern set to his chin, and his hazel eyes held an edge of anger that made Evaine glad she wasn't on his bad side as she wondered what upset him, considering he'd been fine just a few hours ago.

The minute Evaine was alone, she felt vulnerable, and every little noise had her jumping in her seat and ready to leave for the day. By the time she gathered her belongings and locked the office, it was dusk as she hit the sidewalk and hailed the cab that took her straight to Jacob's apartment, and almost completely dark by the time it pulled up to the curb. An uncomfortable feeling chewed at the back of her brain like a foggy memory that wouldn't reveal itself.

Evaine shoved it down and paid the cabbie before heading up the stone steps to the front door and pushing the button. The intercom buzzed, and a few silent ticks passed before the static on the other side hissed, and Julien's smooth, heavy accent said, "May I help you?"

She swallowed, licking her dry lips. "It's Evie. I'm here to see Jacob."

"Ah, yes, Evie. Please come right in."

His tone was pleasant, like she could almost hear the smile, which made her insides warm. She didn't understand why he suddenly overwhelmed her as the door clicked and the lock disengaged. Evaine slipped inside and ran dead into a brick wall, realizing it was Julien's chest when she caught his cornflower-blue eyes, his hands landing on her shoulders to steady her.

Julien grinned as he stepped back and took her hands. "Good evening, Ma Petite Rousse." His cool lips brushed her knuckles when he bent to kiss them. "Jacob and Raven stepped out to get some dinner. I'm sure they will be back shortly; until then, please come in and make yourself at home."

Evaine watched him effortlessly glide up the stairs. *Damn, he's a thing of beauty.* The flex of muscles under his fitted dress shirt and the way his ass looked in those made-for-him dress pants. Guilt crashed over her when she realized there was drool on the corner of her mouth. *What the hell? Why am I so attracted to him?*

At the landing, he smirked over his shoulder, reminding her of an overly satisfied Gage. "Come along, Ma Petite," he beckoned with his long fingers, the gold rings glinting in the overhead light. His white-blonde hair hung around his perfectly sculpted face, making him look even more angelic, the straight, silky-looking strands falling over his shoulders and down the middle of his back.

"Sorry." Evaine fumbled up the stairs to catch him.

"Never apologize, Ma Petite. It is below you. Especially for something so trivial."

"S-," she started but cut off when he raised a golden eyebrow and ticked his tongue. Instead, she snapped her mouth shut and smoothed her hands down the front of her simple black dress and then through her mess of fire-red curls.

"Better." Julien led her through the foyer into the formal living room, gesturing to the oversized leather sofa. "Please sit down." He said and asked, "Would you care for a glass of wine?" as she settled into the seat.

"Yes, please." Her eyes followed him as he crossed the room to the bar and then back again with two glasses of red wine in his hands. Evaine took the one he offered and sipped it, despite the urge to gulp it down. "Mmm," she purred as its tartness tingled her taste buds. "This is very good."

"It should be. It's a 1947 Richebourg Grand Cru." Julien sipped from his glass and sat down in the large wingback chair across from her, and Evaine smiled like she knew what that meant. "Only the best for my guest, Ma Petite Rousse." His words were smooth and seductive and warmed her in a way that the wine didn't quite accomplish. It made her brave as she asked, "What does that mean?"

Julien cocked an eyebrow and sipped his wine, her eyes tracking his tongue as it ran along his bottom lip. "It is a term of endearment, I assure you."

"I got that much, but what does it mean? My little- I'm not sure of the last word." A smile spread across his angelic face. "You speak French, Ma Petite?"

"Un petit peu. I took it in high school and my first year of college. I was obsessed with Paris when I was growing up and have fond memories of visiting with my parents." The thought of them made her smile for a tick and then frown as she remembered she'd never get to travel with them again. Julien leaned forward. "I am sorry for your loss, Ma Rousse. I did not intend to bring you pain." Evaine's eyes flicked to the floor before meeting his. "It's not your fault." She took a breath and asked, "What does Rousse mean?"

"It means redhead. Ma Petite Rousse." Julien smiled.

"My little redhead?" Evaine asked, her eyebrows pulling up in surprise. "Isn't that a little presumptive?"

"I typically get what I want, Evie. So, non." His eyes zeroed in on her, and suddenly she felt like an insect under a scope, shifting and smoothing the hem of her dress before crossing her legs. Julien's sharp blue eyes tracked her like she was prey. It made her lick her lips and take another, larger sip from her glass, swallowing before changing the subject. "How long have the boys been gone?"

"Nearly an hour. As I said, they should be home any minute." Julien sat back and pushed his hair behind his ear, mimicking her by crossing his legs. "Why don't you tell me about your day, Ma Petite?" It was more an order than a request, and she felt compelled to tell him all about the shit storm that was her day, like he'd be a good listener. Instead, she forced a sugary smile. "It really wasn't so bad. I got some work done, and the distraction helped." Which was a full-on lie, but she didn't care.

He frowned. "I'm sure it is difficult. At least you have a tool to help you cope. That is important to your well-being."

Evaine nodded. "Exactly. I've never been a wallower. I need to keep moving forward."

"Everyone copes with loss differently." Julien sipped his wine and watched her over his glass, his eyes piercing her in a way that made her empty hers, which seemed to amuse him because he wore a satisfied smirk when he lowered his. "Would you like a refill, Ma Petite?"

"Yes, please," Evaine managed around the lump forming in her throat. This man drew her like a moth to a flame, and she was pretty sure he'd burn her to a crisp given the opportunity. Nevertheless, she felt the need to touch him, even though it went against every fiber of her being.

His body flexed under his tight-fitting clothes as he stood and reached for her glass. After handing it to him, she watched him move to the bar and pour them another. When he handed it back, his fingers brushed hers, making them tingle, and her face flushed, causing amusement to flicker in his blue eyes as he settled on the couch beside her this time. His arm rested along the back of the sofa, and he was so close that he invaded her personal space as he sipped his wine and made her squirm under his gaze.

"Turnabout is fair play." Evaine gulped down the tart wine, swallowing loudly. "Tell me about your day."

His angelic face lit up. "I assure you; it was nothing to brag about, Ma Rousse."

The intimate way he said the last two words sent a shiver down her spine and made her take another sip of vino to steel her resolve. "Then you should have no problem telling me about it, hmm?" Julien straightened in his seat, tucking a strand of stray hair behind his ear, the tip of his white canine catching his bottom lip when he smiled wider. "Who am I to argue with such a beauty?" Heat flushed Evaine's face as she stared across the space at him, but she held her ground, earning a raised eyebrow when she said, "No one."

"As always, I started the day with a glass of superb wine. Breakfast is the most important meal of the day." He winked and then continued with that smooth, seductive voice that made heat pool low in her belly. "Then I spent a few hours in my office taking care of business. I also went to a meeting downtown, which kept me out until the late afternoon. When I returned,

I spent some time reading one of my favorite books." He cocked a golden eyebrow. "This is all quite enthralling, Non?"

Evaine grinned, her words dripping with sarcasm, "Absolutely riveting," before asking in a more serious tone, "What book was it?"

"Hmm?" He tilted his head as if he hadn't heard the question.

"What book were you reading?" she repeated, clearer.

His cornflower-blue eyes sparkled. "It was actually a book of poetry, Ma Rousse. Les Fleurs Du Mal." Julien dropped his chin at her confused look and explained with a small flourish of his elegant hand, "The flowers of Evil."

"Sounds wonderful." More sarcasm.

"It is quite a good read. If you enjoy the sharp contrast between decadence and eroticism mixed with a touch of death and decay."

"Huh? That sounds intriguing," Evaine mumbled around her glass and sipped her wine.

"You are welcome to borrow it if you are so inclined."

"I might take you up on that."

He tipped his glass and grinned, his words loaded with innuendos. "I do appreciate a woman who's willing to try new things." And the way he said them made her clench her thighs.

Bad!

Before Evaine had a chance to contemplate all the new things she would be willing to try much further, Raven and Jacob sauntered into the room, each with a white plastic bag. Jacob lifted his and smiled, quite proud of himself. "We brought dinner."

"It took the two of you long enough!" Julien pushed to his feet and reached out to assist her. Evaine hesitated for a tick but allowed him to help her stand. He was an unusual character and didn't look a day older than her. But the way he spoke and moved was timeless and elegant, like he'd been royalty in a past life, and somehow his body remembered it.

"It's not our fault the line was outta the building."

"I imagine the food should be quite tasty then." Julien's tone was droll as he passed Jacob on his way to the bar.

Hunger ate at her as she smoothed the front of her dress and then followed Jacob through a large archway. A substantial wooden table sat in the middle of the dining room. It was ornate and looked antique. Julien sat at the head, all long limbs and well-fitted clothes, his blue eyes twinkling as he sipped his wine with languid ease. Raven sat to Julien's right and Jacob next to him, leaving her at Julien's left. Evaine settled into her seat and glanced up when she felt his eyes on her. She couldn't help but track his Adam's apple working as he swallowed until rustling plastic snapped her from the trance and focused her attention on Jacob pulling the food containers from the bag in front of everyone.

"I hope you don't mind. I got you Chick Parm." He set the white styrofoam container before her.

"At this point, I'm so freaking hungry; I'd eat the container."

"Okay, but use your plasticware." When Jacob chucked the wrapped spoon, fork, and napkin at her, Julien shook his head. "Manners, Son, manners."

Jacob's shoulders slumped at the reprimand, and he actually said, "Sorry," first to Julien and then to her. Evaine's mouth hung open in surprise. *Who is this person that body-snatched my best friend?* Jacob never apologized for his inappropriate behavior. Most of the time, he would just flick off whoever complained. She wasn't sure she liked the frown he wore as he dropped into his seat, but a delicious smell tickled her nose when she opened the container, pushing the thought away. Her mouth watered, and her stomach growled.

After watching her fumble with the plastic wrap on her silverware for a tick, Julien took it and opened it easily before handing it back with a wink.

"I almost had it," Evaine half-grumbled and swiped it from him.

"Of course, you did, Ma Rousse. But your stomach was getting impatient."

She wanted to stick her tongue out at him but didn't want to get the same lecture as Jacob. Plus, it was probably poor form to insult her host. So instead, she pulled her plasticware out and cut up her chicken cutlet while Jacob scarfed down his pasta at a break-neck speed. The boy could eat; there was no doubt about that.

Raven seemed far less interested in his food and curled his nose as he shoved it around the container. Julien took a bite or two but seemed more interested in his wine than his meal. Evaine couldn't understand why because the sauce was thick and fresh with chunks of tomatoes and basil, the pasta cooked to a perfect al dente, just how she liked it, and though the chicken was a little dry, she was thoroughly enjoying the meal.

When Jacob finished his food, he shoved his plasticware into the container, wiped his face with the folded paper napkin, and tossed it in before shutting the lid. With a glance in her direction, he finally noticed the necklace and sat back in his chair, crossing his arms over his chest and jutting his chin. "Where did you get that? Cause I know for a fact that Gage wouldn't buy you something that ugly."

Pasta stuck in Evaine's throat, and she had to take a sip of her wine to clear it, coughing softly as her free hand fiddled with the necklace. "It was at the desk in the lobby this morning with a note." Julien watched her out of the side of his eye, sipping his wine with a distracted sort of interest. At the same time, Raven seemed a little more blatant about his disinterest and sighed as he closed his container and stood up, scooping up Jacob's in one hand and his in the other before heading out of the room. "I'll be in the game room," he said without looking back.

Man, she liked him less and less by the minute. *Whatta pompous asshole.* She couldn't understand what Jacob saw in him, which meant it was likely the size of his cock, considering her friend's tendencies.

"Gage's gonna lose his shit when he sees it! You know that, right?"

Evaine caught Julien's eyes over the table, and there was something unreadable about his face as he sat there so still it didn't seem like he was even breathing. When she cocked her head, he shifted in his seat and ran his hand through his loose hair, her eyes tracking his fingers before focusing on Jacob. "What am I supposed to do?"

"Take the stupid thing off before you see him for sure." Jacob's eyes narrowed. "In fact, I'm a little disappointed that you're wearing it in the first place. How can you cave to this asshole after what happened?"

Evaine frowned. "That's exactly why I'm wearing it. I can't let something happen to you or Gage." She didn't enjoy sounding so weak in front of Julien, but it was the truth.

"Not for nothing, Baby Doll, but you need to give this asshole a big F.U. and take that fucking thing off." Anger bloomed in his tone as his open hand hit the top of the table with a thwap.

When Evaine flinched and flicked her eyes to Julien, he gave her a slight nod. "Jacob is not wrong, Ma Petite. Whoever is harassing you is not in their right mind, and wearing that may feed the fantasy and make them bolder."

"See!" Jacob squawked, then said in a much calmer tone, "You should take it off."

Her mind spun as she stared at Jacob, but she couldn't find a valid argument and slipped her hands behind her neck to reach for the latch.

Before she realized he'd moved, Julien was in her ear. "Let me, Ma Rousse." His cool hand brushed her hair off her neck as his fingers deftly found their way past hers to the latch, and he had it off before she could protest, laying it in her open palm. His touch sent a tingle across her skin. Her body responded to him was like a live wire, his touch lingering a little longer than necessary.

Evaine closed her hand around it and murmured, "Thank you," trying to keep the hitch from her voice as her body tightened.

"My pleasure." His words were like silk as he reached around her to grab his empty glass. "I believe I need a refill. Be sure to say goodbye before you leave, Ma Petite." He strode through the large archway toward the bar as she and Jacob silently stared at each other. Concern was written across his handsome face; his brows furrowed, and his mouth turned down in a slight frown.

Evaine mimicked him, crossing her arms. "Don't look at me like that."

"I'm just worried about you, Evie. This whole thing is so fucked up, and I feel like shit for leaving you in the middle of this craziness."

"You didn't know this would happen. It's not your fault. Besides, you're still here for me, so it's all good."

A low chuckle rumbled from him. "I love when you ramble."

"I'm not rambling. I'm explaining in great detail."

This time, he laughed, "Call it what you want, Baby," and climbed to his feet, rounding the table and holding his hand out. "Let's go."

"Where we goin'?"

"My room, of course. So I can recover from the carb-coma."

Evaine slipped her hand into his and followed him as he weaved through the spacious house. When they finally reached his room, she was surprised to see that he'd gotten some boxes emptied since her last visit. It was really looking like his room, which made her kind of sad.

"Is Raven always so quiet?" She dropped onto his bed and curled up with his pillow, catching a whiff of the cologne and shampoo that always made him smell so good. Jacob sat on the floor against the bed, flipping through the television channels, and glanced at her. "He's kinda stoic, I guess. Why?"

"I'm trying to figure out how he deals with you every day, all day. I love you, but you're a bundle of energy, even worse when you've only had a little caffeine and sugar. It seems like that would drive him crazy."

Jacob chuckled. "Is that your nice way of saying that I'm an annoying asshole?"

"Hmmm. I guess it is." Evaine smirked and snuggled into his pillow, enjoying his scent.

With a shake of his head, Jacob mumbled, "You're such a bitch," and then grabbed the T-shirt next to him and chucked it at her.

"Hey!" she scoffed and sniffed it. "You're lucky it doesn't stink like pits."

"No, Babygirl, you are." That Cheshire grin crossed his handsome face as he reached up and snatched it back. When he pushed his long hair behind his ear, she caught a glimpse of his shaved sides and the silver rings lining his heavily pierced ear as he sniffed it before tossing it back on the ground and going back to flipping channels.

Concerned about pushing the subject and her luck, she tentatively said, "Plus, I don't think he's ever said more than two words to me."

Jacob side-eyed her. "Are you trying to tell me something?"

The words were on the tip of her tongue, but she couldn't get them out, so she shrugged innocently instead. "Me? Never."

"You're so full of shit," Jacob shot back before focusing his attention on the television. A couple of seconds ticked by before Evaine found her voice again. "I just want you to be happy."

"All's good, Baby. I'm a big boy, so don't worry about me."

After a couple more minutes, Jacob landed on re-runs of Seinfeld, which was one of his guilty pleasures. To her, it was just eh, at best. Curled in his bed, her eyes drooped, and it became impossible for her to keep them open. But every time she dozed off, the low rumble of Jacob's laugh pulled her back from the edge of sleep until she couldn't fight it any longer.

The next thing she knew, Jacob was nudging her shoulder. "Evie, you ready to head home?"

It took some effort to get her eyes to stay open as she blinked at the blurry outline of her best friend and rubbed her eyes with her balled-up hand before sitting up. "I dozed off, huh?" Jacob rubbed her back and smiled, his long hair bouncing as he nodded, and she said, "Sorry."

"No worries. But it's almost three-thirty, and Gage should be home by the time we get there." Jacob stood and held a hand out, and she took it without a thought, letting him pull her to her feet. "Come on, sleepyhead. Let's get you home to that boy before he has my balls."

Evaine giggled. "That's not likely; he'd have to touch them."

Laughter echoed around his room as he led her toward the door. "That's the truth."

The apartment was quiet as he weaved them through the dark rooms until they passed through the library, where Julien was reading in one of the large, overstuffed leather chairs and glanced up with a smile. "Ah, Ma Petite. I wanted to give you this before you left." There was a small, leather-bound book with gold writing scrawled on the spine in his outstretched hand.

"What is it?" Evaine asked as she reached for it, too tired to read the title.

"Les Fleurs Du Mal."

"The Flowers of Evil," she translated before slipping it into her messenger bag. "Merci."

A smile spread across Julien's thin lips, his angelic face brightening as he reached for her hand and kissed her knuckles. "Je vous en prie, Ma Petite."

Chapter
Fifteen

Death & Morpheus

J acob insisted on walking Evaine up when they arrived at her apartment, and she appreciated it, especially since they found it dark and empty.

"I'll stay until he gets home." Jacob flipped the light on and turned the deadbolt before strolling into the living room. Evaine hung her coat and bag and then took off her boots and padded over to the couch, where she found Jacob sprawled out with his arm slung over his eyes.

Evaine sighed as tension spread through her shoulders. "Maybe Matt kept him late to do inventory or something."

"It wouldn't be the first time."

"I know." Still, her stomach churned and swirled with foreboding. *Maybe the psychopathic killer has him and is torturing him because I refuse to wear that fucking necklace.*

As if Jacob read her mind, he said. "I'm sure he's fine, Evie. Come lay with me." When she stepped closer, he reached for her hand and pulled her down onto his lap.

She settled between him and the couch, resting her head on his chest, and he kissed the top of her head. "He'll be home any minute. So stop worrying." His words were a sleepy whisper, and even though Evaine was just as tired as he was, she couldn't overcome the dread and anxiety fighting to overtake her. So she closed her eyes and tried to slow her breathing as time ticked by at an excruciating pace.

After failing a few minutes, Jacob asked, "Do you want me to get you a Xanax, Baby Doll?"

"Yes, please." His warmth went with him as he slid from the couch with a groan, and she missed it.

"Are they in the medicine cabinet or your nightstand?" Jacob asked as he headed toward her room.

"Nightstand."

It only took him a minute before he was in the kitchen getting water, and when he returned, he shoved a glass in her direction. "Sit up, or you're gonna end up wearing this." He tried to keep his voice light, but she could hear the roughness it got when he was tired and sat up to take the pill, washing it down and handing the glass back. "Thank you."

"No worries." He flashed her a half-smile that didn't reach his eyes and then set the glass on the coffee table and stretched out on the couch next to her. Even though having Jacob there made her feel safe, macabre scenarios looped in her head that made it impossible for her to relax until Gage walked through that door. Still, she tried to calm down and keep it together. She'd been a good girl, worn her necklace all day like she'd been told. *How would he know If I took it off?* She'd been at Jacob's the whole time and worn her coat when they were in the cab. *There was no way.* The dread wound in her guts, and her heart thumped against her chest.

"Breathe, Evie, breathe." Jacob wrapped his arm around her and pulled her closer as she did as he requested.

It took about a half-hour before the Xanax kicked in, allowing her body and mind to relax. Curled against Jacob's warm body, her eyes got heavy, and that wonderful feeling of floating overtook her. Within minutes, she was out, but her dreams were anything but peaceful.

At first, she ran down the empty city streets, yelling for Gage. Then the landscape shifted, and she was at Eucharist, which looked dilapidated and deserted. Lights hung from the ceiling by their cords, and all the mirrors were smashed; furniture overturned and torn to shreds. The entire building felt dark and haunted. She felt like she was being tracked as she searched the abandoned club for Gage, and her skin crawled with the realness of the dream, sending goosebumps up her arms as she climbed the stairs to the darkened balcony.

When she hit the top step, her body tensed as a shrouded figure stepped out in front of her, a sinister grin spreading across its wide mouth. "You won't find him here, Little Poppet, but I'm feeling generous, so I'll give you a head start before I tear you to shreds." Evaine's fight-or-flight instincts kicked in and made her take off back down the steps, the menacing cackle following her as the figure counted down from five. With her rubbery legs, she was only halfway down them before the monster nipped at her heels, kicking up her fear and making her stumble. The monster cackled as it reached for her. "That's right, Poppet, run."

Evaine screamed, tears running down her face as she scrambled to stay out of his ghoulish grasp. *It's just too fast!* She felt the ominous energy it manifested as it bore down on her, Cool breath huffing down her neck as it overtook her. Evaine skittered across the dance floor and barreled toward the entrance as fast as her adrenaline-filled body would take her, pumping her arms, her legs screaming with pain. Still, it wasn't enough to keep her from his clutches.

When he tackled her, she hit the floor with a hard thud, and the monster pinned her under his steel-like body. "You're mine now, Poppet," the creature growled as she squirmed under him and then wrestled her onto her back, smiling in a way that made her feel like she was dinner. His sharp white fangs gleamed in the darkness, his colorless black eyes boring down on her from his shrouded face. "And I will tear you to bits, drink your blood, and consume your soul." The creature gripped her wrists with one hand and then grabbed her chin and jerked her head to the side. Pain shot through her as his fangs tore at her neck, his tongue lapping at the warm, viscous blood spurting from her opened artery.

The nightmare jostled Evaine from her slumber with a scream that made Jacob jolt upright.

"What the hell?" he grumbled and rubbed his sleep-filled eyes.

"Sorry, I had a bad dream." Evaine panted.

"You okay?" Jacob asked, shifting under her.

"No." The last thing she wanted to do was check to see if Gage was home because she knew, in her gut, that he wasn't. He would've woken her up when he got home to take her to bed. Her stomach lurched with nausea as she scrambled over Jacob and almost fell on the coffee table, trying to get her feet under her.

"What're you doing, Evie." He groggily reached out to steady her.

"He's not here." She hated the desperation in her voice.

"Maybe he's in the bedroom?"

"No, he's not here. I know he's not, Jay. I can feel it."

Whatever Jacob saw when he squinted up was enough to get him to sit up and grab her hand. "Breathe, Evie." Jacob swung his long legs off the couch and stood, gripping her hand and tugging her towards the bedroom door. "Let's just make sure, huh?" As they walked to the door, it reminded her of the scene from Poltergeist where the mom was running down the hall at the door that just kept getting further and further away. Terror chewed on her insides as Jacob's hand wrapped around the knob.

When they found an empty room, terror enveloped her. "I told you." And she fought to keep the nausea at bay. "Something's happened to him, Jay. I can feel it in my bones." Tears burned her eyes, threatening to escape and roll down her face, and when he glanced over his shoulder at her, his expression was a mix of pity and concern; she felt like she was on the verge of losing her mind.

"We need to call Matt." Jacob dropped her hand and went to get the phone. Evaine watched him pad back into the living room and then stop in front of her and ask, "Do you know his number?"

"It's in my cell." Evaine glanced at the clock and realized it was almost dawn. Her stomach roiled as she crossed to her bag and pulled it from the side pocket, her fingers shaking as they fumbled over the numbers. Frustration rattled her as she shoved it into Jacob's hand, "Here, just call him on this," and paced in front of him.

"Breathe, Baby Doll." He hit the call button and put the phone to his ear, and she could hear it ringing as she traveled back and forth along the same path. After the sixth ring, someone finally picked up, and Evaine held her breath, unable to shake the foreboding feeling from her dream. *He has Gage. Is he already dead?* She couldn't shake the feeling that something awful had happened to him because of her.

"Voicemail." Jacob frowned as he pulled the phone away long enough to push a button on the keypad and then left a brief message with his name and number before mentioning he was looking for Gage and it was urgent that Matt call him back as soon as possible.

"He's probably sleeping." Jacob tossed the phone down on the dining room table and ran his hand through his hair before closing the distance between them. When he wrapped his arms around her, Evaine melted into his chest, silent tears streaming down her face. "What if he's hurt? Or worse, dead like my parents?"

"Don't say that, Evie." Jacob's tone was harsh as he gripped the back of her head and pinned her against him.

"Maybe we should file a missing person report."

"I think he has to be missing for twenty-four hours to do that."

"Jesus Fucking Christ, Jay. I can't just sit here and do nothing." She wiggled out of his hold. "Maybe we should go by Eucharist and see if he's there by some crazy chance."

Jacob nodded and bit at his bottom lip in a way that reminded her of Gage and sent a fresh wave of anxiety bolting through her.

"I'm gonna change." There was no discussing it; she was determined to find him.

Evaine set a new record with how fast she washed up, got dressed in her black yoga pants and a long-sleeve T-shirt with her purple chucks, and piled her hair in a messy bun. Purple bags shadowed her eyes, but she didn't care because all that mattered was finding Gage.

"Let's go!" She headed toward the door, stopping long enough to grab her coat and bag, and Jacob was right behind her, so close that when she screeched to a halt and stared at the bloody knife stuck an inch into her door, he ran right into her back. Evaine's stomach dropped as he said. "What the hell?" The words died on his lips as he followed her gaze.

The sleek silver switchblade had an ornate mother-of-pearl handle that caught the light from overhead and pinned a large padded envelope to the door, the blood from the blade oozing down the yellow paper and turning it a burnt orange color. Without thinking, Evaine reached for the envelope that had sweeping black cursive that spelled out her name. "Don't touch it!" Jacob barked, ripping her hand away as her fingers grazed it. When she scowled at him, he said, "It could be evidence."

"I'm not gonna know unless I open it, Jay." Her tone was sharp as her insides churned with anxiety, and the icy fingers of adrenaline seeped into her spine, her heart pounding in her ears.

"Good point." Jacob gripped the bottom corner of the envelope and jerked it hard enough to tear it from under the knife. Though it wobbled from the force, it stayed wedged into the wood. "That's fucked up," he said as Evaine reached for the package and jerked it away before she could get a hold. She frowned and crossed her arms. "It's addressed to me, you know?"

"I don't give a shit! I'm opening it! So, take your ass back in the house and have a seat."

The look on her best friend's face told her he wasn't changing his mind as he turned her around and gave her a soft push back through the door. As she crossed to the dining room table, her mind raced, wondering what could be in the envelope. Whatever it was, she was sure it would be bad, very bad.

Blood is never a good thing.

"Just open it already," she barked, wringing her hands in her lap. Jacob shot her his best side-eyes but did as she requested. When he looked into the open end, his face turned ghost-white, and the envelope fell out of his shaking hand, landing on the tabletop with a wet thump.

"What is it?" she asked, already knowing it was worse than she imagined it could be from the look on his face. Jacob snatched the envelope back up as she reached for it, shaking his head. "No," he said to her like she was a five-year-old that shouldn't touch grown-up things. Evaine narrowed her eyes and pushed to her feet. "What is it, Jay?" He hugged it to his chest as she rounded the table toward him. "You don't want to see this, Babygirl. Trust me."

The disgust and sadness in Jacob's eyes scared the living hell out of her. "Yes, yes, I do!"

"Evie, you need to sit down and shut up for two minutes so I can call the fucking police."

Evaine could count the number of times Jacob raised his voice at her in anger in all the years they'd been friends. And now it was two, which told her that something was significantly wrong, and it had to do with Gage. Tears stung her eyes as they welled and tumbled down her face, but she did as he asked.

His glare softened. "Thank you," he mumbled, reaching for the phone and dialing nine-one-one. "Yeah, I'd like to report a missing person I believe might've been murdered."

Evaine's body went numb as the words registered, and she fought to keep the vomit threatening to choke her down long enough to run to the kitchen sink. Convulsions wracked her body as bile poured from her nose and mouth, burning her throat and nasal passages on the way out.

Jacob's voice lowered as he continued to talk into the phone, and after a couple more ticks, he finally set the cordless handset back on the table and came around the corner as Evaine washed her mouth out with water from the tap. "The police are on their way. She said fifteen minutes and not to touch anything else, just in case." The envelope was still in his tight grip as he rubbed her back. "Are you okay?"

She nodded and wiped tears from her face with the kitchen towel as she stared at it. "What is it?" The sobbing started again, despite her efforts to keep it down. "Tell me, please!" Sheer desperation made her voice tremble.

"Awe, Evie. I don't even know how to say it out loud." He glanced down at the yellow envelope and then caught her eyes again. She could see his sadness, making her stomach clench again with the promise of more retching as he sighed. "It's skin, Evie."

Evaine's ears buzzed. She already knew something terrible had happened to Gage, but now there was proof. "Gage's skin?" The question tumbled from her numb lips as panic took over her body.

Jacob gave her a slight nod.

She tried to wrap her mind around it but couldn't accept it as truth. "How do you know?"

Revulsion marred his face, his Adam's apple bobbing as he swallowed. "It's his tattoos, Evie."

Evaine's knees hit the floor, her body collapsing before Jacob could catch her. But the stinging pain was nothing compared to her heart breaking into a million pieces. There was no controlling the sobs that ravaged her. The realization that Gage was gone broke the small piece of her that was left into tiny slivers. *I can't believe he's gone!* She couldn't imagine a future where Gage didn't exist.

"It can't be." Pain tore through her as she chanted the words over and over until Jacob scooped her up off the floor and carried her to the couch. As he ran his hand over her hair, he kissed her temple and whispered soft reassurances as she curled into him and bawled her eyes out. They stayed like this for several minutes until a loud knock at the door jarred them both from the trance. Jacob pulled back and caught her eyes. "I need you to stay here, Evie. I'm gonna go talk to the police, okay?"

Numbness owned Evaine, the buzzing blur of panic and grief choking her. Unable to form words, she nodded.

As Jacob wrapped a blanket around her and headed toward the door, her body felt weirdly detached from her mind, which was so far away she couldn't comprehend what was going on around her. Still, the urge to see Gage's tattoos for herself overwhelmed her, chewing at Evaine's insides like fire ants. It was imperative for her to see them with her own eyes.

When she glanced up, the envelope called like a neon sign from the dining room table, where it sat unattended. *All I have to do is get on my feet and make it to the table before Jacob notices.*

As if the universe shifted to her will, Jacob and the detectives stepped into the hallway to inspect the switchblade still stuck in the door.

Evaine ran her hand through her hair and stood, her legs like rubber as she tried to cross the room. She used the furniture to prop herself until she finally made it to the table, her hand shaking as she reached for the open package. She sucked in a breath, steeling against the rising hysteria, and exhaled before tilting the gaping mouth of the package in her direction.

Inside was a wet mess of red, angry flesh, black ink tracing over the skin. It was all lumped together, but when she jostled the package, the pretty face of death smiled up at her, distorted and covered in smeared blood. Evaine gasped, dropping the padded envelope on the table as another wave of nausea swept through her, and she covered her mouth and ran to the bathroom, barely making it to the sink before it exploded from her in an angry wave of bitter bile and dry heaving. It took her a few minutes to get her body back under control. But once the vomiting stopped, the tears started again, and when Jacob knocked at the door, she was curled in the fetal position on the cool tile with no idea how long she'd been there, trying to cope with the pain that was eating her alive.

"You okay in there, Evie?" There was a brief pause before he knocked again. "Can I come in?"

"Yeah." Evaine sat up, leaning her back against the cool tub.

The door opened enough for him to stick his head in, and he looked down at her, half-smiling with sadness reflected in his eyes. "The detective wants to ask you a few questions. Are you up to talking to them? If not, he said we can come down to the station later today and make a statement."

Part of her wanted to push it off, but she needed to do everything she could to help them find out what happened to Gage. "Let me clean up, and I'll come answer them now."

It only took her a few minutes to answer the detective's questions because they just wanted to verify the information Jacob gave them about Gage, the package, and see if there was anything additional she could share about her stalker, which there wasn't.

The furrow of the detective's brow made it clear that he had nothing, which made her feel even more helpless. He told them that the only hope was fingerprints on the knife or envelope at this point. The team had already collected both for processing. Before leaving, the detective handed her his card and said the standard, "Please call me if you think of anything else."

Evaine nodded as Jacob took the card and shoved it into his back pocket. "We will," he said for both of them.

"I would strongly suggest that you find somewhere else to spend the rest of your night." the detective said as Jacob walked him to the door.

"She'll be staying with me."

"Good. We are going to post a couple of uniforms outside. They'll keep an eye on things for the next few hours."

"Thank you, Detective." Jacob shook his hand.

Evaine's heart ached as she watched him from the hallway. He was the only person she had left, and the idea of something happening to him scared her to death. All he cared about was protecting her, and she hated the helpless feeling of knowing she couldn't save him from whatever twisted freak was out there, tearing her world apart.

Daddy always told her she needed to protect herself and gave her a gun for her eighteenth birthday, so he could take her to the range to teach her to shoot. It wasn't something she enjoyed but did it to humor him. And since then, the gun was locked in a metal box at the top of her closet, forgotten until now. And there was no way she was leaving without taking it. If it came down to killing some crazy bastard to save Jacob's, or her own, life, she'd be ecstatic to put a hole in them. Without a second thought, she headed for her room. The key to the box was in her nightstand, and she had to use a hanger to jimmy the box from the top shelf. But by the time Jacob found her, she was already palming the cold metal in one hand and the box of ammunition in the other.

Jacob's eyes went wide when he saw the gun. "What are you doing with that, Evie?"

"Protecting you," she mumbled and laid it down on the bed with the box of bullets.

"I appreciate that, Sweetheart, but, really?"

"What?" Evaine asked, cocking a brow at him. "My dad taught me how to use it."

"Yeah." He ran a hand through his hair. "Like a hundred years ago."

She crossed her arms over her chest and stared at him. "So? It's not that hard."

Jacob stepped closer, reaching for her hand and tugging her arms loose. She let him pull her into his arms, burying her face in the softness of his T-shirt. He smelled like clove and spice. "I think maybe the aiming part might give you some trouble, Kitten."

"I have to do something, Jay." He was working so hard to avoid calling her Baby or Princess that it made her heartache, made her miss her parents, and long for Gage's deep voice and scent, cigarettes and all. *What I wouldn't give to have his arms wrapped around me.*

"I know. I know." Jacob stroked the back of her head, smoothing her wild red curls. "Let's get a bag packed, and you can come stay with me for a few days while we figure this out."

"He knows everything, Jay," she mumbled into his chest. "It doesn't matter where I go. He's everywhere. Maybe I should just let him come for me. Then at least you'd be safe."

Jacob gripped her shoulders and jerked her away from his warmth, glaring down at her as he ground out, "I don't give a fuck about being safe." And then shook her to emphasize his point. "You're not staying here alone under any circumstances. In fact, I'm not leaving you alone until they catch this psycho." He pulled her back into a hug, and she wrapped her arms around his waist. "I've already talked to Julien, and you can stay with us as long as you need. So, pack a fucking bag, Baby Doll." His large hands scooped up the gun and bullets before he walked out of the room. "And we're leaving this here. Understand?"

Evaine's shoulders slumped. "But."

"No but."

"Fine."

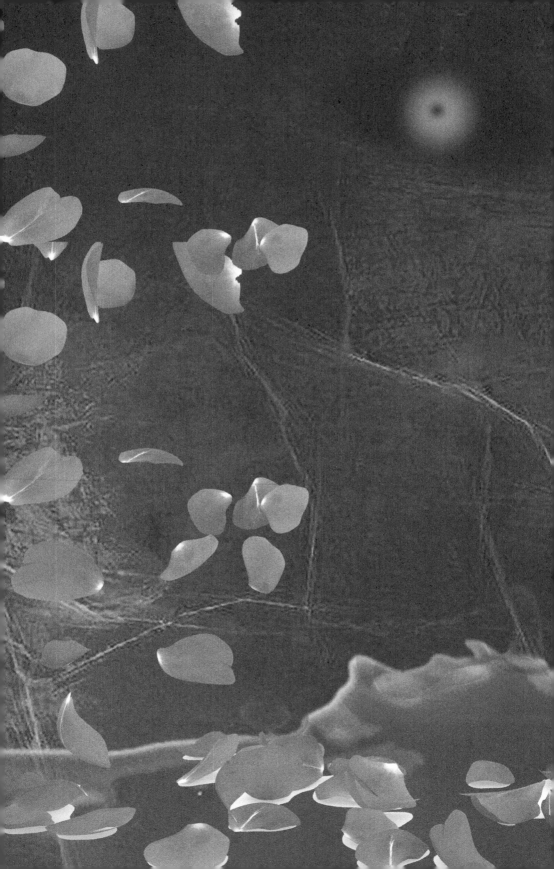

Chapter
Sixteen

Sixteen

Broken & Bent

It was well after dawn when they got back to Julien's apartment. Jacob fell right to sleep, but it took another Xanax before Evaine could get any rest because her brain wouldn't turn off. When she woke up, the sun was setting, and before she even fully awakened, the anxiety and guilt choked her so badly that she didn't want to face the world. It would be easier to hide in Jacob's bed and let it all pass her by.

Her phone rang from her messenger bag for the third time in the last ten minutes, and she was no more motivated to answer now than the first time it rang. Evaine didn't care who was calling or what they wanted. She just wanted them to stop already.

When she rolled over onto her other side, Evaine cracked an eye open and realized she was alone in the queen-sized bed, the shower running behind the closed bathroom door, and she pulled the pillow from under her, covering her head to muffle the annoying ringing. Relief washed over her as the phone stopped, giving her a tiny window of silence. But unfortunately, it wasn't long before the high-pitched ring tone shrilled again. Unable to handle it, Evaine shot up and huffed, "Damn it!" as the bathroom door opened and Jacob emerged with a waft of steam billowing around him.

271

"You, okay?" He glanced up from weaving his studded leather belt through the loops of his tight black pants, his T-shirt draping over his shoulder. The large turquoise towel wrapped around his head was almost the same color as his sea-green eyes.

"Damn phone," Evaine grumbled and fell back into the bed.

As if on cue, it blared again.

"Maybe you should answer the thing." Jacob grabbed her messenger bag from the floor, dug it out, and tossed it at her. "Here." Evaine groaned and fumbled around until she found it, squinting at the screen for a second before sighing and clicking the talk button. "Hello."

"Evaine?" Justin Marcus asked on the other end.

"Yes, Mr. Marcus. What can I do for you?"

As her parents' lawyer droned on about legal detail, Evaine wished she'd never answered because she couldn't care less if the board of directors now ran Daddy's company or that she would receive yearly dividends from the profits as arranged by her father. Or if the apartment would be in probate for a few more weeks. None of those things mattered on a good day. And they certainly didn't matter after last night. "Mr. Marcus. I appreciate the update, really. Daddy trusted you, and so do I. So I would prefer you handle the details and only reach out if there is a problem. I don't expect to hear from you until the apartment is ready to be sold or things are going sideways." When she hung up the phone, Jacob was staring at her. "What?" she asked.

"You're just gonna let him do whatever he thinks is best? You do realize that's how people get robbed blind, right?"

"Honestly, Jay, I just don't have the energy to care and just want some peace and quiet. He can have at it if he wants it that bad. Besides, like I said, Daddy trusted him, so he can't be all bad, right?"

"You say so." Jacob shrugged before pulling the towel from his head and draping it over his other shoulder. Water dripped off his wet hair onto the towel as he shook the ends and dabbed them on the damp material. Evaine watched him stride back into the bathroom.

He was only gone a couple of ticks, pulling his T-shirt over his head and tugging his hair from under his collar when he came back out. It took him a couple of minutes to find clean socks and his red chucks before sitting down next to her on the bed. "What do you want to do tonight, Sweetheart?"

It was her turn to shrug. "Nothing."

"That's not an option. At the very least, I need to feed you."

"I'm not hungry."

He wrinkled his nose. "Maybe I can talk you into washing?"

Evaine shoved his shoulder and stuck her tongue out. "I'm not doing that either."

"Really? I mean, I love you and all, but I draw the line at your dirty ass in my bed. I'll wash you myself if I have to, Kitten."

She appreciated the lightness of his words and that he wasn't tip-toeing around her, but she still struggled with the gaping hole in her chest where her family and Gage belonged. It felt like an oozing wound that would never heal, raw and angry, just like her. *Or worse, just like Gage's bloody tattoos.*

Evaine forced a half-smile for his benefit. "You'll have a fight on your hands."

Before Jacob had a chance to respond, there was a knock on his door. "Entrer," Jacob said in his best French accent, and it was clear he was spending too much time around Julien.

When Raven stuck his head through the cracked door, Evaine was surprised by his solemn expression, but it didn't quite reach his stormy-gray eyes. "How's it going?"

"I'm trying to talk Evie into getting outta bed." Jacob grinned over his shoulder. "And maybe washing."

"I think I'm going to try to call that detective first. Do you still have his card?" She scooted next to him as he jutted his chin at his nightstand and said, "It's right there."

"Thanks." Evaine wasn't expecting much from the authorities, but she felt like she needed to push them because Gage deserved better than becoming just another missing person.

"I'm gonna go make some coffee. Come down when you're done, okay?"

Evaine nodded and then watched Jacob close the door before dialing the number on the card. Dread ate at her, but she needed to know if they'd found anything else about Gage. A small part of her hoped, but the longer he was gone, the less likely that part was right. When the detective's voice mail picked up, Evaine left a message asking for an update and if he would return her call as soon as possible.

As soon as she hit the end button, a sob racked through her, tears streaming down her face. Evaine bawled her eyes out until she was gasping for breath and had snot running down her red, heated face. Agony tore through her insides, making her stomach churn. "Get it together," she mumbled, wiping her nose with the back of her hand and padding to the bathroom to clean up.

Though all she wanted to do was wallow, she forced herself to shower, turning the water up so high that it could cook her flesh, and stood under the punishing stream, trying to get her emotions in check and failing. Evaine sank to her knees, curling into a ball at the bottom of the tub, tears pouring down her face and mixing with chlorinated water as she thought about all things she'd never get to do with Gage. It made her chest ache as sobs racked her lithe body.

All she wanted was to wake up from this nightmare, and she cursed the universe when she couldn't and tried to come to terms with this shit show that was her new reality. "Why?" She tucked her knees closer to her chin as the water beat down on her side and hip, leaving welts of red in its wake until the water finally started to run cold, and she found the determination to climb out of the tub, dry off and get dressed in her black T-shirt and yoga pants. She even brushed her teeth and put her hair up in a ponytail. *That's progress, right?*

It took her a few minutes to find the kitchen, and Jacob was already on his second cup of coffee when she settled next to him at the small, round table, and he grinned over his mug. "You showered?"

"Just for you."

With a swallow of hot coffee, Jacob said, "I appreciate that more than you know."

Evaine stuck her tongue out as Julien walked into the room and said, "Bonsoir." Despite her grief, her insides shivered at his silky, smooth voice, his long fingers gripping her shoulder and making her tense as he leaned in. Sandalwood and copper enveloped her as his stray hairs tickled her face. "I am so glad to see you up." When she caught his cornflower-blue eyes, he gripped her chin. "Did you eat something, Ma Petite?" And she shook her head. "I'm not hungry right now."

"I understand, but you must eat. Please try for me, Ma Rousse. It would ease my concern, knowing you have eaten." His thumb brushed the edge of her bottom lip, making her pull it between her teeth and nod despite her lack of appetite. At the moment, she'd pretty much tell him whatever he wanted to hear to escape his piercing gaze. Not that it was harsh. In fact, it was quite the opposite, which is what made her squirm in her seat and say, "Okay."

Julien flashed her a toothed grin. "That a girl!" And then released her from his cool grip and headed through the large archway of the living room. "I will be checking in with you in a few hours, Ma Petite. Do not disappoint me, Hmm?"

"Yes, Sir," she said without thinking and earned another grin as he stepped back into the arch. "I do like the sound of that." His tone made her body clench, and it troubled her, even more so now that Gage was gone. *Why am I so weak? And such a shitty person?* For something she had no control over and would never act on, guilt took its place at the table next to terror, sadness, and misery. *Great!*

Jacob nudged her with his shoulder. "Evie?" And caught her eye when she broke her gaze to look over at him. "Did you talk to the detective?"

"I left a message." Evaine tracked Julien as he strode back into the room, his hand cradling a large, delicate wine glass filled midway with red wine. As she remembered the taste from the other night, she licked her lips, her face flushing as Julien zeroed in on the slight flick of her tongue and stopped mid-step with a grin. "Would you like a glass, Ma Petite? I would be happy to get it for you this time, but you will have to fend for yourself the next."

Saliva pooled in her mouth, and she swallowed, chewing on the side of her thumbnail. "Yes, please."

"Very well." Julien disappeared for a couple of ticks and then walked over and handed her the glass in his left hand.

She sipped the tasty tart wine. "Thank you."

"You are no longer a guest in my home, Ma Rousse. Now, you are family, and I always take care of my family." His words were smooth and kind, but something flickered in the back of his eyes that made Evaine's breath hitch. Heat flushed her face as she gulped down more wine. "I appreciate you letting me stay. I'll try not to wear out my welcome." She forced a smile.

"You, never," Jacob joked and then glanced at Julien. "I guess that means I have to get my own glass, huh?"

"It does, My Boy." When Jacob rounded the corner, Julien filled his vacant seat, leaning close enough to make her uncomfortable as he invaded her space. "Has there been any updates on your friend?" His gaze pinned Evaine against the rigid chair back, unable to escape his proximity, her voice wavering. "I left a message, but I haven't heard back from the detective."

"Very unfortunate. Please let me know if I can do anything to help you. I have some connections in the police force. If we need to contact them to get you answers, we will do that."

The wine and his silky voice took the edge off, and Evaine's body relaxed. "That's very kind of you, but you've done so much for me already. I couldn't ask you to do that."

Julien's brow furrowed. "Ma Petite, as I said, you are family. You will always have a place here, and I am happy to help. I know that does not take away the pain you must be feeling at losing your friend, but I hope to ease it some. To be a shelter for you in the storm." His eyes darkened. "I would do nearly anything for you, Ma Rousse. All you need do is ask." His words rolled off his tongue like sugary sweet syrup, making her want to agree to whatever he promised. *I need my head checked!* Evaine didn't know this man from Adam and felt like she trusted him more than she should. There was some strange, unexplainable connection, and again, guilt overtook her, making her down the last of her wine before slipping from her seat as Jacob walked back into the kitchen, sipping from his glass.

"Would you like a refill?" she asked Julien.

"Non, Ma Petite. I am quite satisfied at the moment."

When Evaine turned toward the doorway, she ran smack into the tiny, pink-haired girl she hadn't seen since her first visit to the apartment. Skye was wearing a black dress with knee-high white socks and black buckle shoes, looking all of sixteen. Evaine wondered why she lived with her brother, Raven, and not her parents.

"Evie!" Skye's voice was sing-song and edged with excitement. "I'm so happy to see you again. Julien said you would be staying with us." She clapped her hands together, her pink nails glittering in the light. "I am so excited to have a new sister!"

Julien narrowed his eyes at Skye, correcting her with a sharp tone. "She is our guest, Skye, not your sister." His eyes flicked back to Evaine. "You will have to forgive our Skye. She gets confused sometimes."

Skye's large black eyes bounced from Julien to Jacob and landed on her. "Sorry." She wrung her hands together in front of her short black dress. Evaine felt sorry for the girl and closed the distance between them, pulling Skye into a hug. "It's okay. I don't mind being your sister while I'm here." When Evaine stepped back, Skye's face lit up, her smile from ear to ear. "Do you mean it?" She bounced in place.

"Of course."

"That means we can have a sleepover?" She glanced at Julien, whose face was almost unreadable. He nodded. "If Evie desires."

"Oh boy. Oh boy." Skye beamed. "This is the best day ever."

Julien's smooth veneer slipped, his thin lips tightening as he eyed the small, bouncing girl.

Skye cocked her head to the side and frowned. "I'll see you later, Evie." She gave Evaine another quick hug and bounced off in the same direction she'd come from, her bright pink pigtails dancing.

Evaine wondered if there wasn't something wrong with Skye. Sure, she was young, but there was a naivety that seemed unusual, to say the least. When she glanced at Jacob, he gave her a slight shrug, his sea-green eyes flicking to their host when he stood up and emptied his glass.

"I'll leave you two to it. Be sure our Evie eats, Jacob." Julien's eyes landed on Evaine. "If you prefer your own room, the one next to Jacob's is vacant. Feel free to make yourself comfortable."

When they were alone, Evaine asked, "She always so odd?"

Jacob nodded. "I think maybe she had some trauma at a young age. She isn't quite right." He leaned in and whispered, "Honestly, sometimes she's downright scary. But they both keep a pretty close eye on her."

"Huh," Evaine wondered what the poor girl had gone through in her past that left her so off. In some ways, she felt terrible for her. The last few weeks had taken their toll on Evaine, but she'd still kept some semblance of normal, or at least tried. On the other hand, Skye seemed to find peace, hiding behind her child-like naivete.

Just after midnight, Julien, Raven, and Skye left to go clubbing, and Evaine couldn't stomach stepping foot in a club. The thought of it tightened a band around her heart because she knew the smell of dry ice and cigarette smoke would remind her of Gage. The way it hung on his hair and clothes when he'd come home after work. She wasn't sure she'd ever get to a point where it wouldn't trigger memories of him. Maybe someday she'd welcome those memories, but right now, she was fighting to shove them down and keep a tight lid on them so she could function.

Evaine was relieved when Jacob stayed home with her, not that she expected anything less. The thought of being alone right now was also overwhelming, and he was a welcome distraction from all the sadness. It felt good to watch some mindless television and drink Julien's expensive wine, which warmed her belly and made her sleepy as she curled against her best friend in his bed. All she wanted was the painlessness of sleep, so she added a Xanax to the mix. If she could just turn her brain off for a few hours to reset, maybe she could make it through another day.

For some reason, she felt protected at Julien's. Maybe it was the fact that there were three bad-ass boys to protect her from the crazy psycho who was trying to tear her world apart. Or perhaps it was how Julien seemed to keep an eye on her. The more time she spent around him, the safer she felt, which was interesting because her first impression of him was completely different.

When Evaine woke up the next afternoon, she stretched her arms over her head before grabbing her phone from the nightstand. There were several missed calls, but only two voice mails. The first was Tristan asking her to call as soon as possible because he was worried about her since she missed work yesterday. The second was the detective returning her call. He didn't have anything new. The florist was a dead-end, and they still hadn't found Gage. Reality drove a spike into her chest as she worked to keep her emotions in check. It wasn't that she didn't want to grieve for Gage. *Gods!* She did but feared breaking into so many pieces that she'd never be able to put herself back together, and she couldn't let that happen right now. There was no other option; she had to stay strong. He'd want her to keep pushing forward and fighting the psycho.

For his mellow yellow attitude, Gage was one stubborn ass when he wanted to be, and he'd expect nothing less from her. The thought of his tattoos being carved from his body was gruesome, but there was some slight chance that he could have survived and was still alive, and a part of her clung to that, too. She flip-flopped between hope and despair, unwilling to give up.

When her phone rang again, Evaine hit the button and brought it to her ear. "Hello?"

"Evaine. I've been trying to reach you all morning. Where are you, My Dear?" Tristan's tone was frantic and carried a note of concern or maybe more like panic.

It jostled her from her reverie. "Tristan, I'm sorry; I should've called you earlier, but I just woke up and don't think I'm coming-" Before she could finish, Tristan cut in again. "Where are you, My Dear?" His tone changed to a smooth drone that lulled her and made her head feel fuzzy. "I want to know exactly where you are."

And suddenly, she felt compelled to tell him. "Jacob's."

"You mean Julien's, Evaine?" The sharp edge to his question made her nod, even though he couldn't see her. *How does he know who Julien is? Is he stalking me?* After a tick, she said, "Yes."

"I need you to listen to me, Evaine. You will come to my office immediately. There is a critical business matter that requires your assistance. No matter what, Julien or Jacob, or anyone else, for that matter, says I need you here now. Get dressed and come to the office immediately, Evaine. Do you understand me?"

Compliance swept over her as she glanced at her sleeping friend's broad bare back. "Yes."

"Very good, My Dear. You have one hour, or I will come get you myself."

When she hung up the phone, Jacob yawned sleepily and rolled over to look at her with half-open eyes. "Everything okay, Kitten?"

Evaine's brow furrowed as the compulsion to comply with Tristan's demand sparked and burned across her mind like wildfire. "I have to go to the office. Tristan needs my help with a project."

"Now?" Jacob rubbed his half-open eyes and then scrubbed his hand over his mouth before sitting up. "Are you kidding me?"

"No." She pushed off the bed and went straight for her suitcase, pulling out fresh clothes and her travel bag with her hygiene and makeup. "He needs me immediately."

Jacob was on his feet and gripped her arm before she took another step, jerking her against his chest and narrowing his eyes. "What could possibly be so important that he doesn't understand that you just lost one of the most important people in your life, Evie?"

For the life of her, she couldn't explain the compulsion, the drive she felt to follow Tristan's directions. When Jacob mentioned Gage, it was a dull pain that she shoved to the back of her mind, overtaken by the urge to comply. "I have to go, Jay," was all she could manage as she tried to squirm from his grip.

"Nope." Jacob shook his head and leaned in close enough that she could feel his warm breath on her face. "That's not good enough, Evaine. You need to call him back and tell him you can't come in today. He's a big boy. He can handle his shit without you."

The stern tone of his voice made anger churn in her gut. Suddenly, she felt like a cornered animal. "You don't get to tell me what to do!" she half-growled and jerked her arm free. "He needs me, and I'm going. Put your big boy pants on and deal with it." Not allowing him to argue, she stomped to the bathroom and slammed the door.

Trepidation rushed over her as she stripped naked and climbed into the hot water, which drove her to wash her hair and body without wasting any time enjoying the water like she usually would. There was no time to waste as she toweled off.

Thankfully, there was no shortage of scrunchies in Jacob's bathroom. She borrowed one of the many black ones to secure her wet hair into a tight bun and then put on enough makeup to hide the puffiness around her eyes from all the crying before dressing in a simple black long-sleeve blouse and slightly wrinkled burgundy dress pants that she paired with her black platform ankle boots.

When she came out of the bathroom, Jacob was sitting on the edge of his bed; his arms crossed over his T-shirt-covered chest. He'd changed his clothes and was wearing shoes, along with a frown that told her their conversation wasn't over.

"Jay, I'm not going to argue with you! I need to go, and that's it; I'm going."

Jacob pushed to his feet and stepped into her path. "Why are you so hell-bent on doing what this asshole is telling you to do? What is wrong with you?"

"There's nothing wrong with me!" Her voice ticked up a notch as frustration washed over her. "I need to go now!" His hand snaked out, fingers curling around Evaine's upper arm, and his voice matched hers when he snapped, "I'm not letting you go."

Panic crashed over her as his grip dug into her arm. She squirmed and jerked back but couldn't break the hold. "Let go!" Tears welled in her eyes, her breathing quick and labored. "LET. ME. GO."

"Something's not right with you, Evie, and I'm not letting you go anywhere until I figure out what's wrong."

Evaine felt the minutes ticking down as they glared at each other, and the relentless drive chewed at her brain, spurring her to fight. To both their surprise, her hand struck out with a loud crack as it landed against Jacob's cheek, welting with a print of her fingers.

"What the fuck!" he barked, shaking her as she fought his grip as hard as possible. As Jacob rubbed his cheek with his free hand, Raven stuck his head in the door, looking like he'd just woke from the dead. "What's all the noise about?" His stormy-gray eyes held an edge of indignation mixed with drowsiness.

"She's leaving," Jacob said, his tone rifled with irritation

"So what?" Raven rubbed his stomach lethargically.

Irritation plagued Jacob's face, and he took a deep breath. "So, she's not acting like herself, and I'm not letting her go."

Raven narrowed his gaze, watching Evaine struggle.

"I have to go. Tristan needs me!"

Raven closed the door and rested his back against it when he stepped into the room, crossing his arms over his well-muscled chest, his biceps flexing. He shook his head, his long hair mussed from sleep. "Hate to tell you, Sweetheart, but you're not going anywhere." The set of his jaw begged her to prove him wrong, and even though he was twice her size and double her weight, she was ready to take him on.

Evaine stepped toward Raven. "You think you can stop me?"

Jacob jerked her, pinning her back to his chest, and wrapped his arms around her waist as she fought against him. "Get a grip, Evie."

As she kicked and fought, panic choked her. There was nothing but the need to comply, to do as she was told. Desperate, she dropped her chin to her chest and then flung her head back, nailing her best friend square in the nose. He cursed as one hand went to his nose, and his grip loosened enough to allow her to squirm loose. Evaine glared at Raven as he straightened up, shifting his body into her path. "Get out of my way!" She stomped toward him with renewed determination.

Raven moved fast, scooping her up and tossing her over his shoulder. His steel grip held her with ease as Evaine screeched and cursed like she'd lost her mind until he finally smacked her on her ass and said, "For fucksakes! Hold still, you stupid bitch."

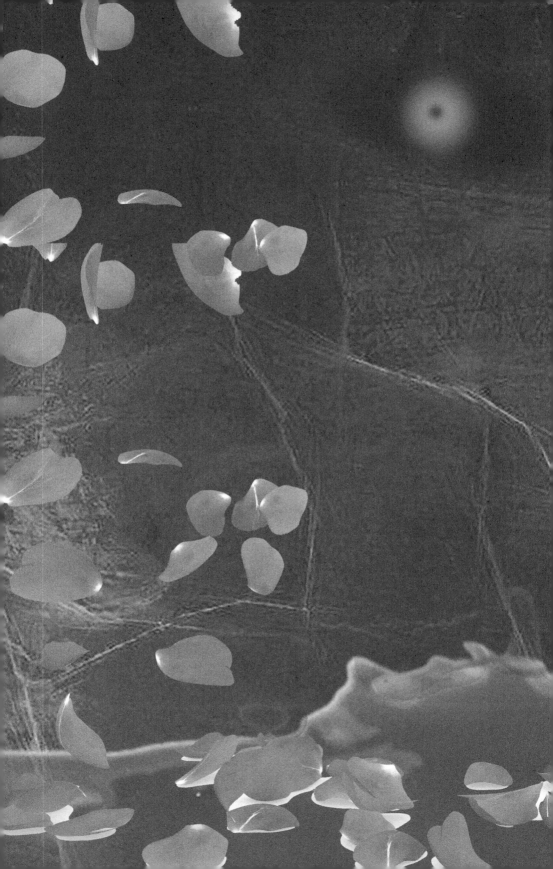

Chapter
Seventeen

Seventeen

Jealousy & Influence

A piercing screech pulled Julien from his thoughts, its anguish drawing him to his feet and the source. Her pain was impossible to ignore, and he would need to remedy it.

When he stepped into Jacob's room, Julien said. "Now, now, Raven. Is that any way to speak to our guest?" Despite the frustration making his body tight, his calm mask was in place. "Our rival has obviously swayed her." He tamped down his annoyance, his tone smooth as he closed the distance between them and gripped Raven's shoulder, his rings glinting in the light.

Jacob furrowed his brow. "You know what's wrong with her?"

There was genuine concern for his friend. *Easy on the eyes, but clueless.* He'd spent days among some of the scariest predators on the planet and was oblivious to the fact that Julien's protection was the only thing keeping him from suffering the same fate as Gage. They were coming down to the wire, which meant it was even more essential to have Jacob tucked on the sidelines out of Tristan's reach.

No matter how many times life knocked Evaine down, she climbed back to her feet and fought on. From the beginning, he knew she was a strong girl and wanted to earn her trust and compliance without using his gifts. It was a challenge, and he believed challenges should have stringent ground rules because there was no honor or fun in cheating to secure the victory. *Non, not his clan.* His clan would succeed despite Tristan's under-handed methods because what started as a mere distraction quickly became an imperative. Now he wanted Evaine as part of his clan and was so close he could taste her. Sure, having her as his newest protégé would be enjoyable, but the real reward was thwarting Tristan's plan to possess her as his thrall.

Julien caught Jacob's gaze and injected an edge of control into his polished tone. He'd marked the boy as his thrall days ago and had considered turning him before Tristan forced him to adjust his plans. Now Julien had to rethink his entire strategy because he wouldn't let Tristan put his binding mark on Evaine and claim her as his thrall. He'd as soon kill her rather than let her spend the rest of her natural life as Tristan's slave. *Non!* The best course of action would be to hasten her turning; then, Consul Law would protect her. She'd be untouchable, strong in her own right, and never have to fear Tristan claiming her because she would have the Dark Blood Clan's protection.

There was only the minor matter of getting her to agree to the change because Julien wanted her consent before moving forward with his plan. Careful to exert the smallest amount of influence possible to manage the situation, he caught Jacob's gaze. "Give me a moment."

Jacob's face smoothed, eyes staring off in a daze as Julien's powers lulled him. Julien hated breaking his own rules, but Tristan was as determined to win the prize as he was. The only difference being Tristan had no qualms with using every available resource to make it happen.

It was bad enough that Tristan's stench had already marred such a perfect specimen because he'd marked her recently. Julien smelled his taint from across the room, and jealousy boiled his blood. He was beginning to regret the restraint he'd exercised in refraining from biting her. It would have been so easy to spell her and have his way on more than one occasion, like Tristan, but he'd chosen not to do it. With a wave of his elegant hand, Julien turned to Raven. "Pose-la, Mon Fils." Raven nodded and let Evaine's body slide down his, holding her forearms tight when her feet hit the floor.

"He needs me!" she ranted and struggled, forcing another wave of anger to wash over Julien.

His mask slipped as he gripped her face and hissed, "The only thing Master Tristan needs, Ma Petite, is a stake through his heart. He is a sneaky lying scoundrel, and I will not- cannot let him have you."

Evaine's head lulled, her eyes rolling back as the compulsion gnawed at her mind, compelling her to fight harder. Tristan's bites made her especially vulnerable to his influence. She was like a rabid dog, out of her mind and out of control. Julien hated seeing her this way and needed to keep her from the bastard's clutches. He scrubbed his free hand over his face and cursed before throwing his hands up and glaring at Raven. "I'm going to have to accelerate our timeline."

"Do you want me to do it?" Raven's tone was riddled with detachment and disinterest, like he couldn't bother to care either way.

"Non." Julien's eyes darkened as he caressed her cheek, a small smile curling his tight mouth when her body shivered involuntarily. He couldn't deny the satisfaction her reaction gave him. "Ma Rousse," he whispered when he brushed his lips along her jawline.

Her intoxicating scent permeated his senses, making his fangs ache for a taste of her, patchouli and vanilla, with that underlying hint of copper all humans had from the blood pumping through their veins. She was a thing of beauty, and he understood Tristan's obsession with her because, if he was honest, he was acquiring one of his own, despite having to come to terms with Tristan tasting her first. He was determined to be the last and would possess her, heart and soul; just as soon as he convinced her that turning would be the best solution to their dilemma. "She is mine. I will do it."

Strands of her blood-red hair pulled free from the bun on her head and hung around her face, softening her perfect features. Despite her young age, there was a fire in her that paid homage to the vibrant color of her curly locks. It was one of the things he appreciated about his little redhead, and he twisted a silky length around his finger, relishing the turmoil that kicked up her adrenaline and made her smell even sweeter as she pleaded with him. "Please, Julien. I need to go. I need to get to the office. Tristan needs me." Tears streamed down her face. Julien swiped one with his thumb and brought it to his lips, sampling the salty wetness. *Surely it isn't as tasty as her blood, but beggars can't be choosers.*

"Just enough to break his compulsion, Ma Rousse, and then you and I need to discuss your future." Julien gripped her chin and brought her exquisite face to his. Her emerald-green eyes were darker than usual, desperation seeping into their ordinary brightness. His thumb traced the underside of her pouting full bottom lip as he forced down the urge to steal a kiss and ordered, "Calm yourself, Evaine."

As Julien's influence forced out Tristan's intentions, she stopped struggling, her body relaxing against Raven's. Her arms fell loosely to her sides.

Julien held a loose grip on her chin as her head kicked back against Raven's chest as she worked to catch her breath as exhaustion overtook her. She'd worn her fragile, weakened body out, trying to escape Raven's iron grip. Influence often affected humans this way, especially when they fought so hard to comply. When she wavered, Raven held her upright.

"That's my girl." Julien cupped the side of her face and purred, "You are mine now, Ma Petite." She leveled her chin and caught his eyes, pulling her bottom lip between her teeth and leaning into his touch like the perfect little pet she would soon become. His tongue darted out to wet his dry lips.

Raven tapped into their connection and pushed into Julien's thoughts. *You need to turn her now*, without speaking aloud, and Skye chimed in, *Yes, Tati, turn her now. Turn them both. I want new toys to play with.*

That is the plan, Les Enfants. Julien heard Skye squeal with excitement over their connection. He loved her child-like enthusiasm.

Evaine gazed at him like he was the sun and stars all rolled into one. He relished the awe sparkling in her eyes, coerced or not, and wondered if she would ever look at him like that for real as he smoothed his fingers along her cheekbone and tapped the tip of her nose with a smirk that made the sharp edge of his fang snag his lip. "I have a couple of requests, Ma Petite. First, I hate to see you so sad, so you will tuck the pain deep inside and move forward with your life. It is what Gage would want you to do, would he not?" When she nodded in agreement, he said, "Also, you will not talk to that sneaky bastard, Tristan, again, Evaine. If he calls, you will ignore it. If he comes to you, you will come to me to protect you from that monster. You feel safe and want to stay here with me, don't you, Ma Rousse?" Okay, maybe he was taking more liberties than he should, but he couldn't help the need to relieve the grief that was eating her alive and keep her safe from Tristan. They were minor concessions and didn't change that she would have to decide to be with him.

"I do," Evaine mumbled.

Unable to resist her draw, Julien leaned into the curve of her neck, her sweet, earthy copper scent intoxicating, even tainted by Tristan's stench. His fingers stroked the contour of her supple waist and hip, and she shivered under his touch in a way that had nothing to do with fear. It made him bolder. "Ask me to protect you from the man who killed everyone you love, Sweet Thing. Beg me to keep you safe from him."

"Will you please protect me, Julien?" Evaine asked as his influence washed over her a second time. The Hollow words weren't as satisfying as they would be if he earned them, but he'd take what he could get in this moment.

"Of course, Ma Petite." Julien grasped her hand, bringing her warm fingers to his mouth to kiss each knuckle. A small wave of pleasure washed over him as her face flushed with heat. Her body couldn't deny the draw he had, which made him smile, despite his disappointment with the circumstances. "But you will need to calmly learn the truth of what we are first." It took every bit of his honed resolve to step from her and focus his attention on Jacob for a moment. Julien gripped his shoulder and caught his eyes, exuding a more substantial wave of influence over him. "You, Dear Boy, will also let go of the loss of your friend and stay with us for protection."

Jacob nodded his compliance. "Yes, Julien."

Julien turned back to Evaine. "Now, My Children, trust that I will take care of you and come back to me." And watched her shake the effects off like cobwebs from her brain.

Confusion washed over her pretty face as she pushed off Raven. "What happened?"

Julien narrowed his eyes. "That villain tried to steal you right out from under us, Ma Rousse."

Evaine cocked her head, glancing at Jacob and then back at Julien. "What are you talking about?"

"It is time I told you both the truth." Julien smiled and beckoned her with a fluent wave of his hand. "Come along, Ma Petite. I believe you will need a large glass of wine for this. Perhaps the entire bottle."

When Raven let go, Evaine stumbled, and Julien reached out to steady her, her hand slipping into his as she clumsily let him lead her from the room. It was nice to see a flicker of fire back in her eyes, even if it was just a touch. Her grief was challenging to watch, and his guilt lessened as she smiled at him.

Jacob and Raven fell in behind them as Julien led her down to the living room. "Please sit, both of you." When he let go of her hand, he went straight for the bar and poured four glasses of 1947 Richebourg Grand Cru, emptying the bottle. Raven stood at his right with his arms crossed over his chest and watched their guests, his jaw ticking as Julien turned and handed him two of the glasses. "For our guests." Raven took them with a nod and gave them to Evaine and Jacob, both sipping from them.

After adding a dash of human blood to the other two, Julien joined the group and handed Raven one of the special glasses before sipping from the other as he sat across from the pair and sighed as he prepared to not only break vampire law but likely scare the hell out of the two of them.

"Did Tristan kill my family? Gage?" Evaine asked before he had the chance to begin.

As much as he wanted to shelter her from the truth, she needed to know. He nodded. "Oui, Ma Petite. He is the reason your family is dead and Gage is missing. He is a vile monster, determined to have you as his slave." Fear and confusion washed over her face. "I will not let him have you, Evie. I will protect you from him at all costs." Her stunned expression made it clear she was only partially digesting the information, and he pushed a touch of influence at them both to ease the onslaught of emotions. "I need you to listen to me, Children, and heed my words. I am putting myself at significant risk revealing these secrets to you. It is against our Consul law to share them with humans, but I feel compelled to help you, Ma Rousse."

They watched him from the sofa, Evaine sipping her wine and Jacob swirling his glass nervously.

"You need to know that we are all vampires. Raven, Skye, Tristan, Keegan, and myself included. So when I tell you Tristan is a monster, it is quite literally that I mean it. He has been my rival for the last three hundred years. I have watched him tear other humans' lives apart to take what he wanted from them. He is obsessed with having a human thrall and will do whatever it takes to have you."

Evaine sucked in a breath, choking on her wine, and Jacob set his glass down on the table and lightly tapped her on the back. "You, okay?"

"Mmm-hmm," she mumbled unconvincingly and took a large gulp of wine, her body tensing.

"I know this is hard to believe, but it is true. Tristan used his influence to wipe your memory at least twice."

"His influence?" Jacob asked for both of them.

"We vampires can influence humans with our will. He has marked her twice and used the influence to erase the memory from her mind. If he marks her a third time, she will be his by Consul law, and there will be nothing I can do to protect her from his intentions. He will make her a slave, his pet." Julien's gaze bore into Evaine's. "He will own you for the rest of your life, Ma Rousse. He will make you do vile things for him- to him- with him, and I will be powerless to help."

Evaine swallowed hard and wiped the back of her hand over her mouth, her eyes filling with fear as the reality of the situation washed across her pretty face. Jacob wrapped an arm around her shoulder and pulled her into his side. "I'm not going to let that happen."

Julien couldn't keep a chuckle from bursting from his chest. "My Boy, there will be absolutely nothing you can do to stop it. He is a three-hundred-year-old vampire, and you are a fragile human. There is no contest. The only reason you have not joined Gage is that I have protected you."

Anger marred Jacob's face as Julien's harsh words made Evaine flinch. "What then? How do we protect her from him?"

"Obviously, he will come for her now that his plan failed?"

"What plan?" Evaine asked around her glass.

Julien's shoulders slumped slightly, but he tempered his tone and softened his words. "Oh, Ma Petite. Do you not remember when he used his influence to make you crazy with the need to go to him? Had I not stopped you, you would surely already be at his beck and call."

"You're lucky Julien was here," Raven said from the chair next to him. "You were out of your mind, so I had to restrain you."

Evaine's face went white as she glanced between them and then at Jacob, who hugged her closer. "I vaguely remember the urge to go to him. It was overwhelming." Her eyes caught Julien's again, panic darkening them to a forest green, her words laced with the acid of hate. "I don't want to be his pet."

Julien relaxed into his chair. "As I promised, I will not let that happen to you. But I worry he will continue to hunt you as long as he believes there is a chance to possess you." Julien tapped the tip of his finger against his lip. "Perhaps, if we found a way to make it impossible for him to..." His words tapered off, and after a couple of ticks of silence, Rave asked, "What if you turned her?"

Evaine's eyes widened, but she didn't disagree, which made Julien lean his elbows on the arms of his chair as he caught her gaze and nodded. "It would make it impossible for him to claim you because you would be part of our clan and under my protection, and the law would hold him accountable for any actions against you."

"That's crazy!" Jacob said.

"It is the only way to ensure that she is safe, Jay," Raven said.

When Evaine's eyes landed on him, Julien nodded, unable to read her thoughts because they were jumbled and erratic. Her expression was vague, far away, like she was lost in thought. *How do I convince her this is the best course of action?* "It is your choice, Ma Petite, but I assure you if you do not do something drastic, you will become his property, and I will not be able to stop it. I need you to let me help you before it's too late."

"I- " Evaine stuttered.

Jacob squeezed her. "I can't believe I'm actually going to say this, but maybe he's right, Evie. That psycho has done some awful shit to get to you already. Maybe we need to do this to keep you safe."

Evaine's eyes widened again as they darted to Jacob's. "We?"

He grinned. "You don't get to become a hot-ass vampire without me, Bitch."

"Are you crazy?" she asked.

"Maybe a little."

Evaine shook her head and cracked a small smile. "I love you; you know that, right?"

Jacob hugged her. "Then do this for me so that Tristan can't hurt you any more than he already has. You won't be alone."

Evaine furrowed her brow and then turned her attention to Julien. "Would you turn us both?"

Julien's fangs lengthened at the thought of making her one of them. He smiled, steepling his fingers. "Of course, Ma Rousse. All you need do is ask." Victory was right there within his grasp, so close he could taste it. He felt Skye's excitement and an edge of disappointment from his jealous right hand as he waited for her to take the next step.

"Are you sure you wanna do this, Jay? I mean, I'm crazy for considering it, so you're definitely out of your mind."

Raven leaned forward, planting his elbows on his knees. "He is safer as one of us, Evaine. If Jacob doesn't turn, Tristan could continue to pursue him. Don't you think he will want to make you pay for escaping him? Hurting Jacob is the best way for him to do it."

"Raven is right, Ma Rousse." Julien shifted in his seat, tapping his long fingers on the armrest.

Evaine was silent for a couple of ticks, staring at the floor. Julien held his breath, anticipating her answer. Something told him she would agree, but he couldn't get too cocky and wouldn't be content until he buried his fangs in her neck, his venom running through her veins.

When she glanced up, conviction consumed her emerald eyes. "Will I be able to avenge Gage and my parents?"

A wicked smile curled Julien's mouth. "I promise you, Ma Petite, we will make Tristan pay for everything he has done to both of us." Minutes ticked by as Evaine seemed to digest what he shared, and for the slightest moment, he was afraid she'd say no.

She mumbled, "Let's do this then, " when she finally spoke, sounding less than sure.

"Are you positive this is what you want?" Julien asked.

Evaine's eyes hardened, and she nodded sharply. "Yes. Let's do this before something else happens, and I end up a slave to that monster."

Elation washed over Julien as he pushed to his feet and closed the distance between them. "I must warn you that turning is not a pleasant thing. There will be some pain as your body changes, but it will only last for a few hours, then you will be reborn as one of us. Powerful and untouchable." He reached for her hand, and she took it with only a slight hesitation. "There will be nothing to fear when you become one of us. I will protect you for eternity."

Evaine stood, forcing a swallow before her words came out as a hoarse whisper. "Okay."

Jacob was next to her, lacing his fingers through hers. "I'm here, Princess. I always will be."

"Come to me, Ma Rousse," Julien said, letting her make the choice to step into his open arms. Satisfaction washed over him when she complied and tilted her head to give him access to her throat. "It is a shame that we will have to rush this, but I will make it up to you," Julien whispered, licking his lips.

In all his years, only a handful of moments made his heart race, and this was one of them. Victory was his, and he would relish his rival's failure. His fangs dropped, his tongue darting out to taste her soft flesh. He could feel the vein pumping just under the skin and slid his hand up Evaine's back before gripping her neck and pulling her head a little further to the side as he sank his fangs into her supple flesh.

Her body tensed, her small hands gripping the front of his dress shirt as she sucked in a harsh breath and whimpered from the pain before relaxing against him when his neurotoxin flooded into her system, and pleasure washed over her. The way her body ground against his was intoxicating, her whimper turning to a moan of ecstasy as he pulled the sweetness from her veins.

Julien was careful not to take too much because she needed to be as strong as possible for the turn, injecting venom into her veins before he pulled back and cradled her. He licked her wound closed and brushed the loose curls from her face as he settled her into the cushion, her head lulling, her eyes glazing with lingering confusion. "Rest, Ma Rousse."

Fear and curiosity reflected in Jacob's sea-green eyes as they locked with his. Julien held his hand out and asked, "Are you ready, Mon Fils?" The boy hesitated before stepping toward him, his eyes shifting to something akin to resolve as he nodded.

Julien shot him a fanged grin before wrapping his arms around him.

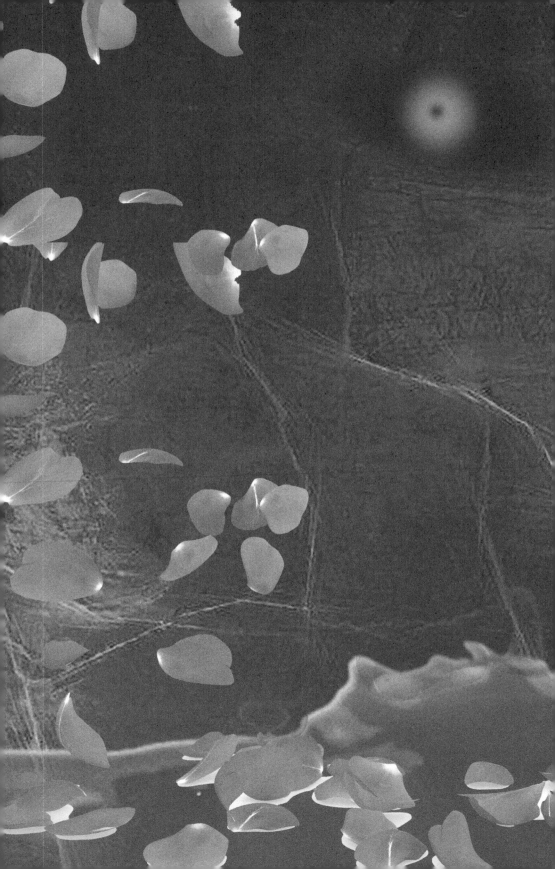

Chapter
Eighteen

Eighteen

Impulse & Frustration

Tristan wore the carpet, pacing in front of his desk as the clock ticked down, and there was still no sign of Evaine.

From the moment he'd seen her picture in Chandler's office, Tristan wanted her, and at the dinner party, he truly understood how amazing she was, how much potential she had. It was nothing for him to decide that he needed to make her his new companion.

Two marks increased his influence enough to force his intentions on her through the phone, and he was glad for the foresight to bite her but knew there was always a chance they would try to stop her because he wasn't naive enough to think Julien would let her out of the apartment if he knew her intentions. Still, he had to try before going head-to-head with Julien because there would be no going back once he crossed that line, and though it wouldn't be the first time they clashed, most of the time, it was over policy or political power, not humans.

Sometimes, you have to break a few eggs to make an omelet, right?

Tristan had no issue breaking Julien's proverbial eggs to topple him from the coveted seat as Ansel's right hand, and he also had no qualms with the role he and Keegan played in sabotaging Julien's efforts here in the States.

They'd played it close to the vest and left no evidence to come back on them and done an excellent job of making Julien's life difficult.

Though Julien couldn't prove it to the Luminary, he whole-heartedly believed that Tristan's hands were in his troubles. He wasn't wrong, and now he was out for revenge, to boot.

Until about two months ago, Julien sat in the First Seat of the Consul and was Ansel's right hand, but recent failures and their consequential punishments forced Julien to the second seat, earning Tristan a promotion. It was Julien's fault for making it so easy for Tristan to muck with his plans for Eucharist and slow down the progress he was making to round up the Lash and increase production for distributing on a larger scale.

Every day, the drug's popularity grew, and with it, the demand. It was getting impossible for the Consul to procure ingredients and keep up with the increased usage. Vampires loved their decadence and extravagance, and this was no different. Everyone wanted a taste of the new drug. Lash was a powerful aphrodisiac that even he'd imbibe a few times. It was the human equivalent of ecstasy times ten and was becoming popular among more than just the vampires.

The increased demand was filling the Consul coffers, so Julien was charged with expanding the supply chains. But finding the commodity proved challenging and became impossible with a bit of tampering, which angered the Luminary, Ansel, the leader of the vampire government and oldest among them. It wasn't unusual for Ansel's anger to result in a fate much worse than being demoted. Julien was lucky to have his head still, but the fact that he did was a glaring indication of Ansel's respect and consideration for him.

So it was pretty easy to see why Julien, a man who didn't take the loss lightly, had a sudden interest in Evaine and stepped in to muck this up. *The Wanker's pissed off!* Tristan couldn't recall the number of times they'd flip-flopped from First to Second, but he knew from experience that Julien would be exact in his payback with the malice and vigor of a serial killer.

Tension knotted Tristan's shoulders and back as he paced, running his hands through his hair. *Where the hell is Keegan?* He needed his right-hand man to help plan his next move because though Tristan never shied away from going up against any member of the Consul, Julien was a different animal, cunning and ruthless, with little regard for human life. Or any life, for that matter.

There was also the matter of staying under the radar because if Ansel caught wind of their squabbling over a human, he would kill her without a second thought. And Tristan couldn't let that happen to Evaine, who was something special and clueless about the situation he'd gotten her into by setting his sights on her.

Tristan's blood boiled from the sheer audacity of Julien meddling with his efforts to acquire a new pet, though it wasn't surprising. Tristan found human thralls alluring. Maybe it was the humanity or their fragility; he wasn't sure. But it was long past time to acquire a new one because it had been years since Summer perished, and her loss took its toll on Tristan.

After all the years together, she was his closest confidant, lover, and even someone he considered a friend, which was hard to come by in the predatory world he was a part of. It left painful loneliness that he hoped Evaine would help to ease, her bright smile and resilience, her brilliance and fearlessness, and the edge of wildness in her emerald green eyes. She would mature into a formidable force, and he wanted a front-row seat when it happened, but something in his gut told him it might already be too late.

Relief washed over Tristan as Keegan strolled into his office, and he stopped in his tracks, crossing his arms over his chest and glaring at the burly Highlander. "What took you so damn long, Mate?"

Keegan wore his usual kilt and linen shirt with a dirk hanging from his belt. This Highlander was a hulk of a man, his broad shoulders and chest making Tristan look like a schoolboy in comparison. He'd pulled back his long red hair and had a freshly groomed beard, his green eyes glimmering as he shot Tristan a mischievous grin. "Are we goin' to battle?" he asked, with his thick Scottish accent, and gripped the hilt of his dirk with his massive hand.

"We very well may be, Ole Friend." Tristan glanced at the clock on the wall and shoved his hands into his pockets to tamp down the nervous energy that ate at his normally calm exterior. It was now five minutes past the deadline he'd given her.

"I look forward to knocking that smug bugger down a few notches. Tis' well past time if ye ask me."

"Knocking him down a notch is exactly how I ended up in this position, Kee. Why do you think he's interfering with my plans for Evaine? He can't prove it, but he squarely lays the blame for losing his seat at my feet."

"He is a ruthless bastard, to be sure." Keegan took two giant steps and dropped into one of the leather chairs in front of Tristan's desk, his dirk and belt clanging as he made himself comfortable. "Are ye sure ye wanna do this, Old Man?"

"At this point, I've gone too far to walk away. Besides, Mate, I'll not leave Evaine in the hands of that man and his twisted clan." Tristan leaned against his desk with a sigh, crossing his ankles and then his arms. "I'm afraid he's wise to my attempt to extract her from his prison and won't be letting go of her so easily."

"Tis' no fun in easy." Keegan rattled the hilt of his dirk. "I prefer to face him on the field of battle rather than playing these political games and back door deals. It is not honorable, though sometimes necessary."

Tristan chuckled. "Always ready for a fight. I hate to disappoint you, Keegan, but the goal is to avoid any more bloodshed and keep the girl alive. He would just as soon turn her than let me have her. The bastard is out for revenge and won't stop until he quenches that thirst."

Bushy eyebrows furrowed as Keegan frowned. "Tis' unfortunate." He caught Tristan's eye, a burly hand scrubbing over his mouth. "Before we go any further down this path, answer me one question."

Tristan gave Keegan a sharp nod, but he already knew his question and waited for his comrade to say it aloud.

"Is the lassie worth all this?"

"There is no doubt in my mind. I will not walk away and leave her to Julien and his clan." He could taste her blood on his tongue, though it had been days, and hear her soft moans as he fed. Tristan craved Evaine like an addict who craved his next hit of heroin and wouldn't stop until he had her, even if it meant destroying her to keep her away from Julien.

Keegan studied him for a couple of ticks and then nodded. "What's da plan, then?"

"There really is only one option here, and that's to go and get her," Tristan said after a moment of consideration.

"Straight at 'im, aye. That sounds like a plan to me." Keegan's green eyes sparkled with the prospect of bloodshed. "Make him wish he kept his tarted arse out of it."

"Something like that, Ole Chap." Tristan grinned.

Keegan stood up and shifted his dirk before shoving his shoulders back. "Let's go get her."

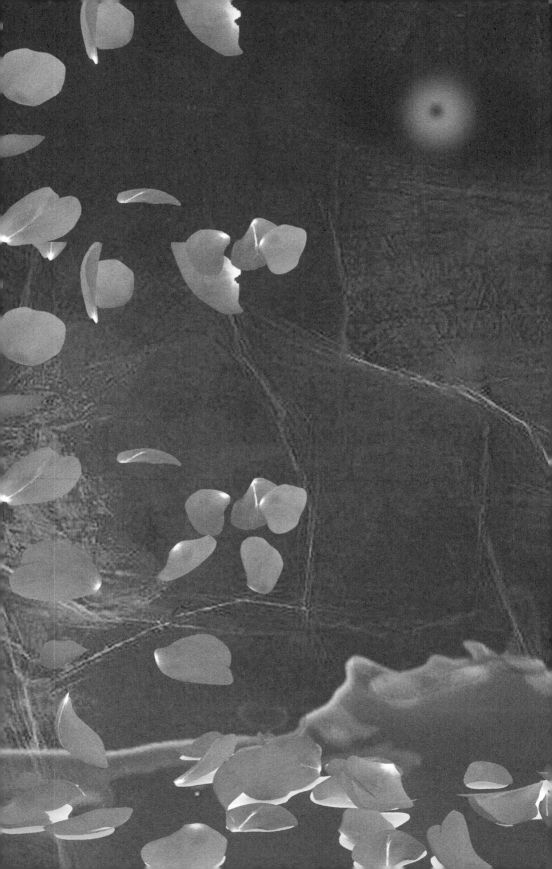

Chapter
Nineteen

Nineteen

Trust & Truth

Fear and anger churned in Evaine's stomach as she sat on the couch, trying to keep herself upright, her head swimming as she watched Julien wrap his arms around Jacob and lean in to bite him. His body tensed when Julien's fangs sunk into him, groaning with pain that quickly turned to pleasure.

She couldn't wrap her brain around the last few hours and wasn't sure they'd made the right choice, but it seemed the only option to escape the monster stalking her. It was so much worse than she ever imagined it could be. Tristan wasn't just some crazy psycho. *No, of course not!* He was a full-fledged monster.

Evaine always loved the darker side of life growing up and had a fascination for all things macabre and supernatural. But she never expected to find out any of it was real and struggled to grasp the truth as Julien settled a dazed Jacob down next to her.

"You will feel a little weak as the venom works. It may also make you run a fever for a short time. It is an arduous process but is typically over within twelve hours. And you have nothing to worry about because Raven and I will be here to help you through it."

When Jacob glanced over, his eyes were almost wholly pupil with only a shiver of sea-green around the outside, and he had that glazed look he got when they did ecstasy or acid. She smiled when he grabbed for her hand but missed his mark, landing on her thigh instead. "This isn't so bad," he slurred and leaned against her, their shoulders touching a minute before he wrapped his arm around her. "I love you, Evie." He kissed the side of her head and pulled her close.

"I still think you're crazy to agree to this for me." Evaine rested her head on his chest, playing with one of the long, silky strands of his midnight hair.

"You're my only family, Evie. I wouldn't leave you to face this alone."

There was no doubt she would do the same for him if the tables were turned, and Raven was right about Tristan using Jacob to get to her. He was her last link and her only weakness. So, she felt relieved to know he would be safe, not to mention the selfish part that wanted him with her forever.

Though forever wasn't something she could fathom as she thought about the utter expanse of immortality. Julien was over three hundred years old, and Tristan was as well. It was too long for Evaine's mind to even process, and the idea that she could live to be that old made her head spin. They'd have an eternity together and never worry about getting old or sick. That was appealing, but it also made her sad.

"I wish Gage was here," she mumbled and earned a squeeze from Jacob as he said, "Me too."

Not that she was vain, but she dreamed of staying beautiful and living forever when she went through her vampire obsession and read every book and watched every movie she could find. She would be one of them soon, which was crazy and scary at the same time. Julien promised to help them through the process, and for some strange reason, she trusted him to be there for them and, when she was stronger, help her find the revenge she so badly craved. Since Julien revealed Tristan's plot, Evaine burned with the need to make him pay for what he'd done to her parents and Gage.

For some reason, her pain lessened and was not as bad when she thought of him. The gaping hole was still there but less jagged and painful. She wanted him back, missed him more than words, and would do anything, literally considering, to avenge his murder. After her turn, she would make Tristan pay, even if it killed her.

Heat flushed across Evaine's face as a wave of pain twisted her guts and brought her from her thoughts of revenge. The pain was sharp but fleeting, and she gripped Jacob's shirt and pushed out a slow breath to manage through it as Jacob held her and told her everything was gonna be okay. When it passed, she looked up to find Jacob doing much the same thing and returned the favor.

"Just breathe, Children. It will all be over soon enough, and you will be on to your new lives." Julien sat in the chair, sipping his wine like it was no big deal. "I would offer you another glass, but it is best for your stomach to be as empty as possible. It will expedite the process."

Evaine glanced at Julien. "How painful is the process?"

Julien swallowed. "Truthfully, excruciating, Ma Petite. You are strong and will make it through. Trust me."

Pain sliced through her, her body tensing against it as a groan slipped between her parted lips. Her stomach roiled and churned, sweat forming around her hairline, the beads running down her face and neck into her shirt as her skin burned with a fire she couldn't escape because it came from under it. Pain strangled her organs as they shifted from human to vampire.

Jacob squirmed and heaved next to her, and when the pain subsided, she gritted out, "I'm sorry for pulling you down this rabbit hole of hell."

Despite the turmoil in his sea-green eyes, he smirked and tried to play it cool. "No sweat, Princess. This is a cakewalk."

"You're a terrible liar." Evaine exhaled as the pain receded.

"Just breathe," Julien said. "As the process moves along, the bouts of pain will become more excruciating. And at some point, your body will shut down, and you will pass out from shock." Julien glanced at the clock on the wall. "But that is a few hours off, Ma Petite."

"See? Cake," Jacob mumbled and clutched his gut, breathing through the pain.

After a couple more minutes, it subsided, and they both sat up and tried to catch their breath. Evaine prayed to the universe that the next one wouldn't be as bad, but she knew it would likely be worse. The only way passed was through, even if it killed her.

Panic coursed through her at the prospect of the pain being any worse. She feared she wouldn't make it through the process and get the revenge she ached for. Sure, it wouldn't bring Gage back, but to be able to end the bastard who skinned him alive, and that was worth whatever came next. It surprised her how easily she'd decided to have Julien turn her into a vampire, but she knew revenge was a powerful motivator. *That, and not being someone's pet.* If there was anything Evaine learned over the last few weeks, it was that she didn't like being helpless and relished the idea of being unstoppable, strong enough to protect the people she loved.

When she glanced at Jacob, his eyes were closed and his breathing soft, like he was trying to calm down before the next round. She reached for his hands that were clasped together on his stomach, his long fingers wrapping around hers as he opened one eye and curled the corner of his mouth in a half-smile. "Cake, Baby." He reminded her of Gage and made her smile, despite the sadness sitting behind some sort of barrier at the back of her brain.

"What did you do to us?" she asked Julien. "Why is the sadness gone?"

Julien's cool gaze caught hers as he waved his hand dismissively. "I took it away for a little while. It was difficult to watch you two grieve, and I wanted to give you a reprieve. Fear not; the effect will wear off when you are fully turned. You will remember everything once you change." His lips snarled. "Including Tristan marking you twice, Ma Petite. And then you will know you made the right choice to join our clan before he could get to you."

Evaine's stomach churned, but she wasn't sure if it was from Julien's revelation or the change. She swallowed and blew out a heavy breath, trying to calm the turmoil. "I'm not sure I want the pain back."

Julien smirked. "Then I will teach you how to shut it off, Ma Rousse."

"It's simple enough that even a fledgling can manage it most of the time," Raven said next to Julien, his eyes narrowing as he watched her breathe. "What you'll need to watch when you are first reborn is the thirst. It will be the hardest part."

Evaine furrowed her brow, and Jacob glanced from her to Raven.

"Do not worry, Children. You will be fine. I will make sure of it."

When Skye skipped into the room, Julien's eyes seemed to sparkle with an edge of triumph, making Evaine think he already knew exactly what she was going to say. "Tati, your guests have arrived."

Julien cocked his head. "Guests?"

Skye twirled, her black dress floating up around her lithe legs and exposing her porcelain skin. When she stopped spinning, her pigtails still bounced. A silent exchange passed between her and Julien, and Evaine wondered if they could read each other's thoughts. Whatever transpired made Julien's face light up like the predator he was, and a fanged grin spread across his angelic face. He licked his bottom lip as he climbed to his feet and adjusted the cuffs of his expensive maroon dress shirt. "Please show them in, La Fille."

Evaine squeaked when he walked over and scooped her from the couch, sitting down and settling her on his lap before wrapping his arm around her waist. His hand rested on her thigh in a possessive manner that reminded her of Gage, and she heard the excitement in his voice as he smiled and whispered in her ear. "Tristan is here to collect you." Her body thrummed with anticipation and dread because she wasn't sure she was ready to face the monster who killed everyone she loved, but deep down, all she wanted to do was show him he'd never have her. To look him dead in the eyes and tell him she was coming for him. Her inside roiled and churned, part anxiety and part wrenching pain.

Jacob squeezed her hand next to her. "You can do this, Evie. I know you can." She was glad he was so sure because she wasn't. It would be so much easier to just run from all of it. *Maybe that should've been plan A!* As she faced the prospect of becoming a monster like Tristan, doubt chewed at her resolve and made her waver. He seemed so civilized, but in reality, he was a blood-thirsty predator that took everything from her, and she wondered if she would be the same.

"Jacob is right, Ma Petite. You can do this. I am here to help you through it," Julien said against the shell of her ear, and her body relaxed with his smooth words, his influence washing over her. It was just enough to calm the turmoil and give her the ability to focus on the present. Evaine squeezed Jacob's hand and then slid her free one over Julien's, lacing her fingers between his, his gold rings cool to the touch.

When Tristan stalked into the living room with Keegan right behind him, his hands fisted at his side. The typical gentleman-like veneer cracked, and his anger was written across his handsome face. His hazel eyes darkened as he glared across the open space, first at Julien and then at her.

Evaine's chest tightened, and she nestled into Julien's lap when Tristan snarled, "You spiteful bastard."

"What are you more upset about? That I won, or that I have your pet?" Julien asked, gripping her chin and running his fingers along her jaw in a way that was nothing but possessive and provocative. He gently nudged her to expose the bite on her neck, and she let him do as he liked, tipping her head to the side as she kept her gaze locked on her enemy but still allowed him to see the tender marks Julien left just above her collarbone.

Tristan stepped forward and sneered, "I wouldn't call one human girl a win, Julien. I would call it a desperate attempt to prove you are not a complete failure after losing your seat to me. I wonder, though, will she be as satisfying for you as being Ansel's right hand?"

Julien's body tensed against hers, his jaw twitching with unspoken scorn. Tristan's words hit their target, and Evaine understood what drove Julien to help her and why he was so willing to protect her from Tristan. He had his own ax to grind, and it was a big one from the sounds of it,

"Considering how badly you wanted her, I am sure you know exactly what she's worth to me." She sucked in a breath when Julien's fingers brushed along the marks, his smile never faltering. "And as you can see, now, she is mine."

Tristan frowned, his hazel eyes boring into hers. "Foolish girl. How could you be so naive to fall for his tricks? I thought you were smarter than that, but evidently, I misjudged you."

Hate flooded Evaine, and she was across the room before realizing her intentions, landing a hard smack across Tristan's face that rang through the large room and made her hand sting. Unable to control the emotions crashing through her, she screamed, "You killed Gage! You killed my family. You're a fucking monster!"

His hand snaked out, gripping her wrist, and jerked her against him. His body was cold steel, his voice seething. "You, My Dear, are mistaken. The only killer here is your Sire. He has blinded you to the truth and tricked you into losing your humanity. Now that he has you, he will never let you go. You will be his plaything, his pet." The edge of pity in his eyes made Evaine's blood boil, and she jerked her arm, trying to get free from Tristan's grip. He glared and tightened it, making her squeak as her bone groaned with pain.

Evaine steeled against the fear bubbling inside and met his hazel eyes, spitting her words like venom. "I don't believe you! I know what you did to Gage. I know you marked me twice so you could make me your slave! You're a liar and a monster! I can't wait to end you and get revenge for Gage and my family!" With her free hand, she pushed off him and swung at his perfect jaw, but his head jerked back faster than she'd expected, and her knuckles only grazed his sharp chin. True, it wouldn't hurt him, but at the very least, it would make her feel a little better.

Tristan twisted her arm and pinned it behind her, wrapping his other arm around her waist and pulling her back into his chest. He bared his fangs and hissed against the shell of her ear, "He is the monster, Pet," as she struggled to get free.

"Liar!" she seethed. "It's you!"

"Need I remind you, Tristan? She is now under my protection. I would ask you to take your hands off my protégé." Something dark glimmered in Julien's eyes as he sat next to Jacob on the couch, his hand on the boy's lap to keep him out of the fray. She could see the effort it took for Jacob to sit there; his body was tight, and his eyes narrowed, his jaw ticking.

Raven sat calmly in his seat, his legs crossed and his arms languishing on the rests. A slight smirk hitched his thin lips, and she wondered if he cared about what was transpiring and if he would do anything to help when Tristan hurt her.

With a growl, Tristan wrenched her arm up at an angle that shot pain down to her elbow, and she cried out despite her efforts to play tough. Her face flushed as another wave of pain stabbed through her insides, and her guts roiled.

"Come get her, Old Friend," Tristan taunted.

"Now, now. Such a sore loser," Julien purred in his smooth tone. "Can you not see that I have won this round? My venom courses through her veins, and in no time, she will be one of us." Julien pushed to his feet, his movements regal and stiff. "There is no reason for this to get ugly, but trust me when I say I have no qualms if it does." It was a thinly veiled threat.

Tristan scoffed and made her squeak again, digging his nails into her side. The sharp points tore through her thin shirt and scored the tender flesh, making her screech as warm blood trickled down her side. For a moment, she wondered if she would make it through this alive. Tristan licked his lips and growled, "Neither do I."

Keegan's dirk clanked as he stepped to Tristan's side. "You're walking a dangerous line, Tris. She's part of his clan now. You need to let her go."

"Let go!" Evaine struggled as panic overtook her and wondered what would happen if he killed her before she turned. *Will I die? Was it all for nothing?* No matter what she did, Tristan's grip held her easily. It was like fighting against iron.

Tristan ignored her plea, holding her closer. "I'm not going to leave her to suffer." He said to Keegan, who nodded but stood his ground.

When Tristan's cool breath tickled her ear, she shivered. "Remember the kindness I've shown you today, Evie. When you realize you have been hoodwinked, I will be here to help you." Tristan gripped her jaw, and Julien growled, though he stayed rooted. Evaine felt the anger wafting off of Tristan as he growled, "You're a cruel bastard, Julien," and fought against him.

He easily held her in place, kissing her temple as he whispered, "Sleep well, My Dear."

A sharp, unexpected pain wrenched her neck with a loud crack, and everything went black.

About the Author

T. Rae lives on the west coast of the stifling-hot Hellmouth, commonly known as sunny Florida, with her husband, daughter, and fuzzy four-legged menagerie. When she isn't busy fighting off Hellspawn, you can find her hiding in the dark corner, writing, reading, or binge-watching anything supernatural or science-fiction-related. This is the author's debut novel.

Made in United States
Orlando, FL
01 September 2022

21829254R00187